SITE

Hope's Return
Book 2
Frozen World Series

Published October 30, 2019
by Mission Critical Publishing LLC

Written by: Jay J. Falconer
Co-Authored by: ML Banner

Foreword

We are happy to see you here at *Silo: Hope's Return,* Book 2 in the *Frozen World Series*. The story continues right where it left off at the end of Book 1, so fasten your seat belts folks. The ride gets intense.

Be sure to check out the **Cool Free Silo Stuff** section at the back of this book for some amazing insider Air Force information, plus a few other surprises.

Also, please join us in supporting our military veterans by joining the **MCP Brigade**. It's free to sign up and **100% of all profits** from the purchase of official MCP Brigade gear will be donated to veterans charities such as the Oscar Mike Foundation for Disabled Veterans.

Our fallen heroes need our assistance, so please join us and show your support at **MCPBrigade.com**.

ML Banner

CHAPTER 1

Summer Lane put her arm out in a jab, slamming it against the side of the transport to keep herself upright as the tires found another wicked rut in the road. She spun her shoulders before leaning toward the access window separating the driver's seat and the bed of the truck. "Are you *trying* to hit every pothole?"

Krista laughed, never taking her eyes from the road. "You said to hurry."

"Yeah, but let's get there in one piece."

"We will, trust me."

Summer ran her hand across the mangled fur of the dog in her lap. "It's okay, boy. Just hang in there. We'll be home soon."

"How's he doing?" Krista asked, though her words sounded less than genuine.

"I think the bleeding has finally stopped. He's weak, though."

"He'll be okay. He's a tough mutt."

"I hope you're right. We've lost enough today," Summer said.

Sergeant Barkley brought his head up from its limp position across her thigh. He let out a whimper, his eyes looking withdrawn and weary.

The animal's pain was obvious. Waves of it, courtesy of Frost and the wound inflicted during the all-out melee at the Trading Post. The bloodstain that had soaked into the temporary wrap on his hindquarters was now a dark red color—a reminder of how fleeting life really is when your insides want to find their way to the outside.

At least the canine was still alive, unlike the other passenger in the back of the truck. They'd covered Professor Edison's body before the trek back to the silo, but the rough nature of the road had vibrated the camo-colored tarp loose, leaving it draped across his body at an angle.

Summer couldn't help but stare at the lifeless face she'd come to rely on ever since The Event.

Her eyes were drawn to his, wishing she was somewhere else. Somewhere where all the blood, death, and misery never existed. Somewhere where a dead mentor and friend hadn't just put her in charge of the families hunkered down in the old missile silo known as Nirvana.

She'd held strong over the years to maintain her status as being a heartless little bitch, something she was sure she needed to continue now that she was in charge of the underground facility.

There are times when an undeserved reputation comes in handy. This was one of those times.

Summer wasn't sure how she was going to pull off being the person in command, but she figured she could fake until she made it, or something along those lines.

In truth, she was good at pretending, but that had always been for her own benefit and only when it suited her. Now she had to become someone she wasn't, for the greater good.

She couldn't stop her hands from shaking, all the while thinking about the men, women and children who would now rely on her to make the right choices. So many hearts and minds, all of them focused on her every move.

The worst part of what was to come was dealing with Krista, her main adversary and the driver of the vehicle. The woman was sure to be riding her ass every step of the way.

In truth, the Security Chief was damn good at her job, commanding her men with the confidence of a dictator. She was also adept at being Summer's chief nemesis, a role they both seemed to embrace.

Summer expected her new position as boss to be an even bumpier road than the one they were on at the moment, especially without Edison to run interference.

"Have you figured out what you're going to tell the troops when we get back?" Summer asked Krista, wondering how the woman planned to explain all the deaths at the Trading Post.

Krista brought her eyes up to the rearview mirror. "That's your job now."

"What do you mean? They were your men."

"True. But like the rest of us, they all work for you. Or worked, I should say. That's part of the deal, Summer. It's what Edison would've done—called a community meeting to relay the news and field questions."

"Maybe this one time you could handle it? I don't know what I'm supposed to say."

"Just tell them what happened. Step by step."

"Everything?"

"Yes, but you can leave out some of the gory details," Krista said, turning the steering wheel to the right, taking a sweeping curve in the road. "Keep in mind there will be kids listening. Young ears and all."

"Great. Just what I need. More pressure to deal with. Saying the right thing has never been my strength. Usually it's just the opposite."

"You can do it. Just be yourself. I've got your back."

"Really? You'd do that for me? I mean, with our past and all?"

"That's my job. Just like it's your job to take over for Edison, per his wishes."

"I appreciate it, Krista. I know I'm not your favorite."

"None of that matters now. We both have responsibilities. There are a lot of people counting on us and we're going to need to work together."

"Despite our differences."

"Roger that. It's the honorable thing to do."

Before another beat passed, the truck's momentum came to a skidding stop, the tires screeching atop the pavement.

Summer lost her balance and shot forward with the dog in her lap, her back crashing into the front wall of the truck. The impact sent a thump into her spine, taking her breath away.

She gasped a few times to recharge her lungs, then slid the dog off her lap before getting to her knees. She peered through the access window. "What's going on?"

"Roadblock."

Summer looked beyond Krista. She expected to see vehicles sitting at odd angles with armed bandits standing guard. But that's not what her eyes reported.

There was a hooded man sitting on the pavement with a body lying in front of him. He had a thick beard and was waving his arms. One of the man's ankles looked to be bandaged with a white cloth. Well, mostly white—there was a prominent bloodstain along the side.

To the man's right was an old VW Bug. It was charred black and burnt down to the frame. There wasn't much left of it—just another corpse along the road—a metallic corpse, long since abandoned.

Summer remembered seeing it on the way in, back when Edison was filling her in on what to expect during their monthly meet with Frost at the Trading Post.

She ran a quick visual assessment, studying the covered body lying from left to right, its back facing the truck. It was centered in the road, with equal spacing to the curbs on either side.

What caught her focus next was the long hair hanging out from under the blanket. The blonde locks were extra frizzy, as if they hadn't been combed in weeks.

Summer's hair was always out of control, but never as bad as what she saw twenty feet ahead. "Is that a girl?"

"Looks like it."

"We should help them."

Krista shook her head, taking one hand from the steering wheel. It dropped to her side. "Too big a risk."

"What do you mean? Look at them. They can't even walk."

"You need to trust me, Summer. Without better intel and a security team to cover our six, we'll be exposed. The right move is to continue onward. This could be a trap."

"We can't just leave them here. They'll freeze to death."

"We can send back help later," Krista said, taking her foot off the brake. She turned the wheel as the truck idled forward, beginning a slow crawl around the victims.

The man on the ground stopped waving his arms. He let them drop to his sides, looking defeated.

"What are you doing?" Summer asked.

"My job."

"I said no!"

"It's not up to you. Not during a threat."

"But Edison put me in charge. You have to do what I say."

"Only if you're giving me a direct order. Is that what you're doing? Overriding my security decision with a direct order?"

"Yes. It's an order. Stop the truck."

Krista slammed on the brakes, then popped the latch on the seatbelt, freeing herself in one motion. She swung her head around. "Fine. But you stay here. Let me assess the situation."

"No. I'm coming with you," Summer replied, turning and crawling past the dog. The blond fur ball looked up at her, then started dragging its body to follow her to the tailgate.

"No. Stay," Summer said, using a hand to stop Sergeant Barkley. "I'll be right back, boy. I promise."

Summer repositioned the tarp covering Edison on her way past his body, concealing his face once again. It was hard enough being this close to him, knowing he would never take another breath. But to see his eyes, empty and meaningless, was just too much to bear.

When she made it to the rear of the transport, she peeled the edge of the canvas tarp up. She swung her legs over the tailgate, then landed her feet on the rear bumper in a double plop. A few seconds later, she was on the ground and hustling around the side of the truck, where she met up with Krista at the driver's door.

"I wish you'd listen to me. It's for your own good," Krista said, racking the slide on her semi-automatic handgun.

Summer ignored the comment. "Come on. Let's get them back to Liz."

Krista sighed, then jogged alongside Summer, the sights of the gun trained on the people ahead.

"Oh, thank God. I thought you were going to leave us here," the bearded man said after they arrived.

"Not a chance," Summer said. It was difficult to see his face inside the hoodie, but Summer thought he looked harmless. She turned to Krista and motioned to lower her gun.

Krista obliged, aiming the barrel at the ground.

Summer knelt down next to the girl. "What happened to her?"

"We were attacked."

"Scabs?"

"No. Bandits."

"I knew it," Summer said, moving the mop of hair from the injured girl's face. That was when reality hit. So did a powerful gasp to her chest.

The girl was missing a nose—frostbite.

"Hold it right there!" a man's voice said, coming at them from the left.

Summer whipped her head around. A second man stepped out from behind the torched VW bug and stood a few feet away with a pistol aimed at her. He looked older than the one on the ground. And fatter. Plus, he wore a Fedora. It was angled slightly on his wrinkled, old man head.

"Hands up," he said, nudging the muzzle of the weapon up and down.

"Damn it, Summer. I told you," Krista said in a whisper, the gun in her hand still pointing at the ground.

"Do something," Summer muttered, hoping Krista had some type of ninja move up her sleeve. Something a commando would use to save the day and get them out of this mess.

"Drop the gun, Missy," the man said to Krista. "Don't make me pull the trigger. Because I will if I have to."

Krista went to bend down.

The man's hands shook with subtle tremors, his index finger resting on the trigger. "Slowly. No sudden moves."

Krista put the gun on the pavement, then straightened up, her hands out to the side. "Easy now. We've done as you asked. How about you take your finger off that trigger? If you engage the sear point—"

The gunman didn't wait for Krista to finish. He pointed with his free hand. "Take a step back."

The blonde girl with crazy hair sat up in a lurch from the bearded man's lap, then got to her feet, snarling with a set of messed-up teeth, looking like a human version of a chainsaw blade.

"Jesus Christ," Krista snapped, moving in front of Summer, taking a defensive stance.

Summer couldn't stop the words from leaving her mouth. "Didn't even know Scab Girls existed."

"That makes two of us," Krista said, scrunching her face. "Can smell her from here."

Summer brought her attention to the gunman. "What do you want from us?"

"Your truck, for one."

Scab Girl helped the bearded man off the ground and to his feet. He looked weak, standing with more weight on his good leg than his bad. He pulled the hoodie back to expose his entire head. That was when Summer noticed the tattoo of interlocking chains on his neck.

Krista must have seen it too. "They're with Frost."

"I thought they were our friends now?" Summer quipped. "You know, on account of he's dead and all."

"What did you say?" the gunman asked.

"About what?"

"About Frost."

Summer didn't hesitate with her response. "He's dead. Scabs ate him. All crunchy-like."

"When did this happen?"

Krista touched Summer's forearm, then spoke in a commanding tone. "At the Trading Post. Hundreds of them. We barely escaped."

"What about Fletcher and the others?"

Krista's tone turned even deeper and more direct, as if she was giving a military report to a superior. "He survived. So did Dice. Can't say the same for the rest. We lost most of ours as well. So did Heston."

"It was biblical," Summer added. "And not in a good way."

"Biblical, huh?" the gunman mumbled, as if the phrase had some special meaning to him.

Krista took a short step forward, keeping her arms up and her voice even and calm. "You should be advised that Fletcher is the one who helped us survive the attack. We are working together now. On the same side."

The gunman's face turned sour. "Why would he ever do that?"

Krista shrugged. "Not sure. But he did. So did Dice. So you can put the gun down. We're no longer adversaries."

"Then he's in charge now," the gunman said in a matter-of-fact way. His face lost its tension for a few seconds as his eyes turned to the left, darting back and forth. When he brought them back up, he shook his hand again, making the gun wobble. "Keys. Now."

Krista shook her head. "Sorry, don't have them."

"Where are they?"

"In the ignition."

The gunman turned his eyes to the bearded man and Scab Girl. "Let's go."

"Wait!" Summer said, ignoring Krista's advice to keep silent. A different approach was needed. "We have casualties in the back. At least let us bury them first." She glanced at Krista with a raised eyebrow, hoping the Security Chief would understand why.

Krista pinched her eyes and sent back a subtle head nod.

The gunman stopped his feet, never taking his aim from Krista, his finger still resting on the trigger. "Fine. Get them out. We don't need to be ferrying a bunch of corpses anyway. But like I said before, no sudden moves. I'll shoot if I have to."

Krista took the lead, setting a path to the transport with her arms raised. Her feet moved with purpose, each foot plant looking measured. If Summer didn't know better, she would have thought Krista was stalling until she could come up with a plan.

Summer followed a few paces behind, feeling the weight of the gunman's eyes on her back. She figured he was close, keeping her and Krista where he could see them.

"Hold on a second," the gunman said as Krista put her hand out to move the hanging tarp on the rear of the truck. "I wasn't born yesterday. You need to take a step back. Slowly."

Krista and Summer moved away, giving the man access to the tailgate. He put his hand inside and pried the tarp up, never taking his eyes from Krista.

Just then a snarl of slobber and teeth came up and clamped onto the man's wrist. The gunman screamed in pain as Sergeant Barkley tore into his flesh.

Krista didn't hesitate when the gunman dropped his guard to whirl around and deal with the dog. She charged him, then jumped into the air with a fist raised above her shoulder. She brought the blow down hard, hitting the back of his head with a wicked strike. It was sheer violence in action.

The gunman's face slammed into the upper edge of the metal tailgate, making a ringing sound. His body went limp an instant later, hanging from the tailgate with his wrist stuck in the mouth of Sergeant Barkley.

CHAPTER 2

Krista bent down and snatched the gunman's weapon from the pavement, then spun to face the Scab Girl and the bearded guy, wondering which one might make a move first. "Freeze!"

Scab Girl kept her snarls in high gear, trying to wriggle herself free from the clutches of the bearded man.

Krista kept the gun aimed at the cannibal, her index finger straight and resting just outside the trigger guard. If she saw so much as a flinch, she'd already decided to shoot them both. Twice to the chest and one to the head—a triple-tap called The Mozambique, something her Drill Sergeant in Basic had preached endlessly. "Better keep your meat-eater in check, or I'll sic ours on her. Trust me, yours will lose that battle. Sergeant Barkley loves fresh meat. Especially young Scab meat."

Right on cue, the dog poked his head out from under the tarp, his chin resting on the top of the tailgate, with teeth showing and drool mounting.

Krista couldn't believe the wounded animal understood exactly what she needed him to do at that moment, all while he was in pain and weak from the knife wound to the hip. "All I have to do is say the word and your pet there is toast."

"Look, we're sorry," the bearded man said. He pointed at the other guy lying on the ground. "The ambush was all Lipton's idea. He held a gun on us, too."

Krista gritted her teeth with her jaw sticking out. "Bullshit. You were working together. Coordinated."

"I'm telling you the truth. Lipton threatened to shoot us if we didn't go along. We just need some help, that's all. Lipton is the one who wanted to steal your truck."

Krista pointed at the blonde with a set of ravenous eyes locked on her. "Yeah, what about her? The last thing on her mind right now is asking for help."

"It's just instinct. If you put the gun down, she'll calm down."

"Yeah. That's never going to happen."

"Trust me. She's one of the good Scabs."

"There's no such thing."

Summer stepped next to Krista and touched a soft hand on Krista's forearm. "It's okay, Krista. Let me handle it."

"That's a bad idea, boss. We need to dispose of these three and get back on the road."

"No, we're not doing that."

"Look, they initiated the threat, so now we end the threat. It's all part of the Rules of Engagement."

"I know what I'm doing, Krista. It's time for you to trust me for a change. I've spent far more time out in the wild than you. I have a good sense for these things. So right now, I need you to put the gun down. I've got this."

Krista hesitated for a beat, working the scenario through her head. Her brain was telling her to shoot all three of the attackers and leave them to rot, but her sense of duty wouldn't allow her. She let her gun hand drop to her side. "Yes, ma'am."

"What's your name?" Summer asked the bearded man.

"Horton," he said, turning his eyes to the Scab Girl. He wrapped an arm around the girl's shoulders. "This is Helena."

"Helena? You gave it a name?" Krista asked, not believing what she was hearing. Or seeing.

"We had to call her something."

"But Helena? Seriously?"

"It's a long story."

"I'll bet."

"It doesn't matter, Krista," Summer said, shooting her a look to back down.

Krista couldn't help herself, speaking again to Horton, only this time with sarcasm fueling her words. "So, what? You two are a couple?"

Horton took his arm from Helena and moved a step away, standing gingerly on his bad leg. "No. She rescued me when Frost tried to kill me. I owe her."

Krista smirked. "Okay, that's a first. A Scab helping a human. Usually, it's teeth first and then ask questions later." She let a round of silence hang in the air, then said, "So let me get this straight. She just shows up out of the blue and saves you from Frost."

"Yes, that's basically what happened. If it weren't for her, I wouldn't be standing here right now."

Krista didn't buy it. Not for a second. "How do you know she's not a plant? Setting us up for some kind of Scab ambush. We've seen it before."

"She's not. Her kind is hunting her as well."

"Why would they do that?"

"My guess . . . because she's unique. Maybe the only one. Girl, I mean. I'm pretty sure they are going to want her back."

"Again, hard to believe," Krista said, flaring an eyebrow at Summer.

Summer motioned to Horton's leg. "What happened there?"

Horton pointed at the truck. "Frost's dog."

Krista laughed. "I'm more impressed with that mutt all the time. That dog has good taste, so to speak."

Summer turned and shot a look at the gunman lying unconscious on the ground, then back at Horton. "What's his story?"

"That's Doc Lipton. Our chief tech."

"One of Frost's guys," Summer said in an affirmative tone.

"Okay, at least I've heard of him," Krista said. "A bit of an asshole, from what I hear."

"That part is true," Horton said. "But he also defected from Frost's camp. In fact, he went out into the cold in search of me."

Krista thought for a moment about believing him, but then her training kicked in, analyzing the ambush and everything that had happened since she'd stopped the truck. "And yet he held a gun on you and the Scab. I'm sorry, but that doesn't jive in my book."

"It was only after we refused to do what he wanted. That's when he turned on us."

Krista shook her head but didn't respond.

"Look, you don't know Lipton like I do. He's more than brilliant, but he has the patience of a gnat. When things don't go his way, he makes bad choices."

"Apparently," Krista said. His story seemed a bit over the top. Summer's face indicated she was cool with his story, but something was off. Krista could feel it.

Horton continued. "Like I said before, this was Lipton's idea. He was the one holding the gun."

Krista pointed with her thumb. "Why didn't you just sick Miss Ugly Teeth over there on him? That would have put an end to the threat."

"She's not like that anymore."

"Yeah, right. So now you're saying a Scab has had a change of heart. Not buying it."

"It's true. Why else would all of us be standing here, together? If she was still all instinct and attack, that would never be the case."

"Nice try. Sorry. Nobody changes like that, least of all a Scab. Even if she's the only female, they can't change their true nature."

"Look, in the end, the three of us are all on the same side. We need each other. Even Lipton."

Krista pointed to Summer and then herself. "And that matters to us, how?"

"We have inside information that Edison can use. That has to be worth something, right? All we need is a little help. That's all. Then we'll be on our way."

Krista angled her head to the truck. "Edison didn't make it."

"I'm in charge now," Summer said.

"I'm sorry to hear that. I always liked the Professor."

"So you've met him?" Krista asked, her gut telling her to continue to vet the man's story.

"Not exactly. But I was part of Fletcher's security team a few times at the Trading Post. I got a good sense. From a distance type thing."

Krista studied the man's face carefully, while searching her memory. "Hmmm. I was there every monthly meet. I never saw you there."

"No surprise. I was usually tasked with guarding the vehicles."

Krista huffed, turning her focus to Summer. "You don't believe any of this bullshit, do you? He's obviously lying."

"I don't know. Sounds genuine to me."

Horton continued. "Just so you know, Helena has saved me more than once. Lipton, too. She can sense when the Scabs are about to attack. I'm sure that kind of skill would come in handy for your group. Right?"

Krista peered at Summer, wanting to make sure their new leader wasn't going to fall for this man's tricks.

Summer let out a thin smile, her eyes obviously asking for confirmation of the claim.

Krista shook her head at Summer, then returned her attention to Horton. "That's all fine and well, until she gets hungry. Then what? We can't have a wild animal running loose in camp, snacking on little kids or whatever."

"She's right," Summer added.

Krista continued, tugging on Summer's shirt sleeve. "We need to leave. Now. They're not our concern. We've wasted enough time already. We've got wounded in the truck, in case you forgot."

Summer took a few moments before she answered. "Okay, I've made my decision."

Krista brought the gun up, hoping to get the order to terminate all three of them. If nothing else, leave them behind.

Summer once again put a hand on Krista's arm, pushing it down. "We take them with us so Liz can patch them up. Then we send them on their way with food and supplies. Give them a chance out there. It's the right thing to do."

"You can't be serious?"

"I am."

"Edison would never have done that."

"Yes, he would. He would never turn his back on those in need. And neither will we. No matter what side they used to be on. That's what June would have wanted."

"That'll give away our position."

"Not if we blindfold them."

"Jesus, Summer. It's still a huge risk."

"You can tie them up, if that makes you feel better."

Krista didn't answer, only shaking her head. She didn't have the words.

Summer's voice turned stout. "You said you'd back me up. Well, right now I need you to back me up. So what's it gonna be, Krista? Can I count on you, or do I need to make it a direct order? Again."

Krista didn't want to agree, but Summer was the boss. There was no denying it, no matter how stupid or risky the decision. In the end, duty called. "The others are not going to like this. Especially bringing back a Scab girl. How are you going to explain that? They'll never trust her. Or you, after that point."

"Not sure yet, but I'll think of something."

CHAPTER 3

Stanley Fletcher took a step back to allow his new second-in-command, Stan Greco, aka "Dice", to lower the front bucket of Heston's backhoe and push the last body into the oversized grave they'd dug with the twenty-four-inch bucket.

Fletcher shook his head, knowing that calling it a body was a stretch. It was more along the lines of a thirty-pound hunk of meat, completely unidentifiable, as were most of the other pieces already in the hole. Many of the parts belonged to friends of his, though it was impossible to know which chunk belonged to which friend.

The Scabs had shredded the men on all three sides of the monthly meet: Heston's, Frost's, and Edison's, using their collective power to destroy almost everyone. It was a strength in numbers approach—their usual tactic.

Or perhaps the correct analogy would be it was a function of physics—an unstoppable force type thing. Fletcher wasn't sure. Regardless, the Scabs' sheer, overwhelming numbers had resulted in an army of scrawny muscles and jagged teeth coming together in unison, mowing down everything in their path.

Even if some of his former colleagues had survived, Fletcher wasn't sure how many of them would have stood behind him when he announced that he was taking over. Some may have stood firm and pledged their allegiance to Frost, even after the man's early demise.

Either way, Fletcher wanted to grieve for them, but he couldn't allow his heart to go there. A warrior must continue on. Never show weakness, no matter what happens.

The four-wheel drive John Deere backhoe had done an admirable job cutting through the hard-packed ground behind the command post, near the rear of Heston's compound.

Its turbo-charged engine and extend-a-hoe upgrade was precisely what they needed to complete the dig. Dice ran the machine with obvious expertise, sitting inside the cab, working the control sticks with ease until the job was done.

"Gotta love life's little ironies," Fletcher said in an amplified voice after Dice throttled-down the hydraulic beast, letting the sarcasm bleed through his words.

Dice turned off the engine and unbuckled the seat belt, then got out of the cab and climbed to the ground. "What do you mean?"

"Just last month, I questioned Frost about the extra fuel delivery to Heston. Had I only known then what I know today, I never would have said dick."

"It was a risk, no doubt. I'm sure there have been plenty of our brothers who wanted to question that man over the years."

"Slayer's name comes to mind, for one. Poor bastard."

"And Horton, too."

"Roger that."

Dice nodded. "At least you took action."

"Almost too late."

"Hey, we're the ones still breathing. That's all that counts, even though things didn't exactly go according to plan."

"True. But the first rule of survival is to stay alive. Then regroup and reassess as needed. We accomplished that, at least."

Dice gave him a fist bump. "Now we just have to convince the others that Frost's death is a good thing."

"They'll fall in line. They won't have a choice."

"Are you sure we should rebuild this place?" Dice asked. "With Edison gone, I'm not sure keeping the Trading Post alive is a good idea."

"There's still a benefit. If nothing else, it stabilizes things. A return to normal, so to speak. That's important until we launch Phase Two."

"I'm still not sure why you decided to use the repellant on Edison's people. Seems a little counterproductive."

"Keeping an enemy an enemy enables them to remain hyper-aware. Never a good thing."

"Ah, you want them to let their guard down. If they think tensions are less now that Frost is history—"

"Roger that. It diffuses their mind-set, providing an opportunity when the time is right."

Dice paused for several beats, then nodded, his face letting go of the concern. "At least we took care of the biggest problem."

"An imperfect plan for an imperfect situation."

"You got that right, boss. On both counts."

Fletcher smiled, appreciative of Dice's loyalty and the man's candor. Both were valuable, more so since he was going to need Dice to rally support within the remaining ranks. There would be resistance. That much he expected, but Dice had the ear of the others, secretly laying the groundwork for weeks, ever since Frost tipped his hand.

Fletcher walked alongside Dice as they walked to their vehicles parked to the east, his mind slipping into analysis mode.

No matter what history might say about Simon Frost and the way he managed his men, their former commander was never afraid to charge ahead and complete a deal he'd made.

That part of his reputation had remained intact until his very last breath, as brutal as it was. However, as it often turns out, a leader's relentless reputation is also that leader's greatest weakness. It makes them easy to anticipate.

In Frost's case, his gung-ho, 'kill everyone who pisses you off' motto was precisely the reason his undoing was possible. The man never saw it coming. He was too consumed with finding a reason to justify taking out Edison and assuming control of everything.

Even his dog saw the end coming and defected. That said something.

* * *

Doctor Liz Blackwell tore through the hallway that connected to the stack of switchback stairs leading to the surface of the silo. She'd traced those same stairs many times before, but never with the type of news she carried today, the weight of it pressing on her chest.

She'd thought about reversing course on the way up as her feet pounded at the metal steps, not wanting to relay the news boiling her heart.

However, that wasn't the only pain in her chest at the moment. She'd skipped her cardio workouts recently, a fact that was all too evident as she stopped to catch her breath. She continued on, taking two more rights once she reached level one.

The shortest of the two guards stationed at the entrance pulled at the interior blast door, swinging it open on its massive steel hinges.

The other man moved forward and stepped into the connecting corridor, then opened the matching outer door, letting her continue her trek without stopping.

Neither man said a word as she passed, a fact she appreciated more than they knew. Her mind was elsewhere at the moment, trying to summon the proper words she'd need when Krista and her convoy arrived.

Liz could have traveled slower to buy herself more time, but for some reason, she felt compelled to push her legs up the stairs. Maybe it was guilt. Or remorse, given that she'd kept Morse's secret for much too long.

She wasn't sure which emotion it was, even though they were her own feelings. Feelings she knew all too well. Granted, it wasn't her decision to keep mum, but she was culpable regardless.

Liz had known a handful of physicians who were never able to get over the agony of delivering bad news to a patient. Of course, that was before The Event, long before she became the sole healer in this underground society.

Now the notification duties were all hers, whether she wanted the job or not. There would be no relief shift to rescue her at the last minute, nor would another doc step up and volunteer to take her place.

Liz had pushed herself early in her career to become desensitized to the process and its related anxiety during the long walks she'd have to make to meet with an unsuspecting patient's family. No medical professional wanted that job, but someone had to do it.

If she stopped to think about it, she was sure she'd remember each and every pair of eyes that had ever waited for her in one of those freezing consultation rooms. Hospitals kept the temperature low for a reason, and it wasn't always related to a medical reason.

She often thought the frigid air was pumped in on purpose, to act as a distraction, refocusing the family's attention on something other than the butchery masquerading as surgery in a sterile room not far away.

A moment later, her mind went into flash mode, showing her a slew of those waiting eyes from her past. One after another they came to her, taking her mind off the chore that awaited her on the surface.

Some of the flashes showed young eyes; others featured old, all of them studying every nuance of her body language as she approached, hoping and praying her prognosis was good. Even the slightest facial twitch, unplanned body motion, or a subtle change in breathing patterns can give the news away.

It's a learned skill that every physician is asked to master. Otherwise, remaining detached while meeting with a family to deliver news would fail. More so when you know the words you're about to speak will stick a dagger into their collective hearts.

One mistake and you amplify their grief. That's something they can never teach you in medical school. You just have to push through it and keep it as brief as possible, then offer hugs to whomever needed them.

She thought she had conquered this task long ago. Unfortunately, those previous efforts weren't helping her today. She knew the next few minutes would be the most difficult of her career.

CHAPTER 4

"What's taking so long?" Summer asked from the covered bed of the truck, kneeling to see through the access window behind the driver. The dog's breathing had changed, becoming more labored than before. Time was not something they needed to be wasting.

Krista was forward in the driver's seat and leaning, with her arms draped over the top of the steering wheel as she peered through the windshield. Her gaze held firm, aimed across the narrow entrance to the valley ahead. "Just give it a minute."

Summer squinted to sharpen her vision, keeping a close watch on the massive wooden barn in the distance. "Come on, already."

Krista pointed at the structure. "There it is."

Summer saw it, too: the signal—a series of light flashes—two long and one short—coming from deep inside the access door on the second floor. The observation scout in the hay loft had just scanned the area around the barn and given his go-ahead to approach. "It's about time. This is frickin' ridiculous. I could've told you nobody followed us."

Krista released the brake pedal and stomped on the gas, taking the transport ahead on a direct path to the barn. "We have to be sure, Summer. It's too important."

"Yeah, I get that. But there has to be a faster way. Especially today."

Krista didn't answer, her eyes focused on the dirt road ahead.

Summer latched her hands onto the bottom edge of the window frame as the uneven terrain slammed into the undercarriage of the truck. The road—if you could actually call it a road—was more than rough, the treads on the tires smashing into rocks and ruts across the surface.

Summer couldn't help but think Edison had designed the approach on purpose to slow visitors down—a fact that was working against them at the moment. Sure, their emergency had to do with prisoners and an injured dog—not an indispensable Seeker or security guard—but it didn't change the need to arrive sooner.

The truck dipped through a sharp depression, then jerked up, sending her airborne. Her head hit the steel framework holding the canopy above her, then gravity took over and sent her back down in a plop.

Summer rubbed her head, then turned to check on the dog.

Barkley looked okay, but she couldn't say the same for the others in the back. The same airborne whiplash effect had sent the blindfolded prisoners into a tumble, their hands still bound behind their backs with paracord. They were now leaning over on their sides and struggling to right themselves.

Horton craned his neck and used the crown of his head to push against Lipton's butt, pushing himself into a sitting position.

Scab Girl was able to accomplish the same feat without any external leverage, probably due to her abdomen being in better shape than the men's. It was obvious—Helena had skills, just not a nose. Or a comb.

Doc Lipton, on the other hand, looked helpless. Or hopeless, the two terms being interchangeable at the moment. It was comical to watch him struggle, his old man's body useless.

Summer thought about helping the man sit up, but decided against it. He didn't deserve assistance, not after pulling a gun and threatening to shoot everyone.

Whether Lipton would have pulled the trigger or not didn't change the fact he was a threat, no matter what the other two had said in his defense after they were in custody.

There was something about the man she despised, even though she barely knew him. Some people just rub you the wrong way, and it wasn't only because of him pulling a gun.

He had an aura that made her skin crawl. It felt black. Malicious. Like some kind of oozing darkness, as if he were hiding a terrible secret. Probably more than one, if she chose to listen to what her gut was telling her. It was a strange sensation, one that made the hairs on her neck stand on end every time she looked at him.

She shook off the feeling, then rubbed the dog's matted fur, appreciating the perfectly timed chomp that Sergeant Barkley had applied to Lipton's wrist.

"Good boy," she said before laughing at Lipton, who was still tussling with himself to sit up.

* * *

Dice turned the steering wheel to the right and drove the four-wheel-drive truck up the slight incline, feathering the accelerator to control the vehicle's slow crawl forward.

He stopped the truck within inches of the front gate protecting Frost's compound. The fortified steel barrier was in the process of opening, its mechanical retraction system grinding away on the chain-driven gears built by the one and only Doc Lipton.

The armed guards on watch seemed unaware that one member of their command team was missing—Simon Frost.

Perhaps they were focused on detecting a tail, as they should be, and hadn't taken a visual head count. He could understand that failure given the circumstances, though it remained a tactical mistake. Head counts are important. So are facial recognition steps, neither security measure having been applied thus far.

Yet what was the most troubling was the fact that they hadn't noticed the rest of the convoy was missing, too—both men and machine. It was a simple calculation, even for the dumbest of Frost's recruits. Far more flesh and steel had departed than what was returning now.

Dice swung his head to the right, checking to see if Fletcher was concerned. It didn't appear so, his eyes tracking the gate's progress with an otherwise blank expression on his face.

"Everything okay, boss?" Dice asked, just to be sure.

"Lipton better be back from wherever the hell he disappeared to. First order of business for him will be to double the speed of this gate. We're sitting ducks out here."

"I'll get him right on it, sir."

"Before that, I want the men assembled in the garage. Word will spread quickly about the missing troops."

"Have you thought about what you're going to say?"

"Working on it. Just sifting through the words at the moment. They need to be right."

"I have every confidence."

"Thanks, Dice. That makes one of us, at least."

"Trust me sir, the men respect you. Hands down. It's not even a question."

"I appreciate the support. But I'm more worried about the few stragglers who are still loyal to Frost. I had them all assigned to cover the monthly meet, but as usual, Simon overruled me and made last-minute deployment changes. Kept a few back for some reason."

"Obviously he didn't suspect anything."

"No. Otherwise, we'd be having a very different conversation right about now."

"The men may want to hold a vigil. You know, raise a glass type thing."

"That's fine, just make sure it doesn't get out of hand like last night. As soon as it's over, I want Lipton's still dismantled. No more moonshine. We're going to tighten up the ranks around here. Especially for Phase Two."

"Yes, sir."

CHAPTER 5

Krista drove the transport through the entrance of the barn, easing the vehicle past the dual doors that served as both a prop and as a sentry to protect access to the oversized structure.

The command vehicle's assigned parking spot was far to one side, leaving room for the rest of the convoy to park next to it, much like a platoon lining up for morning PT.

However, the other trucks wouldn't be making an appearance today. Neither would the rest of her men, a fact that brought a wave of pain to her heart.

The simple task of parking the transport allowed her time to focus on the events of the day. Or take inventory, if you will, of her actions and reactions, even though, as a soldier, she knew better than to dwell on the past, unless you're being debriefed or filing an after-action report with your superiors.

A brigade of shadows stood inside Edison's makeshift command post, waiting with ravenous eyes. Eyes that were backed by something far more powerful than time or space.

Whether it was fate or destiny, she couldn't be sure. But it was real. It was there. She could sense it. Something was judging her every move as she maneuvered the tires across the existing tracks in the dirt, angling to the side as she went.

When a cascade of darkness landed on the windshield, a tingling sensation came with it. It washed over her skin, wafting a cold dampness across her hands.

The chill traveled up her arms and into her neck, as if it was being guided to its target by an unseen adversary. She'd felt the same sensation long ago, back when she was deployed in an active combat zone.

Even watercraft operators experience casualties, usually after the bullets have flown and the boat is tasked to retrieve the wounded.

Many of the troops survive, but some don't, leaving the pilot and her crew to deal with the aftermath. An aftermath involving scrubbing blood off the deck, as well as confronting the ghosts of the dead.

Let's face it, once you've become intimately acquainted with the reaper, you have no choice but to challenge its malignancy head-on—for your sanity, if nothing else.

First you stand your ground to repel its attack. Then, after it pulls back to regroup, you sweep the area, targeting all vectors. Vectors that come in the form of intentions—malevolent intentions—lingering high above, waiting to deliver grief with the precision of a tactical drone.

It's never easy dealing with the savagery of death, but once you're sure the initial threat is over, you can finally turn your back and ignore the possibility of another breech. For a while, at least, because the threat is always there—waiting for a chance to re-engage.

At this point in the process, Krista was sure there was no chance of those malicious feelings gaining a foothold. Not mentally or emotionally. And certainly not until the job was done. A job that was infinitely harder now, with Summer running the silo.

The mere thought of that girl making command decisions for everyone was difficult to justify, despite it being Edison's dying wish.

The staff would soon raise concerns, no matter how Krista chose to spin the news of their newly-appointed leader. Some might decide to balk or threaten to leave.

Not that she would blame them. She'd already had those same thoughts. What concerned her most was the possibility of an eventual mutiny. Or an overthrow, depending on where the majority of Nirvana's population stood at the time.

Krista pulled the transport into its narrow parking spot, making sure the front bumper didn't run into the wooden slats along the wall in front. The last thing she needed was to create a drive-through lane where none was required.

Most of the time, the wooden barn sat alone and appeared to be abandoned. Just some old relic that belonged to a nearby dairy farm with thousands of cows back in the day.

Edison had the barn moved a short distance to this very spot to fool an unaware observer. To them, it would appear to be nothing more than a massive storehouse in the middle of a nowhere. The key word being *nowhere*.

In reality, that term meant a remote field that was now in the process of thawing like everything else. The Event had changed every nuance of life on the planet. Not just with the weather, but each survivor's emotions and goals, plus everything in between.

When Krista heard the rumble of the barn doors closing behind her, she let out the mythical breath she'd been holding in secret, ever since her arrival at the monthly Trading Post meet. It had been a long day, one filled with plenty of blood.

At least everyone was safe, sealed inside the wooden façade built to conceal the silo's entrance, all of it designed with the critical eye of a world-renowned genius. Unfortunately, that same genius was now rotting in the rear of the truck.

Krista fought back the urge to weep for her former boss, a man she didn't always agree with, but a man she respected for his willingness to take a stand, no matter how right or wrong he was at the time. Usually wrong, if anyone dared to keep a tally, his ideals posing a constant threat to security.

Regardless, Edison had thought of almost everything to help sell the backstory of the wayward barn, including constructing stretches of broken-down split rail fencing that gave the appearance of a pasture, one enclosed long ago.

He'd even constructed a dry water well and a few dilapidated stalls, complete with cow pies thrown about, each resembling an ancient fossil, rather than a fresh dropping.

She never understood why there wasn't a main house on the property. She had planned to ask Edison that very question, but never got around to it. Now the answer would forever remain unknown, adding to the mystery of his intellect.

"Concealment Team ready to deploy!" a male's voice called out, snapping Krista out of her reflective state. It was coming from the left, somewhere beyond her view.

The spotter in the loft answered the hail. "All clear. Proceed."

A crack of light erupted along the left side of the building, the sunlight beaming in through the driver's window from an access door.

Krista watched the team leader stand aside as the rest of the squad broke through the exit and trotted outside. Each member carried a custom-made rake, designed with a wide set of tree-like branches made of aluminum. Edison's fabrication teams had made them to his exact specifications, allowing the tire tracks to be erased after each mission.

It normally took about twenty minutes to cover all the signs, smoothing the dirt with sweeping passes. It was a rehearsed production, stretching from the barn's door to the outskirts of the clearing and up the approach hill.

Krista hoped they'd work faster today, not because she was in a hurry, but more because of the knot nagging at her stomach. It wasn't shrinking as it should have been now that they were inside a closed, secure structure.

Something was keeping the pain stoked and alive. Whether it was the universe or something else, she didn't know. The feeling was there, nonetheless.

After the side door closed, Krista put the shifter into park, then turned the engine off and hopped out of the truck. She put her fingers into the corners of her mouth and sent a sharp whistle at the guards stationed near a pair of yellow handrails bordering a staircase that led below ground.

She waved her hand, signaling for the men to join her at the driver's door. They began a jog to her position, the clatter of gear and weapons making a comforting sound. She was home once again, with troops of like minds and similar goals.

Krista whistled at another team of men, only they weren't soldiers. All three wore hardhats and tool belts. They stood bent over, huddled around one of the massive slide rails that supported the blast doors covering the silo's missile bay. The men straightened up and shot a look at Krista.

"A little help, please," she said.

The men stopped their work and began a casual trek to her position.

Her pair of guards arrived first. She pointed to the rear of the truck. "Take the prisoners to the brig. I'll send a medical team down to assess their injuries."

"Yes, ma'am," one of the guards said, turning and taking a direct path to the tailgate. The other soldier followed, his rifle in a standby position, angled from high to low across his chest.

The maintenance workers arrived at the same moment as Summer, who was holding the dog in her arms, her face flushed red and eyes wider than normal.

"I'll meet you inside," Summer said in a stark tone, never stopping her feet. "And for heaven's sake, don't forget the professor. We can't leave him there like that."

"Not a chance," Krista said, holding back a few choice words. Words not fit for the ears of a freshly-minted leader. Nor would they be proper conduct for the second-in-charge of Nirvana. A good soldier keeps their mouth shut and opinions quiet, even when every cell in their body is screaming at them to do otherwise.

Krista wasn't sure why she felt the way she did. It wasn't as if Summer was out of line. It just seemed that way. Maybe it was the sharp tone the girl had just used. Or the fact that they had only just arrived at camp and Summer was already barking orders, with civilians and troops nearby.

Summer continued ahead with the dog hanging limp across her forearms, heading toward the twin handrails that bordered the entrance to the silo.

The hardhat crew formed a semi-circle around Krista.

"What can we do to help?" the fattest man asked, his head covered in a dome of protective plastic.

"I need you to escort the prisoners down to the brig."

"Prisoners? Us?"

"Relax. They're blindfolded and secure. Just make sure they don't walk into any walls, or fall down the stairs."

The men stood there in silence, only blinking, with looks of confusion on their faces.

"Don't think about it. Just do it. My men will cover you," Krista said, grabbing each man by the arm and sending them forward in a shove.

Krista watched Summer travel between the handrails and down the steps. Just then, the top of a head came up the stairs in the opposite direction, climbing higher into view with each step.

It was Liz Blackwell, her shoulder-length hair touching the collar of her traditional white lab coat. Her movements were brisk and with purpose, none of which was a surprise. The brunette always seemed to carry a sense of urgency everywhere she went.

Liz turned toward Krista and picked up speed, arriving with flared eyes. "Where's everybody else?"

Krista didn't have a chance to respond before Liz leaned to the side and peered at the truck, firing another question. "Where's Stuart?"

Krista slid in front of Liz, hoping to keep the physician calm. "He, uh—"

"Did something happen to him?"

Krista paused for a beat. "Liz, I'm so sorry—"

Liz gasped, then used an outstretched arm to leverage her way past Krista. She ran to the back of the truck, sidestepping a pair of arms reaching out from a blindfolded Horton. Lipton was in hand-waving-frenzy-mode too, the maintenance crew escorting him with the two armed guards covering them from behind.

It was the first time Krista had ever seen Liz zip past a wounded person and not stop to treat them. It seemed like that woman was always on duty, no matter the situation—except right now, today.

Krista caught up to the doc about the same time as the woman swung the tarp open on the back of the truck. Krista grabbed at her elbow, trying to pull the healer away before it was too late.

Liz shook off her grab with a flash of her arm. An instant later, reality must have set in, as the expression on her face vanished, leaving behind only a stiff slate of numbness. The doctor's arms and legs froze into place as well, her eyes fixed on the corpse inside.

"I didn't want you to see him this way," Krista said, choking on the words as tears welled in her eyes. She wasn't prepared for any of this. Not the doctor's unexpected arrival on the surface or this meeting at tailgate. "I was going to get him cleaned up first."

Liz didn't respond, her eyes transfixed and energized.

Krista moved a step closer, within an inch of the physician's shoulder. She brought her arm up, planning to wrap Liz in a hug, but she stopped before making contact. She wasn't sure if an embrace was appropriate. They weren't that kind of friends and she wasn't that kind of woman—a woman who knows how to comfort someone in need.

Krista let her arm drop and stood at the ready in case Liz became overcome with grief. The doc's knees might buckle or she could faint. Either way, Krista would have to act, no matter how awkward it felt.

Yet Liz didn't pass out, nor did her legs fail. In fact, she did just the opposite, standing even more firm, resembling a bronze statue that had just been forged. Straight. Strong. Resolute.

Krista figured it was shock.

Liz turned to her with her jaw jutting out and her eyes held tight as she pushed a barrage of sharp words through her clenched teeth. "What the hell happened, Krista? Was it those prisoners? Did they do this? Or was it that dog?"

"No, it was Frost. I wasn't able to stop him."

"So you were there?" Liz asked, sounding both disappointed and pissed.

Krista couldn't hold back the tears. Or her emotions. They came out of nowhere and took over, making her hands shake and her voice crack under the strain. "Yes, I was. When the Scabs attacked the Trading Post, we made a run for it. That's when Frost stabbed Stuart—during the commotion. I never saw it coming, Liz, and I should have. That's my job. I should've been the one Frost killed. Not Stuart. I'm so sorry. I failed everyone."

CHAPTER 6

Franklin Horton took an unplanned step forward after someone tugged hard on his elbow.

He didn't know who it was, not with the blindfold covering his eyes. In fact, he didn't know much at all after being captured when their ambush failed on the road.

The lack of sunshine warming his face told him he wasn't outside. Plus, there wasn't any wind either, leaving only one answer: he was inside a building.

Probably Edison's stronghold, he surmised, a secret location that Simon Frost had wanted to find for years. Eight years, if he remembered right.

The throbbing in his ankle had tripled since they'd dragged him out of the back of the transport truck, each of his heartbeats igniting the nerves around the dog bite.

Yet that wasn't the only pain escalating in his body. The restraints around his wrists seemed to be growing tighter, too, digging into his skin the farther they walked. Maybe it was the constant yanks on his arm by the guards, casing a ripple effect down into his hands.

The escort leading him put a hand on Horton's chest, stopping his advance. "All right, take it slow. There are steps heading down. Eleven of them," the man said, his tone sounding older.

"Where are you taking us?" Horton asked.

Only silence was heard from his escort.

"He's right. We demand to know this very instant," Lipton said.

"Quiet!" a forceful voice said from behind, just as Horton heard an awkward foot plant and the rustle of equipment.

The sharp retort obviously came from one of the guards holding up the rear, precisely where Horton would have been if the roles had been reversed. The guard must have shoved Lipton when he delivered his last command, making the scientist stumble.

Horton took his time with the first four steps, his senses on high alert. There's nothing quite as unnerving as descending an unfamiliar staircase while blindfolded and restrained. It's not just the instability; it's also about being helpless, relying on a complete stranger to keep you from stepping off a cliff—or walking feet-first into a woodchipper.

Since he'd already found himself at the mercy of a woodchipper today—one named Sergeant Barkley—he'd prefer not to land a leg in another one.

Just then, the air around him changed in temperature and humidity. It went from brisk and dry to warm and moist. Damp warmth, actually. And it was stale. Musty, even.

The facts told him he'd just entered an area of recycled air. Probably an underground shelter, he figured, confirming what Frost had suspected in one of their mission briefings a few months earlier.

If Horton had to guess, Edison and crew must have stumbled across one of the doomsday bunkers built by paranoid preppers back in the day, long before The Event.

Or Edison had constructed one himself, using his ability to fabricate something out of nothing. It was a well-known skill, one that had kept the Trading Post in business for years. And Frost's camp, if one cared to be accurate, filling the gaps in technology when Lipton's efforts failed.

Despite Lipton's self-aggrandized view of his talents, the man carried plenty of shortcomings, none of which Horton figured Lipton would ever admit out loud.

"You need to realize that I have a problem with confined spaces," Lipton said right on cue, as if he could hear Horton's thoughts and had decided to rebuff the self-aggrandized assessment. "Unless you're hoping to see a grown man lose it and vomit uncontrollably, I'd suggest you remove the blindfold and liberate my hands so I can deal with the situation head-on."

One of the guards laughed. "Just keep moving, asshole. If you blow chunks, you'll be the one cleaning it up. With your tongue."

"Why, I never—" Lipton answered, not finishing his sentence.

Horton ignored the rest of their useless banter, turning his focus to another task—listening for the Scab Girl. He hadn't heard any of Helena's usual grunts, or her short, powerful breaths since they'd gotten out of the truck.

Perhaps the nose-less cannibal had been taken elsewhere, given that it was impossible to hide who and what she was. That idea made sense since her mere presence would have super-charged the anxiety level of those in sight.

It's one thing to risk bringing members of your rival gang into camp, assuming that's where they were at the moment. But it's an entirely different matter to allow a flesh-eater to mingle with your population. A population that Horton knew included kids.

The term 'appetizer' was probably on everyone's minds.

* * *

Stanley Fletcher finished his business in the shared bathroom of Frost's compound, then tapped his unit twice before tucking everything away and closing the button on his fly. He zipped up with a single pull and turned for the sink.

He'd just finished what some might have considered a world-record-length piss. The ride back to camp had pushed the capacity of his bladder to the edge. The immense pressure had almost kept him from standing upright once he slid out of the truck and landed on the pavement.

Sure, he could have stopped along the way to spray a bush, but he was in a hurry, with his mind focused on other things, mainly the speech he had to give to the remaining troops.

He turned the faucet on and used the trickle of brown water from the tap to rinse his hands, all the while trying not to inhale too deeply. It was always hard to breathe in this room, the reek of week-old piss constantly present.

Plus, it was apparent someone had dropped a deuce recently, leaving the door closed after their evacuation had concluded.

Whoever it was needed to change their diet, or at least light a match in consideration. The hangtime of the fermenting odor was beyond anyone's ability to measure, making him turn his head in disgust.

Now that he was in charge, he planned to have Lipton design a new private head, one that only he and Dice would have access to. He needed a place to sit and think in peace. A place unmarred by the bowels of his brethren.

He dried his hands on the faded towel, ready to deliver the news he carried. He figured that same news had already started germinating on its own, once the waiting members in camp realized Frost wasn't part of the convoy's return.

The words he would speak next needed to be not only accurate but specifically chosen not to raise doubt. He was the new boss and there was work to be done. Efficiency tends to disappear when questions linger. Or uneasiness arises. Neither of which he could afford at the moment.

He turned and stepped out of the head, taking a sharp left toward the main fabrication shop, where he expected the remaining members in camp to be waiting in attendance. That was assuming Dice had done his job and rallied the troops.

Fletcher had been on the other side of this process many times, waiting for Frost to make his appearance and begin one of his rants, usually about something insignificant or overblown. That wouldn't be the case today, on more than one level.

When Fletcher cleared the connecting doorway, a throng of eyes met his. An instant later, backs straightened and chests filled with air, each man energized with anticipation.

Dice shook his head at Fletcher, telling him he hadn't located Lipton. That meant the doc was AWOL, something Fletcher would have to deal with next.

Fletcher held out his hands, palms down. "At ease, guys. It'll be hard enough for me to get through this as it is. In fact, why don't all of you find a seat? There are things to discuss."

"Where's Frost?" one of the men asked from somewhere in the back of the group. His voice was threaded and gravelly, telling Fletcher who it was: Willie Boone, former Army—a six-year veteran of the infantry. A mountain of a man who'd taken shrapnel to the throat in one of Uncle Sam's last skirmishes, only a year or so before The Event wiped out the world's governments and their militaries.

"And the others?" a second member asked, drawing Fletcher's attention a bit to the right. That was when he saw Boone standing in the back with his arms folded.

Next to him was a tiny man Fletcher assumed had asked the last question. One of the new recruits, someone who hadn't had time to make an impression yet. Just another FNG that Frost had drafted off the street; he'd probably wandered into the Trading Post and demanded work.

The new guy was half the size of Boone, but just as irritating. His black goatee held spots of gray, giving him an older look.

Fletcher made eye contact with several of the men to the left, then said, "Just hold on. I'll explain everything. But first I need everyone to plant their ass in a chair."

None of them moved.

"You heard him!" Dice snapped, adding extra volume to his words. "Find a goddamned seat. That's an order."

Fletcher held out a hand, giving Dice the back off signal. He brought his eyes back to the group. "Look, the Trading Post was attacked."

"Was it Edison? That fucking guy—" Boone said.

"No," Fletcher answered, needing to stop the mounting anxiety. "Let me explain."

"Everyone just shut the fuck up," Dice said. "Let the man speak."

Fletcher cleared his throat, wishing Dice would keep his mouth in check. He thought about reprimanding his second in command again, but decided to let it go and forge ahead. "The Scabs hit us. Hard."

"What do you mean, hard?" another man asked, this time from the center of the group.

Fletcher redirected his eyes to find the guy raising concern. It was Sketch, the dark-skinned, thirty-nine-year-old former Army architect, usually the first man with a raunchy joke on his lips, or a drawing pad in his hand.

"He means all of them attacked. Thousands of them," Dice added.

"Dice is right. Our position was overrun and we had to fall back. Unfortunately, Frost didn't survive the second wave. But let me be the first to say our leader gave as good as he got before they got the better of him. Took a dozen of them out, like the true warrior he was."

"Was it before or after the meet?" the goatee-wearing munchkin next to Boone asked.

"During, actually," Fletcher answered, locking eyes on the little guy. "What's your name again?"

"Pepper," the man said. "TJ Pepper."

"What about his body?" Sketch asked, with more urgency in his words than before. "We need a proper service."

"I wish that were possible, but there wasn't anything left," Fletcher said, deciding to spin the truth a bit. It was time to deflect and push forward. "Trust me, we looked. High and low."

"It was like a swarm of termites," Dice said, using his hands to emphasize his words. "They were everywhere. We would've needed an army to stop them."

Sketch didn't hesitate with a response. "Then we mount up and go find those Scabs and take them out. Every last one of them. It's payback time."

"Damn right," Boone added, his chest sucking in air to expand.

An instant later, a smattering of additional comments filled the air, most of them sharp and to the point—everything from "He's right" to "Fuck yeah" and "Roger that, Fletch."

Fletcher held up his hands, preacher-like, shooting a glance at Dice before he spoke again. "No, I'm not putting any more of you in harm's way. Not until we figure out what's going on. We need better intel."

Two of men in the front row looked at each other for a beat, then stepped forward in tandem. "We'll go, Fletch."

Another man on their left joined them out front. "Me too."

A sleeveless man in the middle of the group pushed forward, sliding between the other volunteers, his face covered in streaks of black grease, running at an angle. He wore a black headband, keeping his shoulder-length hair in check. "Count me in."

CHAPTER 7

Rod Zimmer stood from the mess hall chair and moved to the open side of the table after Krista walked into the room.

Krista made eye contact, then changed course, heading his way in a slow walk with her shoulders slumped. Her face looked ten years older, her eyes withdrawn and weary. She'd obviously been through hell today.

Zimmer held out his hand, hoping for a customary handshake, but she ignored the gesture and sat down, plopping her butt in the chair before letting out an air-filled sigh.

"What the hell happened out there?" Zimmer asked, returning to his chair and sitting.

"I'm not sure, exactly. One minute we were dealing with Frost and his bullshit. The next thing I know, we're being overrun by Scabs. Thousands of them. They were everywhere, Rod. Like cockroaches."

Zimmer's mind flashed a visual of what the scene must have looked like. He scooted his chair closer to hers, then leaned in and lowered his voice. "Is it true? About Edison?"

Krista nodded, her face covered in a look of obvious defeat. She changed her tone as well, using a whisper to respond. "That son-of-a-bitch Frost got to him before I could stop him."

"How, exactly?"

"I thought we were all retreating together when all of a sudden, Frost sticks a knife into Edison's neck."

"For no apparent reason? He just kills him? Just like that? After all these years?"

Krista nodded. "I never saw it coming and I should have. That was on me, Rod. Me."

"You couldn't have known, Krista. Not with an all-out Scab attack. Everyone was distracted."

"Well, I should have. That's my job. My one and only job. Keep the boss alive."

Rod put a hand on her shoulder, squeezing with light pressure. "What's done is done. Don't beat yourself up about it. Nirvana is going to need you. Now more than ever."

Krista sat in silence, her eyes dropping to the table, running into a long, empty stare.

Rod took his hand away, extrapolating what must have happened after Edison was killed. "I take it you got payback."

Her eyes came up, more energized this time. "I would have, but the Scabs got to him first. At least he got what was coming to him."

"No doubt."

"Just not how I would have done it. As far as I'm concerned, he got off easy."

"There's going to be a lot of questions. From a lot of people."

She pushed her lips together in a pucker, holding that pose for a few beats before she spoke again. "I don't blame them. I've got my share, too."

"The people will need you to be direct and honest with them, like a strong leader does. That's how Edison would have done it."

"I can't."

"What do you mean, you can't? You're the most honest person I know."

"I mean, I can't address the people. I'm not the new leader."

Zimmer hesitated for a moment, trying to process the words he'd just heard. They weren't lining up in his brain. He must have misunderstood what she said. "I'm sorry, come again?"

"The Rules of Succession, Rod. Edison appointed Summer right before he died. Like you said, what's done is done."

"No, that can't be."

"It is. Trust me. Been trying to wrap my head around it ever since."

"She's a horrible choice."

"Can't argue with you there."

"You need to bring this to the Committee."

Krista rolled her eyes. "What's left of it—"

"Edison obviously wasn't in his right mind. They'll back you."

"Who's 'they'?"

"The others. I'll make sure of it. Though you should probably know that Morse is sick."

"What's wrong with Alex?"

"Not sure. From what I hear, he was in medical for a bunch of tests before Liz confined him to rest in his quarters. Not sure what's going on. But I'll get him to agree, regardless."

"It's not going to matter, Rod. You know as well as I do that Edison *was* the Committee. The last vote. Without him, there's no telling how any of this will go."

"We'll fill his spot, trust me. With someone who is sensitive to our way of thinking."

"I'm not so sure about that. Not when I failed to protect him. His death is on me. Nobody else. There isn't a single person in this place who will back me now."

"Trust me, they'll understand. If nothing else, I'll make them understand. One way or the other."

"What if Summer appoints herself as the head of the Committee?"

"That'll never happen," Zimmer said.

"You say that now, but—"

"We *have* to make this right, Krista. For the good of Nirvana. We can't let her take over. We need to stop her. Somehow. Some way. She'll change everything and we can't let that happen."

"Yeah, maybe, but I'm so exhausted right now, I can barely keep my eyes open. I need to hit the rack, first. Then we can talk about her removal. Like tomorrow or next week. After I get a bazillion hours of sleep. Though I have to say, technically the girl hasn't exactly done anything wrong while she's been in charge. You need that first to impeach. A crime while she's in office type thing."

"Not yet. But she will. Count on it."

Krista let out a slow breath. "You're probably right."

"Can always frame her for something. Make it easy. She's going to fuck up anyway. Might as well just shortcut the process. Probably save lives in the process."

"So what you're saying is the end justifies the means?"

Rod nodded with vigor. "Exactly."

"No, Rod, we're not going there. We play this by the book. Like always."

"Even if someone gets hurt?"

"Look, I get that you're just trying to help. But the rules are the rules and we all live by them. It's what civilized human beings do. Otherwise, we have chaos and I'm just too frickin' tired for any of that shit."

"Okay, okay, I get it. I don't agree, but I understand why you feel the way you do," Rod said, figuring she'd take that stance, though he had to try anyway.

Krista was a lot of things, but she was consistent in her belief in duty, honor, and respect—traits that would make her the perfect leader of Nirvana.

Rod continued, "I heard you brought back prisoners."

"Yep. They're in the brig. I need to head there and start my interrogations."

"I thought you were going to get some sleep first."

"Wishful thinking," she said in a downtrodden tone. "There's work to be done and it won't get done by itself."

"I hear you. It never ends around here."

"And it's only going to get worse with little Miss Snot Nose in charge."

"Hey, we can only do what we can do."

"For you maybe. For me, it comes down to one thing: keeping everyone safe, regardless of who's sitting in the big chair. In the end, Summer and everyone else is counting on me to do my job. Exhausted or not, I have to keep pushing ahead. Need to pay a visit to medical, too. Check on Liz. See how she's holding up with Edison's death and all. Maybe I'll do that first."

Krista brought her hands up from the table and put them on the armrests of the chair, then pushed to her feet.

Rod did the same. "I'll go with you."

Krista gave him a hug out of nowhere. Not her usual response, but she was bushed and he figured she was not thinking clearly.

Krista let go and gave him a thin smile. "Thanks for the support, Rod. I know you've always got my back."

"Even when I'm wrong in your eyes?"

She nodded, her eyes returning to their full intensity. "It's not about who's right or wrong. It's about the greater good."

CHAPTER 8

Fletcher walked into Frost's old office, closed the door, and sat in the chair next to Dice.

It wasn't an office in the traditional sense, more like a dingy storage room in the back of some rundown auto repair shop, one filled with stacks of manuals, screws, belts, hoses, hand tools, and scraps of hardened steel. Layers and layers of grease, too, and a marred flattop surface made of metal.

It wasn't a luxury space by any stretch, but it served its purpose. Plus, it came with a door for privacy, an important security measure that they would need going forward.

"Have you heard from our one-eyed friend in The Factory?" Fletcher asked his number two.

"As a matter of fact, I did. The hunting party just brought back the latest communique with this week's meat supply."

"And?"

"Craven said he's almost ready. Just needs to know when and where."

"That'll depend on what your source has for us. Any word from him?"

"No, but I get the feeling he's close. Said he's been working on it 24/7, whatever that means."

"Good, because we need to get Phase Two moving. The opportunity is now."

"I'll reach out again. I'm sure he's anxious for more fuel."

"He sure burns through a lot for one guy."

"I'm guessing he's not alone."

Fletcher agreed. "Probably not."

"But then again, he's not exactly a Chatty Cathy when it comes to anything outside of business."

"Nor should he be. We all need to tighten things up. It's a new world out there."

"In more ways than one."

Fletcher snorted after a smirk, taking a moment to consider the situation surrounding all that was happening. "Between that crazy son of a bitch in The Factory and your elusive recluse, we are relying on some pretty interesting characters. Not the soundest plan by any stretch."

"That's putting it mildly, boss. They're more like a couple of complete psychos."

"But necessary psychos."

"If you say so."

"You know what they say: gotta dance with partner you bring to the party," Fletcher said, slapping Dice on the back.

"Talk about an old saying from the way back machine."

"Yeah, but it still fits, even if we aren't talking about some skanky slut in a tight dress."

"Been there, done that if you know what I mean."

Dice gave Fletcher a fist bump. "That I do, my friend. That I do."

A pause hung in the air until Fletcher decided to speak again. "I'm afraid it's time to pick our command team."

The look on Dice's face turned sour. "I figured as much."

"We need to be one-hundred-percent sure of each and every one."

"Agreed. I'd start with Sketch for sure, plus a few other guys I have in mind."

Fletcher knew where Dice was going with the conversation. "The hunting party—"

"Absolutely," Dice said before letting out a prideful smile.

"One of the perks, when you keep the freezer full."

Dice laughed. "Even though we both know that isn't tough, by any stretch."

"Like shooting fish in a barrel," Fletcher quipped, letting a chuckle free from his lips.

Dice rolled his eyes, with a full-on grin smothering his face. "More like stabbing corpses in the morgue. Freezer burn notwithstanding."

"I like that better."

Dice raised an eyebrow. "Which part? The morgue or the freezer burn?"

"Both."

"Yeah, they both apply when you think about it."

"Anyone else?"

Dice ran his hand across his chin for a few beats. "I'd also toss Boone into the mix, and that little wiggler, Pepper."

"Damn, he's annoying."

"And then some. But I think he's a stand-up guy. Plus, I know for a fact he hated Frost."

"What about the Indian?"

"Longbow?" Dice asked.

"He seems capable. I hear he's one hell of a tracker and can sling a blade."

"That's the word in camp, though I haven't had a chance to vet the claims yet. He's relatively new."

"Either way, that's got to be a plus. Not much time to form a loyalty to our old boss."

Dice nodded, his eyes pinching a bit. "I'll feel him out."

"Make it quick, though."

"You got it."

"Any more?"

"No. That's about it off of the top of my head."

"Then everyone else will need to go," Fletcher said, having to force the words from his lips. It was the last thing he wanted to say, but there was no other way. There couldn't be any doubt about what came next.

"I'll arrange it."

"Just make it seem legit. Then we can move forward with that business out of the way."

"Should we use Craven again?"

Fletcher gave Dice a single head nod. "Worked once. It'll work again."

"Will do, boss."

* * *

Zimmer followed Krista through the door leading into the medical bay, where they found Summer sitting in a visitor's chair between two stainless steel medical tables. Her shoulders were only inches from both tables with her head hanging low in a slump of frizzy hair.

Zimmer could just see her eyes. They were trained on her lap and dripping with tears.

Liz was in the corner of the room with her back to the entrance, her hands fiddling with a glass vial near the prep station covered in medical supplies.

Krista cut in front of Zimmer and headed to where Liz stood in her traditional white lab coat.

Zimmer continued straight, stopping at the foot of the closest stainless-steel table.

A ratty-looking German shepherd lay on its side with its eyes closed. Some of its golden fur had been covered in a bloody wrap, though most of the redness looked dark and dry. There was a portion of it glistening a brighter red.

At first Zimmer thought the animal was dead, then he noticed its chest taking in air in short, rapid bursts.

Summer had hold of one of its front paws, her thumb stroking it from side to side in a measured rhythm.

Her other arm was outstretched in the opposite direction, reaching across the narrow space to the other table that contained a body under a sheet.

The face of the victim was covered but Zimmer knew who it was. Or more accurately, he knew what it was—Edison's corpse.

The fingers on Summer's left hand were intertwined with the Professor's as his lifeless arm hung below the edge of the table. The man's skin was a pale white.

Zimmer bent down to get a better view of the girl's face, hoping to catch her attention. He waved his hand in the path of her eyes, but she never looked up or blinked, her focus remaining transfixed on her legs. He could see her lips moving with purpose but no words were coming out.

Zimmer cleared his throat. "You okay, Summer?"

She stopped her lips, then brought her head up and made eye contact. She didn't respond, only shaking her head with streaks of tears on her face.

"Is there anything I can do?"

Once again, Summer shook her head in silence, her eyes holding his with a glazed look.

If she hadn't just been appointed the new leader of Nirvana, Zimmer might have been more forceful with his attempt to connect with her.

Instead, he took a step back and turned, making a path to Krista and Liz at the prep station.

When Zimmer arrived, he caught the tail end of a phrase that Krista had just said: "—had your training, maybe I could have done something."

Liz gave Krista a short hug, then pulled back, looking less like a doctor and more like a friend. "The blade severed his carotid artery. There was nothing anyone could've done, short of having a vascular surgeon on standby in a trauma center."

"But *you* could have saved him, right?"

"I'm afraid not. That's beyond my abilities. At least he passed with friends around him. That's all anyone can ask for. It wasn't your fault, Krista. Trust me on this."

"I appreciate the kind words, Liz, but he's dead because I failed. Me. Nobody else."

Zimmer decided to interrupt the pity party to see if he could change the subject to something a little more productive. He pointed at the canine on the table. "Excuse me, Doc. Do you really think we should be wasting valuable resources on some junkyard dog?"

"His name is Sergeant Barkley and he's no junkyard dog," Summer said from her seat. "And yes, we *are* saving him."

"That's a big-time waste," Zimmer said, peering first at Summer, then at Liz and Krista. Surely one of the last two would back his stance.

Krista shrugged, her face looking more dead than alive.

Liz said nothing, returning her focus to the loaded syringe on the table, picking it up with the tips of three fingers. She brought her eyes up, leaning toward Krista.

Zimmer closed the gap as well, wanting to hear their conversation. It was possible the doc just needed time to consider his concern and would now back his request to stop treating the dog.

Liz lowered her voice as she spoke to Krista. "I'm sure you're wondering why I was up top when you returned today."

"Yes, actually. I was going to ask about it, but then the whole thing with Edison's body came up."

Liz glanced at Zimmer, then back at Krista. "There's something you both need to know."

Krista shot Zimmer a look before returning her eyes to Liz.

Liz continued, "It's Morse."

"Rod told me. He's sick, right?"

"It's worse than that, I'm afraid."

"Then why isn't he here, instead of in his quarters?" Zimmer said, interrupting. "Don't tell me we're already out of medical supplies."

"Well, yes and no," Liz said. "We still have plenty of supplies, just not the ones he needs."

"What does that mean?" Krista asked.

"It means there's nothing I can do for him. Not anymore. I've done all I can."

Krista flared her eyes. "Come on, Liz. You need to quit beating around the bush and just tell us. What the hell is going on?"

"He didn't want anyone to know. Not even Stuart."

"Morse is dying, isn't he?" Zimmer added in a whisper. He shot a glance at Summer, who was still tending to the dog and Edison. Everyone knew the girl was very fond of Morse, which was why he figured Liz was keeping the volume low. "And you haven't told Summer yet."

Liz nodded. "Right on both counts."

"What is it?" Krista asked.

Liz exhaled, taking a moment before she spoke. "His pancreas."

"Cancer?"

"Yes, very aggressive."

Krista looked up at the ceiling for a beat, then brought her eyes back down. "I knew something was wrong the past couple of months."

Zimmer smirked. "What was your first clue? The walker? Of course, he was sick."

Krista's voice dropped an octave. "Could have been anything, Rod. Bad back or whatever."

Zimmer rolled his eyes. "Sometimes I think you live in a fantasy world, Krista. It was pretty obvious to anyone paying attention."

"Yeah, maybe. But everyone has to find a way to cope."

"With blinders on?"

"Why dwell on something you can't control? Besides, I really didn't think it was anything serious, other than old age. People use walkers for all kinds of reasons."

Liz cleared her throat, then touched both of their arms. "Look, this isn't about you two. This is about Alex."

Krista nodded. "Agreed, but I still can't believe you kept all this secret. Even from Stuart."

"Alex is a proud man who's endured more than most. This is how he wanted it."

"He's not alone in his quarters, is he?" Zimmer asked.

"A younger couple volunteered to sit with him. She used to be a school nurse."

"Better than dying alone, I guess," Zimmer said, shaking his head.

"It's been getting progressively worse the past few months," Liz said, "but he asked me to keep it confidential. He didn't want anyone feeling sorry for him. But now that he's near the end and Stuart's no longer with us, it's time for you to know. And Summer. We have to tell her. Together. I can't do it alone. It's going to crush her."

Krista shook her head. "I don't know, Doc. She's been through hell today."

"Which is why I haven't said anything. Yet. But we need to. Soon."

Krista hesitated before she responded. "You're right. Word's going to get out. It always does. Summer needs to get in front of it and make a public address."

Zimmer agreed. "About everything, not just Morse."

"Hey! What's all that whispering over there?" Summer asked from her chair.

"Nothing," Liz shot back, "just filling them in on the treatment for your dog."

When Liz turned toward Summer, Krista grabbed her arm, then shook her head with only a slight wobble.

Liz paused for a beat and nodded, not looking happy about the subtle gesture, then carried the needle to the mutt.

Krista and Zimmer followed, taking positions next to Liz as she held the tip of the syringe an inch from the underside of the dog's hind leg.

Summer let go of the professor's hand and stood up from the chair. She leaned in and kissed the dog on the forehead, then used a gentle voice when she said, "It'll only hurt for a moment, boy. I promise. Then you'll start to feel better."

Zimmer watched Liz stick the needle into the mutt's leg and engage the plunger to deliver the medicine into the animal's bloodstream, doing God knew what.

He still couldn't believe what he was seeing—for a dog. A feral dog that looked like it was about to die anyway, before the injury to its hindquarters.

He turned to Krista, his previous concern about supplies roaring back into his brain. "What about the prisoners? Are we going to waste even more on them? Or are *you* going to help *me* stop this insanity? Our supplies need to be for our people. Nobody else. And certainly not for some mangy animal."

Krista answered without missing a beat. "That's up to Summer. She's in charge now."

"Actually, it's up to me," Liz said, "as chief medical officer. When I'm done here, I plan to go to the brig and treat both of them, and I don't want to hear another word about it. We help all of those in need, just as June Edison would have done. Is that clear?"

Krista nodded, then her eyes flared an instant later. "Wait a minute! You said both? Only two prisoners?"

Liz nodded. "In the brig. I'm heading there next."

Krista yanked on Zimmer's shirt sleeve, pulling him toward the door. "There were three, Rod. Three!"

CHAPTER 9

Krista broke through the door to the brig with Zimmer right behind her. When her eyes landed on the holding cell ten feet away, she couldn't believe what she saw: only Horton and Lipton sitting on the cement floor. Both men stood an instant later, looking apprehensive.

Krista turned her focus to the guard on duty, Nathan Wicks—the same guard who had just been cleared for active duty after his short suspension for manhandling Summer. "Where's the girl?"

"Sorry, Chief. Who?" the 6'6" mountain of man asked, the massive scar across his forehead pinching along its seam.

"She was in the truck. Where the hell is she?"

Wicks didn't hesitate, glancing at the cell then back at Krista. "I can't say, boss. Security only delivered these two. I've had eyes on them the entire time."

"Must have taken her somewhere else," Zimmer said, breaking his silence.

"Damn it," Krista said in a terse tone, the beat in her chest thumping hard. "I gave them explicit orders to bring everyone here."

Zimmer's tone turned sarcastic when he said, "Obviously that didn't happen."

Krista took a moment to search her memories, drifting into the scene where a whirl of activity happened all at once.

First there was Summer and her injured dog walking past her in the barn. Then the strain of Liz arriving unexpectedly and having to explain to her what happened to Edison.

A moment later, the scene changed again, this time with a focus on Liz's emotional reaction and her flying past Krista on her way to Edison's body. Then it showed the lab geeks showing up and her tasking them to help the security team escort the prisoners to the brig.

When the vision showed the detainees walking past her while they were under escort, she could see the faces of everyone involved, but there were only two that belonged to the prisoners—neither of which was the Scab Girl. "Shit! She wasn't there."

"What?" Zimmer asked.

Krista turned her eyes to the cell, looking through the bars at Horton. "I was so focused on Liz the whole time, I missed the fact that only these two assholes walked past me."

Zimmer shook his head. "The girl was in the truck, right?"

"She had to be, Rod. Otherwise Summer would have said something. She was back there the whole time, with everyone else."

Zimmer's voice turned sharp. "Unless she helped the girl escape."

"You're reaching, Rod. Summer is a lot of things, but she would never do that."

"But if she did that would be grounds for—"

"What's going on?" a new voice asked from behind, interrupting Zimmer's statement.

Krista turned to see Summer arriving in the doorway.

Summer stopped and put her hands on her hips. "Grounds for what?"

Krista didn't want to answer the question. It would only lead to more questions and raise suspicions, tearing down what little trust Summer had in her. And Zimmer. She decided to redirect everyone's focus, pointing at the cell. "Helena escaped."

"What do you mean escaped?" Summer asked, not waiting for an answer before she turned to Wicks. "It was you, wasn't it?"

"No, ma'am," Wicks said, standing at attention with his chest full and shoulders back.

Summer looked at Krista. "I thought he was on suspension."

"That ended this morning."

"And you trust this guy?"

"Wicks said only two prisoners were delivered and I believe him," Krista said, remembering a conversation she had with Edison years earlier.

She had tried to convince the Professor to install security cameras throughout the complex, but the old man denied the request. They would have come in handy today, had she only known and convinced him to spy on the community. Maybe Summer wouldn't be as tough to convince. She was a rookie leader, after all.

Summer's eyes lit up, as did the redness in her face. "There were three in the truck, Krista. I was there."

"Yes, exactly," Zimmer said. "You were there. Alone. With all three of them."

"What the hell does that mean?" Summer asked, also shifting her eyes to Krista.

"He's just pissed off like we all are. Don't pay him any mind," Krista answered, not wanting to add to Summer's paranoia, as justified as it was.

Zimmer never should have said what he did, but there wasn't time for any of this.

Krista gave Summer a head nod as more facts surfaced in her mind. "We *did* leave them alone for a minute or two."

Summer paused, her eyes dropping to the floor. They darted left and right for a few beats before she brought them up to Krista. "—when I carried Sergeant Barkley to the stairs."

"—and I was dealing with an emotional Liz, telling her about Stuart."

Summer stepped to the bars of the cell, putting her hands on the metal as she addressed the bearded man with the injured leg. "You need to tell me right now, where the hell did she go?"

Horton shrugged. "How should I know? I was blindfolded, remember."

"You have ears, don't you? You must have heard something."

"Not with Helena," Horton said, looking as though he was proud. "Think about it for a moment.

She's been out in the Frozen World, alone, all this time and somehow, she's survived. That should tell you everything you need to know about who you're dealing with."

Krista joined her boss, though she didn't make contact with the bars, only peering at Lipton. "You're apparently some kind of know-it-all. Why don't you tell us what happened?"

"Yeah, right," Lipton said with a twist of his mouth, motioning to Horton. "Like he said, that girl's a ninja and we couldn't see dick."

A pause hung in the room until Lipton spoke again, this time laughing as the words left his mouth. "Looks like you geniuses were outsmarted by a scrawny little cannibal. Now that's what I call funny. Scab Girl: one. Braintrust: zero."

Zimmer grabbed Krista's arm. "A Scab Girl? Are you kidding me?"

"No, I'm not kidding, unfortunately," Krista replied, wishing she could deny it. She motioned at Horton and Lipton. "We found her out there with these two."

"They tried to ambush us, but it didn't work," Summer said to Zimmer. "Lipton was holding the gun."

Zimmer let go of Krista's arm and angled his head back, apparently in shock. "Female Scabs?"

"Yeah, who knew?" Summer said.

"Not us, obviously," Krista added.

"Just for the record," Horton said. "That girl—she saved me. More than once after Frost left me out there to die. She's not like the others."

"Like they care," Lipton snapped, rolling his eyes. "You just don't get it, do you?"

"They need to know, because she's not who they think she is."

Lipton shook his head, looking annoyed, before turning his attention to Krista. "There's something else you might find interesting. That little old Scab Girl has stretch marks around her midsection. Layers of them, by the looks of it."

Zimmer threw up his hands, shooting a piercing look at Krista. "She was pregnant?"

Krista nodded but didn't respond.

"That's right, folks, they're breeding," Lipton said. "Just what the world needs, more ravenous meat-eaters." He pointed to Wicks, standing at attention. "Other than Mr. No-Neck over there."

"If there's one Scab Girl, there's probably more," Zimmer said.

Lipton smirked, looking at Horton. "Well, what do you know? They actually get it. I didn't think there were any brain cells still functioning in this place."

"Speaking of which, where are we, exactly?" Horton said, his eyes gazing up at the ceiling as he surveyed the brig and its support structure.

"Obviously, we are somewhere deep underground," Lipton said. "You can smell it in the air."

"I know, but where? Don't we have a right to know?"

Lipton smirked, looking amused. "Good luck with that argument. They're never going to tell us shit. Or trust us."

"That's all thanks to you. I told you the ambush was a bad idea," Horton snapped.

"Sure, you say that now. But I don't remember you raising even a hint of a protest when we were out there freezing to death."

Krista ignored the men, keeping her focus on Summer. "Helena knows our location, boss."

Summer nodded, tucking a lip under. "We have to find her."

"Before Fletcher does. If someone reports a Scab Girl running loose, he'll send out search parties."

"Or the rest of her kind follows her back here," Zimmer said.

"You should take me with you. I can track her," Horton said.

"Why should we believe you? You'd say anything at this point," Krista said.

Horton pointed at Summer. "I tracked you, didn't I? Couple of times."

"I thought that was the fat Rambo guy?" Summer asked.

"Who, Slayer?"

"Yeah, that asshat."

"He was team commander, but I did all the tracking."

Summer brought her focus to Krista, her eyes indicating she was looking for advice.

Krista shrugged. "No way to know for sure. Even so, it's a bad idea."

Horton continued. "Seriously, I know how she thinks. You need me out there."

"That's the last thing we need," Krista said, wanting the man to shut the hell up.

"Without me, there's no chance you'll ever find her."

"I doubt that. We're pretty good at finding people on our own."

"Well, she's not exactly people, now is she?" Horton asked in tone that sounded rhetorical.

"True," Zimmer quipped, looking at Krista. "He's got a point."

"We'll find her. Count on it," Krista snapped.

Horton threw up his hands, his face twisting a bit as he spoke. "Even if you do, she'll never come in willingly. You need me to talk her down and convince her to come in peacefully. I can do that. She trusts me."

Krista looked at Summer, then back at Horton. "Even if I decided to break protocol, which I would never do, that ankle of yours would just slow us down."

Horton lifted his leg and put it down. "It's not that bad. Really. Just need your medic to patch me up and throw in some pain meds. I'll be good to go."

"I hope you realize there's zero chance Helena stands up to Fletcher's interrogation," Lipton said. "I've seen what that man can do. You have no idea."

"He's right. She'll talk," Krista said to Summer.

"Or grunt," Lipton added, beaming a twisted smile. "All depends on your definition of talking." Lipton peered at Wicks, scanning his size from bottom to top. "I'll bet Gigantor over there would understand what she was saying. He looks grunt-capable."

Krista shot Lipton an intense stare, holding it for a full beat. "You think this is all funny, don't you?"

"That it is, ma'am. Sometimes life provides you with a little unexpected entertainment. I'd say this situation qualifies. It's all about doom, gloom, and boom around here. Gotta love it."

"What's wrong with you? We have families here. Women. Children," Krista said, wanting to send a sharp jab his way, but she held it back.

"That was Edison's first mistake. One of many, I'm sure. Just look at you three right now," Lipton snarked, his face pushing in close to the bars with his hands on either side. "It's nothing short of comical. I can literally see the smoke rising from your ears as you try to wrap your minds, as insignificant as they may be, around what's really happening here."

Zimmer stepped forward and landed a punch on Lipton's face. The blow caught the scientist in the jaw, sending him backward in a stumble, his butt landing on the floor in front of the cot along the back wall. "I've heard just about enough out of you!"

After Zimmer whirled around, Krista sent him a single head nod, appreciating his quick response. He did what she couldn't.

They say rank has its privileges, but not in this case. Not when every cell in your body wants to pummel a mouthy asshole standing right in front of you, running his gums for amusement, all the while taking shots at everything you stand for.

Horton walked over and helped Lipton off the cement and to his feet, then returned to the front of the cell. "You really need to listen to me. You don't know who you're dealing with out there. She's not some helpless cannibal. I can help you bring her back without anyone getting hurt."

"You need to give it a rest," Krista said, waving a finger at him. "No chance that's ever going to happen."

"So just give it up, already," Zimmer said, faking a punch at the man behind the bars. Horton flinched before Zimmer spoke again. "You're going to spend the rest of your days in that cell, so you might as well get comfortable."

"You were right," Summer said to Krista in a downtrodden tone.

"About what?" Zimmer asked.

Summer took a deep breath before she answered him. "We should never have brought them here. Krista knew something like this would happen. Damn it, I should've listened."

CHAPTER 10

Summer made it up the stairs and to the surface inside the barn, skipping over the top-most step as she exited the silo.

Krista was right on her heels with Zimmer somewhere below, his feet only taking one step at a time instead of two.

When Summer turned for the transport truck, Krista caught up and passed her on the left, using one of those freakish Olympic fast-walker techniques, her hips rolling in conjunction with her arms.

Summer tried to match Krista's style and speed, but couldn't get her shorter legs and less-experienced hips moving fast enough. She broke into a full sprint instead, tearing past Krista in a rush of wind.

Seconds later, she tagged the tailgate on the truck first, then whirled around with a mile-wide grin on her face, watching Krista arrive a moment later, her face blanketed with an intense grimace.

"That's cheating," Krista said, gasping for air as she peered back at the stairs for a moment, just as the top of Zimmer's head came into view.

"Cheating? How do you figure?"

"You ran."

Summer shrugged, feeling damn proud to have finally beaten Krista at something. "I don't remember anyone mentioning any rules."

"Well, there were. You saw me."

"That walk-thing you were doing—that was your choice. Not mine."

Krista shook her head, still struggling for air. "Not cool, Summer. Not cool at all."

"Don't take it so personally. It's not like that race was planned or anything. It just happened."

"Still," Krista said as Zimmer trotted in, his old man knees making his steps ragged and uneven. The noise his mouth made as he gasped for air reminded Summer of a freight train engine chugging away.

His cheeks beamed red, with sweat streaming from his forehead as if he'd sprung a leak. He put his hands on his knees and bent over with his head angled up, maintaining eye contact. A few beats later, his knees went into a tremor and his face turned a pale white.

"You okay?" Summer asked, wondering if the man was about to pass out. Or worse.

"I'm fine," he said between deep, powerful breaths. "Just need a minute. Old bones and all. Been a while, you know."

Yeah, like forever, is what Summer wanted to say. "Sorry about that but we were in a hurry."

"I get that, but next time, how about a little warning?" Zimmer said, his words puffed with extra air. He pointed at the back of the truck. "Go on. Get to it. I'll be fine."

Krista took another few gulps of air, then pulled her sidearm and began to circle the vehicle, bending low and inspecting the undercarriage.

Summer turned and tore open the tarp on the back of the truck, then hopped in and scanned for clues. The area was how she remembered, except for a strip of cloth and a coil of paracord in the corner closest to the driver's seat.

There were also red stains dotting the steel surface below her feet. It was blood, most of it belonging to Edison, pooling where his body had lain covered. The rest was from the dog and the prisoners, based on the locations of each.

There was, however, one smear of red that was out of place—to her right. It was higher up on the vertical framework supporting the canopy.

She ran a finger across the metal strut, feeling a rough spot. The protrusion held a sharp edge along its top, from a poorly-finished weld. She leaned in and inspected the defect, realizing someone had repaired the framework, welding in a new piece and not grinding it as smoothly as it should have been done.

There wasn't anything else of interest, so Summer slid out of the truck and planted her feet in the dirt, landing about the same time as Krista finished her exterior vehicle sweep.

"Well?" Zimmer asked both of them in a breathy voice, the color in his face back to normal.

"Not sure," Summer said, still working through the facts in her brain.

Krista pointed at the driver's side door. "There are some footprints leading away. Bare ones. They start near the gas tank."

"That's where she must have dropped down," Summer said.

"From above or below the truck?" Zimmer asked.

"Could be either," Krista added, aiming her finger at the side of the barn. "The tracks lead to the door from there."

"She obviously hid when Horton and Lipton got out," Summer said. "Otherwise the guards would have seen her."

"How?" Zimmer asked.

Summer thought for a moment before responding, aiming her thumb at the back of the truck. "I found her blindfold inside. She must have worked it loose like some kind of magician."

"Probably used her toes," Krista said in a matter-of-fact tone. "Should've bound her feet as well. That one's on me."

Summer shook her head. "I don't think so. I found some blood on a sharp weld. She must have used it to cut the rope from her hands, then pulled the blindfold off."

Krista shook her head. "Actually, it was just the opposite. She used her toes to remove the blindfold, then cut the paracord on the metal. She had to see the bad weld first, in order to use it."

"Still doesn't explain how she got out without anyone seeing her," Zimmer said.

"What about Stuart's body?" Summer asked Krista, remembering the camo-colored tarp they used to cover his body.

Krista paused, then said, "She must have hidden under the tarp right before my men got there to escort Lipton and Horton, then slipped out later when nobody was looking. There *was* plenty of time before anyone came back for the body."

"Clever girl," Summer said, seeing a virtual replay in her mind. It showed Helena's steps one by one.

First, her toes removing the blindfold. Then scrambling to the weld and using it to slice the rope free, before tucking herself under the edge of the tarp, hiding her skinny frame between Edison's corpse and the edge of the truck bed.

If the tarp was angled out and held loose, it would have appeared natural to the guards, while their attention was elsewhere, helping a blindfolded Lipton and Horton out of the truck.

Summer had experienced her share of amazing escapes over the years, but nothing like what Helena had done. The Scab Girl had skills. Just as Horton had said. Unfortunately.

"It's time to send out a search party," Zimmer said in a sharp tone. "She could be anywhere by now."

Krista put her pistol into its holster. "Couldn't have gotten that far, Rod. Not barefoot over uneven ground and not in this cold. I'm thinking a five-mile search grid ought to do it."

"Maybe we shouldn't assume anything at this point," Summer said.

Zimmer nodded. "I agree."

"Okay," Krista answered. "Let's make it ten. We'll need to draft some volunteers to help."

CHAPTER 11

"Please, Krista," Summer yelled out, pushing her legs into a trot down the neon green corridor that connected the command center to the old missile bay.

Krista stopped ten feet ahead and turned, her cheeks filling with red. "For the last time, I said, no."

Summer caught up and stood a foot in front of her. "Come on, I really need to do this. The only reason she escaped is because I talked you into bringing her back here. That was my mistake. I should be the one to go out there and make it right."

"We've already talked about it and nothing you say is going to change my mind," Krista said, turning to resume her fast-walk.

Summer grabbed her shoulder and spun her around. "What if I made it a direct order, like before, on the road?"

"Oh, you mean that order that took us right into an ambush?"

"Yeah, that one. You had to listen to me, right? Even if it was wrong?"

"Not this time, Summer. All security decisions regarding Nirvana are my sole responsibility. Even you can't override them. That's how Edison wanted it."

"Yeah, well, Edison's not here now, is he?"

"Still, the rules are the rules. We all follow them or we have chaos. Even you don't want chaos, do you?"

"No, of course not, but—"

"Well, then, there you go. Issue settled."

"What if you and I changed the rules? We could do that, right? If we really wanted to?"

Krista stood there blinking and didn't respond.

Summer continued. "I mean, who's going to stop us? Really?"

"No. That's never going to happen. Like I said before, the rules are the rules and what happens security-wise around here is up to me."

"Well, technically, the mission is going to be outside the silo. So that means it's my decision. Like before, right?"

"Not when it comes to sending our search parties. I alone am responsible for who goes and who stays. Same with guard rotations, security perimeters, patrols, armaments, disciplinary actions, and Seeker

Missions. We all have a job to do. Yours is here, as the new leader. Where it's safe."

"But what if I decide to go anyway? What are you going to do about it? Throw me in the brig with those other two?"

"If I have to, I will. But you're not coming with us. That's final."

"You don't seem to understand that I have way more experience out there than you do. You need me. You really do. You heard Horton. That girl is like a ninja. She's going to be tough to bring in."

"Trust me, we can handle her, regardless of her supposed skills."

"But what if there are more of them?"

"Scab Girls?"

"Yes, girls—well, I don't know. Maybe the men, too. You know, another attack. You're going to need more help."

"That's exactly why you need to stay right here. I'm not losing another leader on my watch. This is the safest place for you. End of discussion."

"I get that, but what if you're wrong?"

"You're the leader now, Summer. Your duty is here," Krista said, pointing at the south wall of the silo. "Mine is out there, looking for the escaped prisoner. We all know what will happen if Fletcher finds her first."

"What if I don't want to be the new leader? Ever think of that?"

"It's what Edison wanted. You know the Rules of Succession as well as I do."

Summer held back a wince when a sharp pain slammed into the center of her chest. It was followed by a tingle across her skin—a cold, clammy sensation, like she had just been caught stealing money from her mother's purse. "I don't think I'm cut out for any of this. You'd be a way better leader. Maybe you should take over? Let me go back to being a Seeker. I'm good at that."

Krista put her palms on Summer's shoulders, squeezing gently. "You'll do fine, Summer. I have every confidence in you."

"Yeah, you say that now. But what if—"

Krista shook her head, not letting her finish the sentence. "—Edison wouldn't have put you in charge if he didn't think you were ready."

"Well, I'm not ready. In fact, I'm scared to death. Everywhere I look I see people staring at me. Even the kids. What if I screw up and someone gets hurt? How am I supposed to live with that?"

"Trust me. You are ready."

"How can you say that? You wanted to have me banned from Nirvana."

"A lot has happened between then and now."

"And that makes a difference?"

"Yes, it does."

"Bullshit."

"Look, I've been doing this a long time. All you need to do is stop dwelling on the fear and put on your big girl pants. You're a smart girl. You'll figure it out. The people of Nirvana need a strong, confident leader."

"See, that's the problem. I'm not that person."

"Of course you are. You're one of the strongest people I know, even though you can be a little snot sometimes, and a bit selfish."

"Not exactly the qualities of a great leader, now are they?"

"But you have the kind of bravery that most only dream of."

Summer pinched her eyes and didn't respond. The comment caught her off guard, especially coming from her number one nemesis. It was tough to accept that an enemy could turn it all around in an instant like Krista had done.

Krista continued. "How many times have you gone out there, unarmed and alone, and run into trouble?"

Summer shrugged, running a quick count in her head. The number was larger than she cared to admit. "I don't know, kind of lost track."

"That's exactly what I mean. Going out there, mission after mission, knowing that you'll probably end up risking your life for nothing more than a can of soup."

"Actually, it was two cans of soup."

"Exactly. That takes a special kind of bravery. The kind that makes a great leader. One who's willing to put her ass on the line for others."

"I guess I never looked at it that way."

"Like I said before, you can do this. Just give yourself time to settle in and get a handle on things."

Summer took in another breath, but didn't respond.

"If we change things up again now, this place will fall apart. People need consistency, Summer, even in the face of tragedy. Trust me. I've got your back, no matter what happens. But you need to step up. I can't do that for you."

Summer paused, feeling some of the tension in her chest fade. "Okay, I'll try."

"The number one thing is you can never let anyone see that you're the least bit hesitant. They have to know you're in charge, every step of the way. Can you do that? Please? For everyone's sake, especially the kids."

Summer nodded, though her heart wanted her to run to the surface and go hide in her favorite bookstore across the No-Go Zone. "I'll do my best."

"Everyone around here knows that you and I haven't always seen eye-to-eye, but deep down, I know you can do this. You have to. You just need to believe in yourself. Like I do."

"Thanks, I appreciate that."

"If they see us standing side by side as a team, in total agreement, they will believe in us. And that's what matters. They must trust us and know we will keep them safe, no matter what."

"You're right. A united front type thing."

"Precisely."

"Okay. I can do this. I think."

"Oh, and while I'm gone, you need to go have a talk with Liz."

"About what?"

"I'm not at liberty to say. But it's important. She's been waiting to speak to you ever since we got back."

Summer didn't like the tone of those comments, but she wasn't about to show it. Not after Krista's speech about stepping up. "Sure, I'll head to medical next."

"Actually, she's in the brig."

"Patching up the prisoners?"

Krista nodded. "You also need to get your speech ready. It's time to bring everyone up to speed. I'm sure the rumor mill is working overtime. The citizens of Nirvana will need answers."

"All right. I'll work on it. When do you think you'll be back?"

"Not sure. Depends on how well the tracks hold up. The wind is whipping around pretty good out there."

"Okay, but be extra careful. I need you back here in one piece. I can't do this alone."

"I will. That's my job," Krista said. "So now I have to ask the hard question. What if the fugitive won't come in peacefully? What am I authorized to do?"

Summer thought about it for a moment, then felt a sudden rush of confidence as the answer became clear in her mind. "Put her down. Our people come first. We can't let Fletcher get his hands on her."

"Now that's the mark of a good leader. Making the tough decisions. Most could never do that."

Summer nodded. She was starting to believe.

Krista continued. "You just need to accept your new role and grab it with both hands."

Summer smiled, appreciating the woman's support. "Maybe you should think about taking Horton along, like he suggested. If Helena really does trust him—"

"Already ahead of you. Decided that ten minutes ago."

"Good, do whatever it takes to complete the mission," Summer said as the pain in her chest vanished.

"Roger that, boss."

CHAPTER 12

Dice waited to speak until Fletcher was done stuffing a high-capacity magazine with three more 7.62 caliber bullets, clicking the rounds in one at a time with a press of his thumb. "Finished our search, sir."

Fletcher spun the magazine around in his hand and put it on top of another six that Dice assumed he'd already checked.

His boss then picked up a fixed-blade knife from the table and stuck it into a sheath next to it. There were three more Ka-bars like it sitting side-by-side, each nestled into their sheaths as well. "It better be good news."

"It's not."

"Damn it! Doc has to be here, somewhere. Did you check his quarters?"

"Just came from there. Nobody has seen him since about the time we went to the monthly meet."

"Is he AWOL or did something happen to him?"

"AWOL, most likely. His travel pack is missing and so is his fedora."

Fletcher nodded as if he expected that answer. "He never goes anywhere without that stupid thing."

"Found some empty hangers in his closet. Must have slipped out while we were away."

"Slipped out to where?"

Dice shrugged, wishing he had better intel. "Good question. It's not like he can survive out there on his own."

"Hell, he can barely survive in here."

Dice laughed, but didn't respond.

Fletcher shook his head, his lips in a thin line. "What the hell was he thinking?"

Dice took that question as rhetorical, deciding to deliver the next bit of news instead. "Armory reports a handgun is missing. Plus a box of hollow points."

"Lipton?"

"That's my guess. Though I'm not sure he knows how to shoot."

"What about the refinery? And the vehicle mods?"

"Jeeps are done, but the refinery is still offline."

"Shit."

"Do you think that's why he took off?"

"To avoid fixing it?"

Dice raised an eyebrow. "Or because he couldn't fix it. He had to know Frost wouldn't have put up with any more delays."

"That would explain his sudden disappearance."

Dice agreed. "He certainly *was* acting a little more squirrely than normal right before we left. He must have been planning his exit for a while."

Fletcher shook his head, looking as though he was ready to pummel someone. "That's why the threat of a knife is the wrong motivator, Dice."

"Couldn't agree more, boss."

"Men make mistakes. There has to be some leeway on occasion. Otherwise, this shit happens."

"Plus, Frost hated that guy," Dice said.

Fletcher smirked. "Who didn't?"

"I'm sure Lipton thought his days were numbered either way."

Fletcher nodded. "He obviously didn't know Frost wasn't coming back from the meet."

"True, but it's also possible Doc might have still bugged out, even if he did."

"Because of me?" Fletcher asked.

"Not sure how he views your disciplinary techniques, sir."

"Good point. Though most of the time, I was just following Frost's orders."

"I doubt Doc would understand the difference."

"Of course not. All he saw was the result. Men like him can't handle all the violence. More so when it might be aimed at them."

"You should know I ran a quick inventory of the fuel reserves."

"What's the status?"

"Only ten percent left."

Fletcher sighed, then blew out a long breath of air. "The timing couldn't be worse. Need to start rationing."

"Already in place, sir."

"I guess there's no choice, now."

"Craven?"

"I want a meet—ASAP."

"I'll let him know."

"In the meantime, send out a patrol and see if we can locate Doc. Drag him back here in chains, if you have to, but I want him alive and still able to work. Understood?"

"Copy that. Do you want me to use our men or Frost's?"

Fletcher's tone turned sharp. "Ours. You know what needs to happen with the others."

"Just wanted to be sure that was still the plan, in case something changed."

"What needs to be done needs to be done. This bullshit with Doc has nothing to do with any of that. Just sped up the timetable a bit, that's all."

"What's the backup plan if we can't find the asshole?"

"Same as if we do find him. That refinery will take time to get working again, so we need more fuel either way. Go to the Trading Post and grab what you can from Heston's stock. Don't forget the tank on that old backhoe. And his generators, too. Syphon off everything you can."

"I'll get right on it, boss."

'Oh, and Dice?"

"Yes, sir?"

"Double the men assigned to each truck, too. We need to get lean and mean to make the fuel last," Fletcher said. "And press that damn source of yours. Whatever intel he has for us, we need it now."

"And if he has nothing?"

"Then he has nothing. We are out of options at this point, other than Craven's trackers."

"Assuming they're reliable."

"Craven says he's tested them."

"He said that before about the spray and we know how that turned out," Dice said.

"He did eventually get it working."

"But at what cost? We can't afford to lose anyone this time."

"You're right. But unless your source comes through, we really don't have any other options."

"He'll want payment, regardless of the reliability of the intel."

Fletcher pinched his eyes, looking the part of an old wise man, someone who was always ten steps ahead of his adversary. "Now that's not really up to him, is it?"

"He won't trade without the fuel."

Fletcher took a minute before he spoke again. "Does he check the drum before he leaves?"

"Not that I recall."

"I'm guessing it's all about the weight."

"And our history."

"Then there's your answer, Dice. It's all about the eye test. What he doesn't know won't kill him."

Dice paused, making sure he heard the words correctly and understood Fletcher's meaning. He thought he did. "At least, not until we decide."

"Exactly. Might just need him later."

"Understood. I'll get that arranged as well."

CHAPTER 13

The Nomad hiked up the next hill as he crisscrossed the south side of his patrol area, looking for signs of activity. So far, he hadn't spotted much on this frigid day during what he assumed was one of the summer months. July maybe. Or August, closing in on summer's end.

Then again, that was only a guess, having lost track of the calendar long ago. He wondered if anyone else knew the true date, their lives awash in a blanket of gray, each new sun climb a carbon copy of the one that came before.

His days were just like theirs—filled with malaise—only for different reasons: his endless treks across the landscape, looking for more of the disadvantaged who needed his unique skills.

When the world is besieged by misery, there comes a time when someone has to rise up and bring about a modicum of balance, otherwise there's no chance of hope's return. Without balance, only the strong will get stronger, while the meek disappear from existence, with nary a whimper.

That was the rule that applied to everyone unlucky enough to have managed to draw breath this long, even if they didn't recognize it as such.

In truth, though, when you live in an unforgiving place such as this, these types of journeys were nothing more than a wandering haze of cold and loneliness.

Hours turned into weeks, and days ran into years, everything blurring together in an expedition to nowhere in particular. Only when he found himself facing the unexpected did it make getting up each morning worth it.

His quest wasn't a normal one, but it was exactly that—his. A quest he thought important enough to dedicate what remained of his life to it, even if it meant occasionally compromising his own principles to achieve the mission. Today was one of those occasions.

A half a mile back he had come across a fresh trail, leading him here. It hadn't been made in a straight line. More in a snake-like pattern, winding from left to right and back again, as the owner of the footprints battled their own paranoia in a tentative advance forward. A bleak, empty existence can do that, turning purpose into nothing more than random desperation. Or the hunt for one's own end. He wasn't sure.

The trail eventually led him to a scattering of snow, still clinging to life after the overnight drop. The trail only held small footprints from a four-legged rodent—another desperate creature foraging alone for its very existence.

He hadn't run across anything yet from two-legged creatures, but he knew they were in the area. Both the hostile variety and the friendly types, though sometimes it was difficult to know which was which.

Motivation was usually the tell, but that assessment required a prolonged reconnaissance to make certain he didn't misread a target's intentions.

A misread usually meant someone would experience the edges of his blades when they didn't deserve it, or a villain slipped away unscathed.

He wasn't sure what was worse: maiming an innocent or freeing the guilty. Neither met his agenda, though his purpose had evolved in recent months, transforming into a new mission, as if he were closing in on something profound. Whether that change would lead to some kind of defining moment in history—his or the world's—he didn't know and wasn't noble enough to judge or quantify.

It may have only been a lingering premonition of his own death, confusing his thoughts in such a way as to morph his terms of duty and honor.

The Nomad worked his way down the hill, then hauled his legs up the next incline, getting a sense he was close to his destination.

GPS satellites were long since extinct, as was the technology that took advantage of them, forcing him to become adept at navigating by the stars at night and using his heightened sense of location during the day.

Daytime was the more difficult, more so now than before The Event, with the landscape missing many of the landmarks he'd come to know and trust during his formative years.

Before his next step, a gust of wind smacked him in the mask, attempting to lift the cover from his head. He brought his feet to a halt and grabbed hold of the homemade disguise to secure it in place. Once the burst was over, he resumed his march.

"Should be there by now," he mumbled in a less than confident tone, wondering if his sudden need to reassure himself was an attempt to provide optimism for his impending arrival. Or perhaps it was a warning to his suspicious self.

Either way, one thing was clear. He was late for this meeting. A meeting with someone important. Someone he trusted. Someone who needed both his guidance and his protection.

He pushed his legs to the top of the next rise, bringing a new scene to his eyes—a snow-covered depression the size of a football field, with a half-buried school bus smack in the middle of the lowest point. It sat at a steep angle, the hood at least ten feet higher than the rear axle.

Snow drifts had buried the back half of the bus, much like he remembered when he chose this location as the rendezvous point. The front of the bus was less encumbered, with its twin doors near the front hanging open on the side, flapping in the wind on their battered hinges.

He closed the distance in a short minute, expecting to see the face of his waiting friend. Unfortunately, the bus appeared to be abandoned, much like he felt after his disfigurement ten years earlier.

All it took back then was a single run-in with an angry volcano to change his life in an instant.

The Nomad didn't understand any of it when it happened, not just with the accident, but with the people around him. Everyone he knew seemed to withdraw from his life, as if the generals in Washington had ordered their collective retreat.

He was still the same man, other than what he saw in the mirror each night when he removed his mask. Duty had taken its toll, leaving him less than his former self, not just on the surface, but deep inside, too.

Thirty-three steps later, Nomad's assessment changed when he came across a myriad of tracks in the snow—barefoot tracks, thousands of them, heading in every direction at once.

The Scabs had been here. An entire herd. All of them drooling in search of their next meal. If they'd been successful, he'd most certainly find blood belonging to his friend. Or possibly nothing at all.

The Nomad pulled his twin swords and brought them up in a striking position as he bent down on one knee to scan the area with a keen eye.

It's always wise to minimize your profile when you walk into an uncontrolled sector. Not so much to reduce your scent from the creatures with a taste for flesh, but rather to give the men with high-powered rifles less to shoot at, assuming they were nearby.

History had taught him that the Scabs were often hunted by the men with the chain tattoos. Men who ran with the soulless leader known as Simon Frost. A man the Nomad despised like most others who were still alive in this hellhole, but a man everyone came to tolerate, for no other reason than to make it through to one more sunrise.

The rules of survival had elevated Simon Frost to the rank of bearable, if that was even the correct term. Of course, for that to happen, one had to choose to abandon every moral, every ethic, and every decency that made them who they were.

He'd learned firsthand that it doesn't take long for your moral compass to change direction when death is on the hunt for you every minute of every day.

More recently, though, the roles between Frost's crew and the Scabs had reversed, with the hunters now the hunted, despite their superior intellect and firepower.

He'd seen the change in tactics live, when he held back and witnessed the cannibals overrun the Trading Post, tearing through those who opposed their advance. It was an unbalanced war to be sure, but a conflict with clear skirmish lines and differing rules of engagement.

The Nomad knew the Scabs had been growing in numbers, but he had no idea how effective a mass attack would be when it was unleashed with precision.

The tactics employed meant one of two things. Either their collective intelligence was growing or someone with superior skills was coordinating, acting as puppeteer for the damned.

The Nomad took a quick measurement of the track next to his boot. Size eleven was his guess, roughly an inch smaller than his. He ran a visual check of the other footprints nearby. None of them were noticeably smaller, though one set seemed deeper and flatter than all of the others, without much in the way of toe prints, except one—an odd-shaped big toe on the right foot. It was overly large, as if it had swelled to double its normal size.

His eyes came up as he studied the area from left to right, looking for signs of a threat along the ridgeline that surrounded him. There was no movement among the shadows. No unexpected blurs. No random grunts. No prolonged growls. No clatter of boots or gear, or the determined breaths of men with a live target in their sights.

It was time to move ahead.

He rose from his knee, but remained in a crouched position as he swung around to the left, deciding to work the perimeter in a clockwise direction. Not because it was the proper tactical choice, but rather because he'd chosen counterclockwise the last three times he performed this maneuver.

"Got to mix it up," he mumbled in a tone barely above a whisper, his eyes tracking the horizon beyond the bus. If there was an ambush waiting, it would come from the rise at his ten o'clock, matching the path of the sun. He figured somewhere beyond it was a throng of meat-eaters, or a patrol of men with M-Spec rifles.

He advanced another thirty yards left and swung around, putting the bus at his five o'clock position. Still nothing. No blood. No signs of a struggle, either, just the sea of footprints etched in the snow, including the deeper set with the mutant big toe.

Someone else might have wondered if the footprints had been staged as part of some kind of ruse. Yet he knew better, having seen this same mass set of tracks before, minus the big-toe print. The Scabs had worked the area like a squadron of ants, carpet bombing the expanse in their quest for food.

Just then, he heard a rattling thud behind him, followed by a series of grunts. He spun with his curved weapons leading the way, their razor-sharp blades in a forward position.

When his eyes tracked the sound, he spotted someone inside the bus. A girl. Young and blonde. Hair like a rat's nest. Her hands were pressed up against the window on either side of her nose-less face. An instant later, her grunts resumed, as did her pounding on the glass, making an awful racket.

He held out his hands with the blades aimed at the ground. "Shhhhh!'

She stopped the racket, bobbing up and down on her legs, looking as though she were about to open her very first present on Christmas morning.

The Nomad held up a hand, releasing two fingers from his grip on one of the blades, then pushed his palm down a few inches in a repetitive manner to send her a command.

She ducked down to a point where he could only see her eyes, plus the crown of her frizzy mop, her hands no longer in view.

He gave her another hand signal, telling her to hold position while he worked his way around the bus to check the area.

She rose in the window and bounced up and down again, this time waving at him to come closer.

He ignored her request, working the area with his swords at the ready.

First, he made his way to the top of the ridge ahead, then leaned up and peered beyond. There were scores of tracks leading away, heading toward a pile of rubble in the distance.

As before, they were all barefoot tracks, size eleven or so. No small prints or any signs of men in boots. The odd thing was, the deeper set of tracks with the big toe had disappeared.

The Nomad worked his way to the right, repeating the same scan multiple times until he confirmed there were no threats. He returned to the bus, this time approaching the doors hanging open along the side.

He climbed the steps and went inside, where he was greeted with a flying leap from the blonde girl. She wrapped her scrawny arms around his neck, with her equally thin legs latching onto his waist.

"I missed you, too, Seven," he said, peeling her off his body before her strength suffocated the life out of him. "Sorry I'm late. Any trouble?"

Seven grunted once.

He knew that to mean no, even though that went against conventional thinking. "What about those tracks?"

She held up her hand and swirled it, then shrugged with a fast shake of her head immediately thereafter.

He understood. "Happened before you got here."

Seven confirmed with a double groan.

"Better to be lucky," he said, pulling out a hunk of meat he'd smoked back at camp. "Even you couldn't escape that many."

The Nomad tore the piece in half and gave it to her, needing her to take the nourishment in slowly. There was no way to know when she'd eaten last, or what she might have eaten. Plus, smoked meat was her new favorite, something he was sure would count as the first step in evolution among her kind.

She stuck it in her mouth and bit down, her jagged teeth making quick work of the food. A school of piranha had nothing on Seven. After she swallowed, she pointed at the remaining section his hand, then gestured to his mouth, looking concerned for him.

"No, this is for you," he said, offering her the remaining portion. "But I need you to eat it slower, so you enjoy it." He wanted to add the words "like a normal person" but knew that would be pushing the bounds of their relationship a bit. She'd taken great strides recently, but finding your humanity doesn't happen all at once.

"Come on," he said, dangling the food in front of her, watching her eyes track the sway of the treat. "I know you want it. Go ahead. I brought this for you."

She refused with a push of her hand, snarling and waving at him to eat it.

He shook the food harder, regaining her focus. "This is not open for discussion, Seven. You need to eat. Now take it. Please."

She paused for a beat, then grabbed the piece and brought it to her face in slow motion. However, just before it found her lips, she changed course and jammed it into his mouth, pressing his lips together with her fingers.

Seven then leaned up on her toes and flared her eyes, looking imposing as she chomped her teeth together several times, exaggerating the motion.

"Fine," he said with his mouth full, starting to chew. "But remember what I told you. Eat more. Every chance you get. You know how I worry."

She leaned back and puffed her lips, while bobbing her head from left to right as she pranced on her toes in an odd collection of steps. She twirled around several times, showing him a cartoon-like snarl of shark teeth at the end of each rotation.

He couldn't help but laugh as he watched this feral creature act out of character. He would never truly know what she was thinking, but it was clear she wanted to entertain him.

Humor is something all humans share. So is joy, even between differing species of humans. It meant there was a sliver of humanity hiding inside the skinny girl, buried deep under all that scavenging for blood.

Her odd nature and willingness to evolve always seemed to bring a strange sense of satisfaction to his day. In many ways, she was more human than all of his friends who had abandoned him after his skin and face were transformed in a flash of fire and fury.

The Nomad finished the food, then pulled open the homemade leather coat he wore as armor. Inside was a canteen attached to the belt of his thermal pants. He pulled it free, took a swig, then offered Seven the water.

She took a sip, then spit it out in a spray of angst.

"What's wrong?"

She grabbed his hand and tugged him toward the exit doors. He allowed her to lead him outside to the rear of the bus, where the snow drift had buried the vehicle up to the middle of its windows.

Seven let go, then bent down and scooped up a handful of snow. She looked him in the eyes, then put the frozen precipitation into her mouth and began to chew, nodding as if he was supposed to understand what she was thinking.

A beat later, he did. "Ah, that's right. You like it frozen. I won't forget again."

She motioned for him to look down at her feet.

When he did, he saw them wrapped in burlap with brown shoelaces holding the cloth in place. He studied the tracks she'd made from the bus. They looked just like the size eleven footprints he'd seen on the way in, though deeper and flatter. Plus, her right foot made the same big toe impression.

Nomad smiled, appreciating her resourcefulness. "Clever girl. I thought maybe you had a big, fat brother with mutant feet that I didn't know about."

She took another mouthful of snow and worked it down her throat, looking content. Well, as content as a cannibal can be. At least he'd broken her of the taste for human flesh. Rats and rabbits were now her favorite.

"What do you have for me?"

She pointed at one of his swords and held her hand out.

He gave it to her.

She turned and used the tip to draw in the snow. It took several minutes for her to complete the sketch, then she gave him back the blade.

Nomad studied the drawing, recognizing two of the larger markers she'd drawn: the old church four miles east and the bridge over the canal just beyond it. "Show me exactly."

She bent down and dabbed her finger next to a circle shape she'd drawn. It held a triangle in the middle of it. To one side were dozens of trees she'd sketched, plus a row of what he assumed were houses.

"That's where they took you?"

She slipped the tip of her finger under circle, then started drilling lower, emphasizing the depth.

"Underground?"

She grunted twice.

He searched his memories for something in the area that fit her description and was near a huge orchard. The answer roared to life in his mind. "One of the old Titan II Missile sites."

She confirmed again, then drew a large house symbol next to it.

"Another house?"

One grunt.

He took a moment before speaking again. "A barn?"

Two grunts, then she covered her eyes with her hands.

"The entrance is hidden."

Two grunts.

"In a barn. A big barn."

She responded with two grunts, then washed out the drawing of the big barn with a light touch of her hand, patting the snow as she went. When she was done, she expanded her motion, sweeping a much wider area flat.

"A clearing?"

Two grunts.

"Okay, it's in a clearing. I think I know where that's at. Took a tour of that place once, thanks to an old friend of mine in the Air Force."

She bounced on her heels and started panting, pulling at him to head in the opposite direction of the silo.

"No, you can't go with me this time."

She stopped her excitement, looking lost, then grabbed his right hand, wrapping her fingers in with his and squeezing.

He pried her loose before taking a step back and pointing at her feet. "I need you stay here, Seven, and carefully walk through all my tracks with those fake feet of yours to cover them up. Nobody can know I was here. When you're done, make sure you end up next to the steps, then go inside and take the burlap off. That's where you need to wait."

She grunted once, but it was a short, loud burst. Not her usual tone or volume.

"Do as I say, Seven. It's important. They have to find you and can't know we talked."

Seven grunted again, then took a break before doing it again and again, each time making a single, sharp noise with her eyes flared.

"I'm sorry, but it has to be this way. Everything will be okay. I promise. It's the safest place for you. Trust me."

CHAPTER 14

Summer cruised into the medical bay and went to the first table, where Sergeant Barkley lay on his side. The blonde mutt lifted his head to greet her and wagged his tail.

Summer couldn't hold back a smile as she rubbed his neck with both hands, then leaned in and kissed him on the forehead. "Look at you. Someone's getting better already."

"I'm always amazed at how fast animals recover," Liz said, leaving her worktable and walking to Summer.

"That's because they don't know how to wallow in self-pity and beg for sympathy, like us humans. They are only focused on one thing, getting back to normal. All that other stuff is a waste of energy."

"That's true. Never thought of it that way."

Summer rubbed him a few more times, then turned her head away in a flash. "Phew, somebody really needs a bath!"

"As soon as he's able to walk on his own, but you'll need to keep that dressing clean."

"I can do that," Summer said, leaving the dog's side to walk to the empty table next to him. She put her hand on the cool metal surface, leaving it there for a three-count.

Liz followed her and put a soft hand on Summer's back. "Stuart's down on seven, being prepped."

"Do we really have to cremate him?"

"It's what he wanted."

"Still, maybe we should bury him next to June by that old tree in town. I'm sure that would be okay."

"No, Summer. It's important that we abide by his wishes. Stuart would've never wanted us to expose our numbers or our location, simply to put him to rest. It's too big a risk."

"I get that, but it just feels wrong, that's all. He should be with June."

"Any idea when you want to have the service?"

Summer paused, waiting until the twinge in her heart faded. "I suppose the sooner the better. Everyone needs closure."

"I'll make the arrangements," Liz said, wrapping Summer in a hug and squeezing.

Summer returned the favor, using her arms to send back her half of the embrace, only much harder. "I know you miss him, too. I'm so sorry."

Liz pulled back and let go, her face wet with tears. "We all miss him, sweetheart, but these things happen. What's important now is that we never forget him or what he stood for. He'd want us to carry on in his name."

"And June's."

Liz moved her hands to Summer's elbows, holding gently like a mother would do in support. "Of course. She was his rock."

"And he was mine."

"I hope you know Stuart saved a special place in his heart, one that was only meant for you. I know that for a fact. He loved you, Summer. Never forget that."

"I won't," Summer said, feeling a stream of tears leak from her eyes. "It's just hard. I miss him so much. I keep expecting to see his great big smile around the next corner, but then I remember what happened. It breaks my heart every time."

"Just be strong and finish what he started. That's all anyone can ask. You'll find your way through it. We all will."

"I'll try."

"Unfortunately, there will be some who don't think you're ready."

"Yeah, I'm one of them. But Krista said she'd help."

"She did?"

Summer shrugged. "I'm as surprised as you. I thought she hated my guts."

"She did have her moments, that's for sure."

"Not that I could blame her. I did go out of my way to piss her off sometimes."

"People can change, Summer. On all sides. And it's never too late to do so."

"Yeah, I'm starting to learn that," Summer said, not wanting to ask the next question. But it was time. "Krista said you wanted to talk to me about something?"

Liz pointed to the rolling stool in the corner. "Why don't you have a seat?"

"I don't know if I like the sound of that."

"Please, Summer. It's important."

"Okay," Summer replied, walking with heavy feet to the chair and pulling it away from the wall.

She sucked in a deep breath and sat down, feeling the twinge in her chest return, only this time it was deeper and more profound than before.

Something bad was coming and it was making her dizzy in the process. Just then, the air in the room seemed to disappear, making it hard to breathe.

She bent over, resting her elbows on her knees, giving herself time to work more oxygen into her body. It took a dozen or so breaths, but the lightheadedness finally went away.

Summer looked up to find Liz leaning against the worktable, with her butt pressing against the edge. Her fingers were laced together and resting against her thighs, just below the bottom of her medical smock.

The look on Liz's face was one Summer hadn't seen before. Withdrawn. Red. Numb-looking. Her eyes more round than normal.

Summer gulped and sat upright, then wriggled her butt to the left, finding the exact center of the stool for balance. Not that it mattered in the least, but it felt like the right thing to do.

Liz raised one eyebrow before she spoke. "Have you heard anything about Alexander?"

"No, should I have?"

"Wasn't sure if someone might have told you."

"I haven't heard anything. Is something wrong?"

Liz took a few seconds to respond. "He's sick, Summer."

"What do you mean sick?"

"He's very sick, Summer. The kind of sick that I can't treat."

When those words landed on her ears, Summer closed her eyes as she felt the energy drain from her body, almost as if someone had just pulled the drain plug.

Summer grabbed the edges of the stool to keep herself upright as a vision of Morse's gentle face flashed in her mind, his smile aimed at her from his walker, while standing in front of one of the chalkboards in his office—the same board with the strange calculations on it, written in red.

She'd been too busy to notice that he hadn't been around since they'd gotten back. She should have known something was wrong. He always seemed to go out of his way to greet her after one of her missions. Somehow. Somewhere. But he hadn't. They were more than close. Best friends, actually, and best friends know when something is wrong. It's part of the connection you share. You just know. And yet, she didn't. She'd been too per-occupied with her own shit—selfish shit.

Summer took another moment to collect herself, allowing some of her strength to return. She opened her eyes and aimed them at Liz. "He's dying, isn't he?"

"I'm afraid so."

Summer couldn't hold back the tears. They came all at once, flooding from her eyes as if a dam had broken.

Liz came to her side, knelt down, and wrapped her in a hug. "Just let it out, dear. It's okay."

Summer melted into her arms, her body falling limp as she lost all control.

Liz held her upright as Summer cried into her shoulder, each burst followed by spasms from her stomach and chest, pushing out air and tears together in uncontrollable heaves.

Summer felt Liz's hand on the side of her hair, stroking it gently as she began to rock the two of them from side to side, keeping Summer close to her chest.

"Shhhh. It'll be okay, honey," Liz said.

The tears and pain continued for another minute, but somehow Summer fought through them and found a way to regain her voice. The words were choppy, but her tongue was able to set them free. "Is it something with his legs?"

"No, honey. It's cancer. He's had it for a while now."

"Cancer?" Summer replied, letting the word soak in and find meaning. "Why didn't somebody tell me?"

"He didn't want anyone to know. I'm sorry I couldn't tell you before."

Summer couldn't believe what was happening. First Edison and now Morse. "What kind of cancer?"

"Pancreatic. But it spread to his spine a few months ago."

"That's why he had the walker?"

"Yes, he fought hard, but he knew this was coming."

"I thought he was just getting old. But cancer? Seriously? How did he hide something like that?"

"He's a prideful man, I'm afraid. The last thing he wanted was anyone's sympathy. He wanted to go out on his terms. You need to understand that, Summer. This was how he wanted it. We have to respect that."

"There has to be something you can do."

"I wish there was, but we don't have the drugs or the facilities. Plus, I'm not trained for this. Oncology is a very specialized discipline. It takes years of study."

Summer broke free of Liz's hold. "Then we send out Seekers to find what you need. It's out there somewhere. I'll go if I have to, but we have to try."

"I'm afraid it's too late. The cancer is now in his bowels. It won't be long."

"Don't say that!" Summer said, not wanting to hear any more bad news.

"I wish it weren't true, Summer. But it is. We have to accept it."

Summer slid off the stool and worked herself to her feet as anger swelled inside her body at a rate she hadn't experienced before.

It felt as though someone had just stuck in a hose from an air compressor and turned it on full blast. She wasn't sure where the rage was coming from, but it energized her body from the inside out. "Where is he?"

"In his quarters, resting," Liz answered, standing as well.

"You just left him all alone?"

"A family's there with him. They volunteered to help keep him comfortable."

"I need to see him."

"Of course. I'll go with you."

CHAPTER 15

"Hold it right there," Krista told Horton, tugging on the paracord binding his wrists together behind his back.

The prisoner let out a grimace as the rope cut into his skin. She'd laced the restraint extra tight, wanting to send a message. And, to be honest, to cause him some pain. It was her form of payback for what the man had attempted to do during the ambush, now that Summer wasn't around to run interference.

Krista pulled the blindfold from his eyes, letting the sunlight bombard his vision.

He squinted and turned his head, blinking rapidly in a wash of tears.

Krista ran a visual check of the terrain, scanning the depression ahead. There were footprints everywhere, crossing over each other and heading in different directions.

All of the prints were barefoot and petite, made by someone with feet much smaller than hers.

Their diminutive size ruled out a herd of male Scabs, unless they were a herd of adolescents, something Krista doubted, despite what Doc Lipton had mentioned about Helena and the possibility of her breeding.

The knot of trails covering the area meant only one thing—Helena had spent time here. A lot of it, doubling back over her tracks at least a dozen times and in as many directions, making a mess of the evidence.

Krista yanked on Horton's hands again. "Okay Mr. Tracker, you said you could help, so help. Which way?"

"Untie my hands so I can inspect everything up close," Horton said, beaming his focus at Krista. He twisted his back toward her. "Can't do that like this."

Krista motioned for her biggest and most trusted guard, Nathan Wicks, to come forward.

He responded with a quick step, taking position behind Horton. The other men she'd brought along remained behind at their post by the truck, covering the area as they were trained to do.

"If he even flinches," Krista said.

"With pleasure, boss," Wicks replied with a tense jawline, bringing his rifle up and aiming the muzzle at the back of Horton's head. He pulled the charging bolt back and let it snap into place.

It was refreshing to have her most loyal guard on this search and recovery mission. Wicks always seemed to know what she wanted, sometimes before she did, eliminating the need to explain every command in detail.

Krista leaned in to Horton's ear. "I swear to God, just give me a reason."

"I'm here to help. Nothing more. You have my word."

"Then get to it," she said, pulling a knife and cutting the cord from the man's wrists.

Horton brought his hands around to the front, rubbed his wrists for a few seconds, then stepped forward and bent down on one knee.

Krista followed behind, still carrying the knife in her hands, wanting to keep the man within striking distance.

Wicks was positioned on her right, looking ready to fire if Horton made a false move.

The index finger on Horton's right hand found its way to a pair of trails crossing in opposite directions, only inches from the front of his shoes.

He tested the walls of the first print with the tip of his finger, then did the same with the one perpendicular to it. He continued to examine a few more, leaning forward and reaching what he could.

Krista was tired of waiting. "Well?"

"Everything looks just a little too random, don't you think?"

"What do you mean?"

"I mean it looks like Helena was trying to make it appear she was traveling through here for all different reasons and did so over time. But the tracks are all the same age. Plus, there's a pattern here, if you know where to look."

Krista took another gander at the tracks around her. She couldn't identify the pattern he mentioned.

Horton stood and walked about ten yards to the right, bending down and testing another set of footprints.

A minute later, he got to his feet and rubbed his hands together, as if he were washing the dirt from his hands.

He pointed to the right, at the top of the hill thirty yards ahead. A trail of prints led in the same direction. "That way."

Krista grabbed the hair on the back of his head, yanking hard on the mop of gray. "You only get one chance to be wrong."

"She went that way. I'm sure of it."

Krista let go of his hair.

Horton took a step forward, nodding. "Looks like she was in a hurry, too. Just look at the space between the prints, plus the deeper depressions around her toes. She was running."

"Don't they always run?" Krista asked in a glib tone, not expecting an answer.

"Not her. She never just reacts. She always moves with a purpose. If she ran, there was a reason. A damn good one."

"Isn't it obvious? Someone was chasing her," Wicks said. "That's why animals run."

"Look around, dumbass. Do you see any other footprints?" Horton said to Wicks after pinching his eyes. "There's only hers. That means she wasn't being chased; she was in a hurry."

Krista didn't buy it. "Hurry for what?"

"A meeting of some kind would be my guess."

"Or the dinner bell," Wicks added. "Could be anything. No telling with these things. They're all balls and instinct, so to speak."

"Trust me, she was late for something," Horton said with a firm confidence in his voice.

"You're reaching, Horton. Scabs don't have meetings," Krista said, shaking her head. "These things are not that organized."

"Like I said," Wicks said. "All balls and instinct. Attack first and ask questions later."

Horton's tone turned cynical. "Though she did manage to outsmart all of you and get away."

"Well, there was that," Krista said, not wanting to admit the man was right.

"There's more to this girl than any of you realize. She's not some crazed animal. She thinks. She plans. She's smart."

"Enough debate. It's time to see how right you are," Krista said, shoving Horton forward. "But remember, if there's an ambush waiting, you'll be the first one into the meat grinder and none of us are going to lift a finger to stop it."

* * *

Summer stood in front of the door to Morse's quarters with stiff knees and a lump in her throat. Liz was there, too, looking somber and strong, holding her medical bag.

Neither of them had said a word since they'd left the medical bay. The silent walk wasn't planned, nor was it customary, but sometimes no words at all is the better response.

Summer had often wondered why people felt compelled to say something during times like this. In truth, it rarely helps having to endure an earful of forced rhetoric or stale platitudes when your heart is breaking for another.

True strength comes from within and not from meaningless words. Strength requires experience, meditation, and sheer will, none of which can happen when someone is flapping their gums simply for the sake of not being silent. It's even worse when all you want to do is be left alone, so you can curl up in a ball and cry.

Summer wiped the tears from her eyes, hoping she would make it through the next few minutes without breaking down. When she looked down at the wetness on her fingers, she realized that if she'd been wearing eyeliner like the normal girls before The Event, the black would have been smeared across her cheeks, making her look like an emotional racoon.

Who knew one of the few benefits of life in the Frozen World would be a complete lack of makeup?

"You ready?" Liz asked.

Summer sent her a thin smile before sucking in a deep breath and letting it out in a slow, controlled manner.

Liz continued, her tone gentle. "Remember what I said, sweetheart. He doesn't want sympathy. Let's keep it positive, for his sake."

Summer nodded, then looked down at her hands, both of them wobbling like an out of balance front tire. "Okay, I'll try. I just can't seem to stop my hands."

Liz put her medical bag on the floor, then wrapped her fingers around Summer's. "It'll be okay. We'll do this together."

The warmth felt amazing, taking some of the nervousness away. "Thanks."

Liz let go, picked up her bag, and opened the door with a twist of the knob, allowing Summer to walk in first.

A dark-haired family of three sat in chairs next to Morse's bed—a mother and father, both slender and in their 40s, plus a teenage boy with curly black hair and a wide nose.

Morse's bunk was pushed up against the wall to the right in an understated room of plain cement. His desk and dresser stood together on the left, with a free-standing bookcase beyond them, each of its shelves stuffed with reading material and journals—each of them spiral bound and worn.

Most of the books were thick hardbacks, but there were a few paperbacks mixed in. Three of them carried the title *SILO*, which Summer found interesting, given where they were at the moment.

She wasn't sure if the *SILO* books were fiction novels or textbooks, but their matching blue and white color schemes made it obvious they were a set. He'd kept them together on the middle shelf for a reason, she figured, since Morse never did anything without a plan.

"How's he doing?" Liz asked the mom upon arrival, putting two fingers on Morse's wrist. She looked down at her watch, her lips moving in one-second increments.

"Been asleep for hours, but he doesn't seem to be in any more pain," the woman answered. "That last dose really helped."

"It's time to turn him again," the father said, leaning forward and motioning to the boy to help. The kid followed his father's lead and the two of them turned Morse from his back onto his side, facing the middle of the room.

"Can we have a minute?" Liz asked the family, motioning with her eyes at the door.

"Right, no problem," the father said, standing up and corralling the other two in his hands before escorting them to the door.

"God, I thought they'd never leave," Summer said after the door closed behind them. She sat in one of the open seats, then picked up Morse's hand and held it.

There was a faint pulse across his cold skin, running at a pace much slower than Summer expected. She adjusted the blanket covering his body, pulling it up to cover his shoulders.

"Go ahead. Talk to him," Liz said, "while I take the rest of his vitals."

"Will he be able to hear me?"

"Does it really matter? If you have something to say, say it. Might not be another chance."

"I'm not sure what to say."

"Just speak from your heart, dear. That's all that matters. Just keep it positive, like we said."

Summer nodded, then leaned in to his ear. It took a few seconds for the words to line up. "Hey Alex, it's me, Summer. Liz is with me, too. Just wanted to let you know that we are both here and everyone is taking really good care of you. Hope you get better soon. We have a lot of catching up to do. A lot happened at the monthly meet. There's so much to tell you, I don't know where to start."

Liz motioned with her hand for Summer to continue.

Summer continued after another breath. "We found this ugly dog named Sergeant Barkley. He tried to protect me from Frost, but got hurt in the process. He's down in medical right now, resting. Liz is taking good care of him, just like she is for you."

Liz continued checking more of the man's vitals with instruments from her medical bag as Summer continued to fill Morse in on the happenings of the day. Since she wasn't allowed to tell Morse anything that wasn't positive, she decided not to mention Edison or what happened to him.

When Liz was done with her tests, she wrote a few sentences on a notepad, then put it away in the medical bag.

Summer leaned close to Liz, whispering in her ear. "How long does he have?"

"Not long. His heart is very weak."

When those words landed on her ears, Summer took in a huge gulp of air all at once. Tears started to well again, only this time she found the strength to stop them from overflowing down her cheeks. She sniffed hard and turned her head away to collect herself, jamming her lips together and pushing her jaw out in defiance.

When she brought her eyes back to Morse, she saw that his eyes were open and his lips were moving ever so slightly.

Summer smacked Liz on the shoulder and pointed. "Look! He's trying to say something."

Liz leaned in close to his mouth and turned her head, holding that pose for what seemed like an hour. When she sat back in the seat again, Morse's eyes were closed and his lips were no longer moving.

Liz brought her attention to Summer with eyes thin and forehead creased. "That doesn't make any sense."

"What did he say?"

Liz paused for a beat. "Red radio thirty-five."

"What?"

"He kept saying the same thing over and over. Red radio thirty-five."

"What does that mean?"

"I don't know. Probably just random gibberish," Liz said.

"But his eyes were open and he looked right at me. He knew I was there."

"I don't think that's the case, Summer. He's heavily sedated. It's more likely his mind and body are just reacting involuntarily."

Summer shot Liz a confused look. "And speaking real words?"

"It does happen on occasion."

"No, that can't be. He was trying to tell us something. Something important."

Liz shook her head but didn't respond.

Summer couldn't let it go. "He has a radio in his lab. Maybe that's what he meant?"

"Is it red?"

"No."

"Then I'm afraid it's just—" Liz said, stopping in mid-sentence when Morse suddenly turned over onto his back with his eyes open once again.

Summer grabbed his hand. "Alex!"

A second later, his entire body tensed in a straight line like a pencil, right before his chest took in one massive breath and held it for a three-count. Then, just as quickly as it came in, the air escaped from his lungs and so did the stiffness from his body. His arms and legs fell limp and so did his head, turning to the side with his mouth and eyes still open.

Summer squeezed his hand, hoping for some kind of reaction. "Alex? Please, talk to me!"

Liz listened to his heart with her stethoscope, then shook her head with tears streaming down her cheeks. "I'm sorry, Summer."

"No! God! No!" Summer said, putting his hand to her cheek. "Please, Alex, don't go! Please! Not yet! I need you!"

CHAPTER 16

Krista came to a stop when the trail reached the pinnacle of the rise ahead. She held up a closed fist to her point men, then worked herself into a prone position with her rifle at the ready, its barrel just beyond the edge of the ridge. She brought the optics mounted on the top rail of her weapon into position in front of her eyes to survey the area and take a risk assessment. Her men slid in next to her and did the same.

"See something?" Horton asked in a low tone, holding a few yards behind her, still under guard by Wicks and his always-at-the-ready assault rifle.

Krista turned her head, using a whisper to respond. "An old school bus in the wash ahead. Half a click out."

"Seriously? Way out here?"

"Been there a while by the looks of it. The girl's tracks lead straight toward it."

"Do you see her?"

Krista scanned the snow around the vehicle, but the low-powered scope wasn't helping her identify any more detail. "Not yet, but there may be more tracks in the snow. Hard to know for sure, but there are shadows. Don't see much else."

"She's probably in the bus, staying warm," Horton said.

"Wouldn't surprise me, though tactically, hunkering down at that location would be a mistake. The sight lines are a problem and there are too many elevated positions surrounding her. She'd be a sitting duck. If she's there, it's more likely an ambush. Trying to draw us in."

"Orders, ma'am?" one of the point men asked, also in a whisper.

Krista pointed to the right. "You two are on overwatch. Work your way around that ridge and cover our advance. Shoot anything that moves."

"Other than the girl," Horton said, his tone filled with urgency.

"Unless she attacks, then put her down," Krista added.

"Roger that," the man answered, getting to his feet in a crouched position, then scampering with his squad mate in the direction she'd ordered.

Krista waved Horton and Wicks forward, sliding back a few yards before getting to her feet and meeting them halfway down the hill, their heads out of sight from the bus.

The fourth member of the patrol team arrived, too, and Krista addressed him. "Remain here and cover our six. I'll bring you forward when it's clear."

"And if it's an ambush, ma'am?" the guard asked.

"Fall back and get word to camp. They'll want to send reinforcements, but tell them I said not to risk it. They are to hold position and cover Nirvana."

The man stood without a response, looking confused.

Krista continued. "Make sure they understand. Nobody is to follow us here. If something goes wrong, we can't afford to lose anyone else. Is that clear? They are to protect the camp at all costs."

"Yes, ma'am."

"All right, take your position."

"So it's just us?" Horton asked, looking at Wicks and then at Krista.

"Time to nut up or shut up. As soon as my men are in position, we're going to see if you're as good as you say. Otherwise, this is where we bury your ass, once and for all.

Wicks grabbed Horton by the collar and yanked him back hard. "And the first bullet is from me."

"Stand down, Wicks. We'll get to that soon enough," Krista said.

Horton flared his eyes wide. "You don't think any of this will work, do you?"

"No, I don't. It's a total Hail Mary, if you ask me. I doubt you could track down a drunken toddler in the snow, let alone someone with skills and a decent head start."

"Then why did you go along with it?"

"Because it's what Summer wanted. But you and I know what's really happening here."

Horton threw up his hands. "I wish you would trust me. I'm a man of my word. I can do this."

"Look, asshole, you worked for Frost. Not exactly a ringing endorsement about someone we should trust."

"Not my best decision. I'll give you that. But a guy's got to stay alive. At the time, that meant joining Frost."

"And doing whatever unspeakable acts he ordered you to do along the way."

"It's not like I had a lot of choices."

"We always have a choice, Horton. It's those tough decisions that define us. One way or the other."

"I get that, but—"

"For all we know, you're some kind of plant, sent here to infiltrate our camp."

"Except Frost obviously wanted me dead when he left me out there for the Scabs. That should tell you all you need to know."

"Yes, it does. You are not one to follow orders."

"Actually, just the opposite. I can follow orders. But with Frost, if you fail, you die."

"What was the failure?"

"Tracking your boss," Horton answered before a mumbling stutter hit his lips. "I mean, bringing her in. Tracking her wasn't the issue."

"That girl made you all look like fools, didn't she?" Krista said.

"And she cost our team commander his life in the process. Like I said, with Frost, failure is not an option. Not after Summer gave us the slip more than once."

"If all that's true, then why should we trust you with tracking the Scab Girl? Seems to me failure is your middle name."

"Because Helena is not your boss."

"But you said she's smart."

"She is, but there are varying degrees of smart."

"Sounds like a complete spin job to me," Wicks said, rolling his eyes at Krista. "It's all about CYA with this guy. We should just burn him now, beat the rush later."

"Actually, it's not about spin. It's quite simple," Horton said. "When Summer got away the second time, I became expendable, like everyone else under Frost's command. That's how the man rules. Through fear."

"Ruled—" Krista corrected.

"Yes, ruled. Now that Fletcher's in charge, there's no telling how this is going to go."

Krista smirked. "I trust him a lot more than I trust you."

"That'll change, if you just give me the chance. Let me prove it to you."

Krista pulled her knife again, aiming the tip at Horton. "So I'm curious—what makes you think I'm any different than Frost?"

"Well, uh, not sure."

"I guess, then, we'll see what happens. But don't think for a second I won't do it. If it were up to me, we would've left all of you on that road to freeze to death, so factor that into who and what you think I am."

Horton didn't respond this time, clamping his lips together in silence.

Krista put her knife away and looked at Wicks. "Overwatch should be in position. Let's move out."

* * *

Summer lifted Sergeant Barkley from the medical bed and lowered him to the floor, letting his legs touch gingerly. Once she was sure he could stand on his own, she let go and took three steps back, then bent down and slapped her hands against her knees. "Come here, boy. You can do it."

"Are you sure about this?" Liz asked.

"Yeah, I need something to take my mind off all the crap going on," Summer said, seeing flashes of Edison's and Morse's faces in her mind. "Besides, he needs to move around a little, like you said."

"I meant later, as in tonight or tomorrow."

"I'm pretty sure he's a lot stronger than you think. I saw what he can do when he wants to," Summer said, turning her focus back to the dog. She slapped her hands again. "Come on, boy. Come here. Show Liz how strong you are."

Barkley looked at her and blinked, his face peppered with matted fur. He took a tentative step with one of his front paws, wobbling as he ventured forward, his other legs reacting in concert with the first.

"That's it. Keep going."

Barkley took another step. Again, it was filled with instability. Then he took another and another, each one a tad faster and more confident than the one before.

"See, I told you," Summer said to Liz. "Just needs to push through it, like we all have to."

"Okay, but take it slow," Liz said. "He should drink some water and try to eat a little something, too."

"I'm sure the chef has something he can nibble on," Summer said as Barkley arrived. She rubbed his neck, then gave him a hug, ignoring the stink that went along with it. His tail wasn't wagging yet, but she figured that would happen eventually. He just needed to get his footing and find more strength.

"If you decide to give him a bath, make sure the dressing stays dry. We don't want an infection settling in."

"Okay, got it, Doc."

"And be careful around the kids. They might get a little too rough with him and we don't know how he will react."

"That was my plan," she said, leading him to the door that opened into the hallway.

CHAPTER 17

"Looks like a swarm of ants hit this place," Krista said as they approached the myriad of tracks in the snow around the abandoned bus.

There was no telling how many Scabs had made the tracks, especially since they looked to all be barefoot and about the same size, though there were a smattering of odd tracks, too—all of them flatter and deeper with an oversize big toe. She'd never seen that particular type of track before. Perhaps a pair of Scabs were purposely walking in each other's steps, but for what purpose, she had no idea.

Krista kept her rifle in a defensive position, aiming just short of Horton's feet with her finger resting on the metal surrounding the trigger guard. "Wicks, you're on point. Clear the bus."

Before the man could step forward, the bus doors rattled on their hinges and out came the Scab Girl.

"Hold your fire!" Horton said, his arms out high.

Helena scampered up the front bumper, then climbed onto the hood of the bus and scurried to the top of its roof.

Krista was about to give her overwatch team the order to shoot, but instead held up a closed fist when the girl sat down cross-legged and put her hands up over her head.

"She's surrendering," Horton said, looking at Krista. "Let me talk her down."

Krista gave him a nod, then tossed him a length of paracord to use as a restraint. "You get one chance to bring her in and she needs to be secured. That's non-negotiable."

Horton didn't hesitate, nodding and then taking steps in the Scab Girl's direction. "Everything's okay, Helena. They're not going to hurt you, if you just hold still and let me come up there. Can I do that?"

Helena grunted twice, indicating a yes.

Horton glanced back at Krista for approval.

Krista nodded. "No sudden moves, either of you." She turned to Wicks. "Keep an eye on that bus. There could be more of them."

"Roger that, ma'am," he said, swinging around to the right with his rifle in a firing position.

Krista figured if there were any Scabs hiding in the bus, Horton would act as the bait. Expendable bait, giving them the needed sightlines to take out the threats. Horton included.

Horton was now at the foot of the bus, not far from the double doors hanging open. He brought his head up to speak to Helena. "I know you're worried, but they're just doing their job. They're not going to shoot as long as you do exactly what I say."

Helena's gaze bounced between the rifles pointed at her, huffing as she moved her eyes from Wicks to Krista and back again.

None of that was a surprise to Krista, who considered the cannibal more animal than human. When you're trapped in a compromising crossfire position, your heart is going to race, regardless of what species you are, or what species you used to be. "Bring her down slow."

Horton took another step forward, his hand still carrying the paracord. "Okay, Helena, now you need to put your hands down slowly and keep them at your sides."

When she complied, he continued, walking to the front of the bus and taking position a foot away from the front fender well. "Now scoot toward me, but keep it slow and steady."

Helena hesitated, then grunted once, confirming what Krista already assumed—Horton couldn't deliver. "Thirty seconds, Horton. Then we finish this."

"Just give me a minute," he snarled back. "She's frightened. Can't you see? She'll come in."

"Clock's ticking. Twenty-five seconds."

"Please, Helena. Come down. You can trust me. It's important. Please."

Helena's face softened a moment later, her look of fright dissolving into something else.

Krista wasn't sure what to call the new wide-eyed expression or how to describe it, but it appeared as though the Scab Girl had just fallen in love with Horton. It didn't make any sense, but that didn't change the fact about what happened next.

Helena pushed with her hands at the steel behind her, providing the momentum to slide down the windshield, then the side of the angled hood. She landed in the snow feet first, with her torso wrapped in Horton's arms.

"Secure her!" Krista said, not believing what she just witnessed.

Helena spun toward the bus on her own and put her hands behind her back, allowing Horton to lash them together with the rope, using an over-under multi-knot technique.

When Horton turned her to face Krista, he said, "I hope you believe me now. She was never going to attack. She surrendered, just like I said she would."

"You're lucky she did."

"It's not about luck. It's about who she is and her predicament. You just need to get to know her a little first. She's not like the others."

"Trust me. I know exactly who and what she is."

"No, you don't. She's just a frightened girl who's out here all alone. She doesn't know what's going on or who to trust."

"That goes both ways, Horton. Maybe next time, she needs to not take off and make us hunt her down. She put everyone at risk. Her included."

"I'll give you that, but look at it from her perspective."

"Compassion is not my job. Security is," Krista said, giving Wicks a head nod, telling him to move forward and clear the bus.

Wicks stepped forward, working his way up the steps of the bus and through the open doors. His rifle led the way, sweeping from side to side as he worked his way down the center aisle of the vehicle, checking each seat and crawl space underneath.

When he made it to the rear of the bus, he punched out the nearest window and reported in a loud, clear voice, "Clear, boss. Nothing but junk everywhere. Looks like someone's been living in here."

"Probably her. She must have been looking for something," Horton said. "That's why she came back. It's the only place she feels safe."

"Doesn't matter why. The Scabs obviously know about this place," Krista said, opening her canteen and taking a long drink of water. She closed the lid, then held her hand up and gave the rally command wave to her men on the ridge. "Let's move out before they decide to double back."

CHAPTER 18

"There he is," Dice said to his boss from the driver's seat of their truck, pointing at a trail of dust heading their way.

The broken-down buildings on either side of what used to be the gateway to the Interstate cradled the billowing dust, keeping it trapped inside the brick-lined corridor that ran straight at them. "Looks like he made some changes since the last time we met."

"That's an understatement, even for Craven," Fletcher added.

"I guess they had to eat the horses," Dice said after a half-chuckle, counting a team of twenty Scabs with ropes around their necks, pulling Craven atop an old-fashioned covered wagon. "Scab power. The gift that keeps on giving."

Fletcher laughed. "So much for that trade last year."

"Where does he come up with these ideas?"

"Who knows? But they always seem to work."

Dice knew the one-eyed scientist was eccentric, but using Scabs for horses was a new twist he never saw coming. "I get that he hates modern technology—"

"Except when it suits him," Fletcher said, popping the passenger door open with the handle and swinging it ajar. "Lucky for us, he feels that way."

Dice nodded. "Otherwise, things would be a whole lot different right about now." He, too, opened his door, sliding past the steering wheel and planting his feet in the dirt.

A flap of wind smacked into him from the side, kicking up dust that landed on his face. When it worked its way into his eyes, tears came next, lots of them, filling his vision with squiggly lines of blob and light. He turned his head and wiped the skin around his eyes with his sleeve, focusing more on the corners than the middle.

He knew there would be more dust. It never stopped on days like today, but he couldn't wait for his eyes to rid themselves of the irritant. He needed his sightlines clear for this meet. Especially with a herd of Scabs headed their way. "Maybe we should have brought the repellant?"

"Agreed. Needs to be part of our standard load out from now on," Fletcher said, pulling his sidearm and making sure a round was in the chamber of his semi-automatic. "Eventually, I'd like to see each man assigned a supply."

"If Craven ever gets us the rest," Dice said, checking his pistol as well, seeing a .45 caliber bullet ready to be fired. He put it back in his holster, but kept his hand on the leather, just in case this meet wasn't friendly like all those that came before.

Fletcher was now out of the truck and had moved past his open door, taking a position next to the hood. "Next time, we expect the unexpected. Bring an extra team, too."

Dice agreed. "Seems like he's getting worse all the time."

Fletcher advanced, his voice changing in tone to one of cynicism. "Like they say, the lights are on, but nobody's home."

Dice also took a step forward, matching Fletcher's new position next to the front bumper. "Actually, I think it's more like the lights are flickering on and off, ready to set themselves on fire."

"Gotta love his ingenuity."

Dice agreed. "The man knows how to think outside the box."

"An insane box."

"Or a Scab box."

Fletcher nodded. "But his shit works."

"I'll give him that."

"Just need to start taking precautions until his resourcefulness is no longer of use to us."

"You got it, boss," Dice answered as Craven's old-time convoy arrived after a wide swing around and pull in.

"Well, hello there, ladies," Craven said, dressed entirely in black, except for the red, white, and blue patch he wore over his right eye. "Miss me?"

Fletcher pointed at the man's covered eye. "Feeling a little patriotic, are we?"

"Thought I'd go old school. You know, in a star-spangled banner sort of way," Craven answered, turning his attention to Dice. "You getting taller?"

"Not hardly," Dice said, holding back the words he wanted to say about Craven getting crazier. "But thanks for asking."

Craven lifted his patch, giving Dice a clear view of the empty socket underneath. "Remember, boys and girls, don't play with explosives when you're shitfaced and feeling silly."

Dice laughed, even though he'd heard the same gag a dozen times before. No reason to upset the one-eyed pirate by not going along with his worn-out joke. "Good safety tip, Craven, though I don't think that will ever be a problem."

"That's not what I've heard."

"What do you mean?" Dice asked.

"Lipton's moonshine. One-eighty proof. Impressive."

"How did you hear about that?" Fletcher asked.

"Oh, a little birdie told me," Craven said, tying the leather leads controlling the Scab team to a curved hunk of metal under his seat. The man rose to his feet, then climbed to the ground, plopping his feet in the dirt.

"Tired of horses?" Fletcher asked.

"Actually, trying something new," Craven replied, motioning to the team of Scabs standing in a loose huddle. "They eat less and pull almost as hard."

"Except it takes five times as many," Dice said.

"True, but got an endless supply. Almost."

Fletcher stepped forward and shook Craven's hand. "Breeders working overtime, I take it?"

"What's left of them."

"Is there a problem?"

"Nothing I can't handle."

"Seriously, if there's something we should know about, now's the time," Fletcher said.

"Got it under control, Fletch. Just a little setback, that's all." Craven yanked on his waistline, pulling up his sagging pants. "You guys wanted to meet, so let's get on with it."

"It's time for your services again," Fletcher said.

"How many?"

"Couple hundred ought to do it."

"We'll make sure the targets are easy marks," Dice added. "Keep your losses down."

"When?"

"Soon," Fletcher said. "We'll know more after we meet with our source and firm up our plans. Gotta make it all seem natural, though. That'll be key. Dice will coordinate, since he will be leading the mission."

Craven raised one eyebrow, leaning back a bit on his hips. "It's going to cost you boys."

Fletcher's voice dropped in tone. "I figured as much. Name your price."

"Well, with the Trading Post out of commission, I'm going to need to boost the meat supply some other way."

"Damn it, I was right," Dice said, shooting a look at Fletcher. "I figured that's what happened to the horses."

"And the stragglers Heston didn't want," Fletcher added.

Craven paused. "True on both counts. Some things can't be helped, not when my army has to eat."

Dice couldn't hold the words back. "Something other than themselves."

"You are correct, my red-haired friend. At some point though, that becomes counterproductive. In the end, it was a simple choice. Those fifteen-hundred-pound slabs of horse went a long way."

A memory of the Scab attack on the Trading Post flashed in Dice's mind, filling his thoughts with images of blood and guts.

Fletcher spoke next. "The indigent supply will resume again, once we get the Trading Post back up and running. Plus, you can keep whatever bounty remains from the new mission."

Craven paused before he spoke. "Assuming you're able to make the targets easy marks, as you say."

"Won't be a problem," Fletcher replied.

"At least you won't have to deal with Heston anymore," Dice said. "Acquisition will be a snap now. So will delivery."

Craven seemed to like those statements, his eyes perking up. "I take it things went well?"

"Perfectly."

"And your boss?"

"No longer an issue," Fletcher said.

"Edison took it in the shorts, too. Well, the neck actually, but you know what I mean," Dice said.

A thin smile grew on Craven's lips. "Sounds like we've cleared the deck—precisely how you wanted it. Should be smooth sailing going forward."

"As long as your prices don't skyrocket," Dice said.

"I think we can work something out. Just need to know when and where and I'll take care of my end."

"As will we," Dice said, turning his gaze to Fletcher.

Fletcher continued. "Like I said before, as soon as our source comes through, we'll let you know the details. After that, we'll need a much bigger army in a day or two for Phase Two."

"Deal," Craven said, shaking Fletcher's hand again. "Though there is one thing."

"What?"

"My most prized breeder."

"What happened?" Fletcher asked.

"She escaped. You wouldn't have happened to have seen her, would you? She's this little blonde with crazy hair and a skanky body full of whip marks. Can't miss her."

"No. Not that I recall," Fletcher said before looking at Dice.

Dice shrugged. "Haven't seen her."

"Are you sure?"

Fletcher nodded. "Positive. I think we'd remember something like that."

"How'd she escape?" Dice asked.

"Don't know, but she's not the first one."

Fletcher shook his head and threw out his hands. "You've lost others?"

"Yep."

"How many?"

"Seven."

"Will that change things?"

"No. Got plenty more in the pipeline. Like I said, just a little setback."

"What do you need from us?"

"If you find her, bring her back to me."

"Alive, I take it."

Craven nodded. "But you can have some fun with her first, if you'd like. A little reward for your help. Ain't much to her but she's a fertile little thing and that ass of hers is world class."

"For a flesh-eater and all," Dice said. "Assuming you can get past the whole missing nose thing."

"That has its uses, too," Craven said with a confident tone in his voice.

"We'll keep an eye out," Fletcher said.

CHAPTER 19

"Slow down. There's a sharp curve coming up," Krista said to Wicks as the man turned the steering wheel a few degrees to the right.

"Sorry, boss," Wicks said, pulling his foot off the gas. "Adjusting speed."

"Keep the center line through the next section and watch that damn crater on the left. I don't want to lose another tire like last time."

"Roger that," Wicks said, angling the truck around the bend. He worked the wheel back and forth to dodge a parade of abandoned cars on the road, keeping an even distance from each one. The thick volcanic ash after The Event rendered them useless after suffocating their engines, leaving nothing but relics behind.

The old horse track was to the right, its roof caved in near the middle. Its parking lot was also full of combustion engine junk, like the roadway. A few of them were old semis, the climate taking a toll on their proud stenciling. All that remained of the lettering on one of trailers was a star icon and the word "mart" after it.

"We stop for nothing until we're back at the base," Krista said. "Is that clear? I want to beat sundown this time."

"Crystal. Stopping for nothing, boss," he said after swinging wide to miss the crater she warned him about. He pressed on the accelerator to resume at a speed somewhat less than before.

The transport had made good time thus far, thanks to the weather cooperating, even though the sky had filled with ominous-looking clouds the last hour and the wind had resumed its wail.

The last thing you want when hauling a couple of prisoners through an uncontrolled sector is to get stuck in the mud or slide off the road due to excessive speed or some other negligence. More so with the light fading, leaving more shadows than normal to cover with a light fire team, and a nightly freeze sure to wreak havoc.

Horton and his pet had behaved themselves thus far, both of them blindfolded and restrained in the back. Her overwatch team had them covered.

Krista planned to personally oversee the unloading of the prisoners and their delivery to the brig this time. They'd been fortunate to capture the

Scab Girl once. She didn't want to tempt fate with another search and detain of the same target.

Something in her gut nagged at her that the capture had gone a little too smoothly, though Horton did struggle to talk the girl down from the bus. Krista knew it was possible she was simply paranoid about the whole thing, but she knew better than to make assumptions about anything that happened in the field.

Regardless, there was something off about the entire encounter. Yet Krista couldn't pinpoint what it was. It felt like the answer was just out of reach in her mind, hiding in one of the dark spaces, tucked behind a mountain of doubt and suspicion.

At least the prisoners were secure and the return to the silo was well underway. Her only problem at the moment was her bladder. It was full and building pressure with each roll of the tires.

It felt like a volcano ready to blow—a whole string of them—supervolcano like. It was all she could do to sit upright in the passenger seat without crossing her legs.

Another thirty minutes went by before she couldn't stand it anymore. Just ahead was an overpass, its four-lane blacktop caved in on the left side. Rebar hung from the interior support structure, with chunks of cement attached to some of their ends.

Krista craned her neck and checked the sky. The clouds were still building and getting darker. She pointed to the right side of the structure coming up fast. "Stop under there. It's time to find a bush somewhere before the sky opens up."

"What about the others?" Wicks said. "Been a long ride for everyone."

"You, too?"

"And then some, boss."

"All right. Everyone can take five. But we do so in pairs. Stay sharp, Wicks. We don't want a repeat of what we just went through."

Wicks pulled to the side of the roadway and slid the truck under what remained of the elevated roadway.

Once the transmission was in park, Krista slid out of the truck and walked to the tailgate, grimacing to keep her bladder in check.

The guard who'd covered their six during the capture of the Scab Girl stuck his head out from under the tarp first. "Problem, ma'am?"

"Gotta take a leak. Wicks and I are going first. You three, cover the prisoners."

"Ten-four."

"Do not take your eyes off them for a second. Understood?"

"Eyes-on, boss. Got it."

"If they give you any trouble, shoot them."

"Gladly, ma'am."

"If anyone else needs to use the head, they can go next."

The man nodded, but didn't respond.

"We'll be back in two shakes," Krista said, swinging around to the driver's side of the vehicle where Wicks was standing, scanning the countryside through the optics on his rifle.

She waited until he finished his sweep. "Anything?"

"All clear."

Krista ran a visual check of the area beyond the overpass, looking for possible squat and drop locations.

A flat area with scores of trees was on the left—dead trees, remnants of what she assumed was an orange tree orchard. It was about twenty yards below grade with a gentle slope leading from the highway to the first row of trees.

The other side of the highway featured a dilapidated wooden structure about the size of convenience store, with train tracks running in front of it.

Weeds littered the ground between the rails, though none of them were green in color—more of a brownish-gray. Sticks mostly, but there may have been some struggling to push out a new crop of leaves.

The building must have been part of an old train depot, possibly the last stop for vacationers heading to the big city up north. Its walls used to be white, though there wasn't much of the paint still holding onto the wood, most of it peeling in streaks of chunky flakes.

What stuck out the most were the windows. They were intact. At least those she could see from her position. An oddity for sure. Only the door facing the tracks was missing.

Krista pointed at the orchard. "Looks promising over there. Let's move out."

A few minutes later, Wicks walked six rows deep into the tree line before running a quick security check. When he was done, he waved her ahead.

Krista joined him, then leaned her rifle against the closest tree to free her hands in preparation for taking care of business.

Wicks moved to the south, selecting a position two rows away with his back to her.

When she was finished, she closed her pants and laced the camo belt back into place, then adjusted her tactical vest, making sure everything was in its proper place and secure.

She picked up her rifle and put two fingers into her mouth, whistling at Wicks.

He spun his head.

She waved for him to proceed.

He nodded, keeping his back to her. It only took seconds for his hands to find their way down to his fly, then his spine arched, indicating he was enjoying his relief. Even a man of his size could only hold it so long, leaving no choice but to stop and empty the tank.

If Krista remembered right, Wicks preferred to call it *splashing the trash*, though she didn't understand the meaning behind those words. It must have been a man thing, she decided.

She kept the sights on her weapon active, sweeping the area from one side to the other, looking for movement as her mind slipped into analytical mode.

Over the years, she'd passed through this area countless times, but she didn't remember there ever being an encounter with Frost's men or the Scabs. In fact, this might have been the most peaceful stretch of the entire highway, if she had to classify it into one category or another.

Sure, it was dozens of miles from Frost's territory, so that explained part of it. However, the Scabs didn't claim a specific zone, roaming to eat wherever they could find accessible meat.

Those facts told her there was something unique about this segment of roadway—something that was keeping them away. Assuming, of course, it wasn't a random happenstance to begin with.

Perhaps it was a unique feature of the terrain?

Or the smell of the decaying vegetation?

Maybe it had something to do with the Earth's magnetic lines and how they may have been charging the steel tracks?

Or some other natural repellant?

When her mind focused on the word "repellant," a vision flashed in her head, taking her back in time to the Trading Post ambush.

The scene showed her Fletcher using his unknown compound to keep them safe. Everyone except Frost and Edison, of course, or a list of others from all sides. Fletcher had acted as if it were a new invention, possibly experimental in nature.

Just then, Wicks finished *splashing the trash* before bouncing on his heels twice, then assembling his pants. He spun and marched in her direction, joining her position with his rifle in hand. "Damn, that might have been a new world record."

She laughed, nodding for him to follow her back to the truck. "When we get back to camp, I want you to assemble a team and get ready to go meet with Fletcher."

"Is that today already?"

"No, but I think we missed something."

When he gave her a curious look, she remembered he wasn't part of their team during that meet. "Oh, that's right, you were on suspension."

"My mistake, ma'am. Won't happen again."

"Not what I meant," Krista said. "He had some kind of repellent that kept the Scabs off us."

"Like bug spray?"

She nodded. "Except it didn't have that weird smell. But it worked. For most of us, anyway. I should have asked him more about it, but I was distracted with everything going on."

"It happens, boss."

"That's no excuse, Wicks. Situational awareness is key to keeping everyone safe. That can never be compromised, no matter how bad things get."

"Roger that," Wicks said, taking a few more steps in tandem with her. "I guess everyone is working on new tech these days. Even Frost."

She nodded. "Probably thanks to that Lipton guy in the brig."

"Maybe an interrogation is in order? See what else they might be making over there."

"I agree. Good idea."

"Now that Edison's no longer in charge, will we be able to use more effective measures? Or will they still keep us in check, making us hug everyone to death?"

"Well, soldier, that'll be up to Summer. She's in charge now."

"Excuse me for saying so, boss, but that's fucked. You earned that post."

The man was right, even though she could never agree out loud. "I appreciate the support, Wicks, but the rules are the rules."

"I'm not sure everyone realizes that Summer is not what she appears to be. I know firsthand. She totally jacked me and everyone bought it."

"I hear what you're saying, but we both know there was plenty of blame to go around."

"That doesn't change the fact that she's a terrible choice. Especially if we have to continue all the diplomatic, wishy-washy crap. We need to get tough before it's too late."

Krista couldn't argue his point because he was right. But regardless, it was time to rein in her man, while still supporting him and his feedback. "We'll see how it goes, but for now, Summer is the boss and we follow her orders. Is that clear?"

"Yes, ma'am."

Before their next step, a string of gunshots rang out.

POP! POP! POP!

Krista stopped in her tracks and took a defensive posture in a low-profile crouch. Wicks did the same, both of them listening for direction and distance.

When another barrage ripped through the air, Krista realized it was coming from dead ahead—on the highway—up by the transport. There weren't any indications that the rounds were being fired in their direction, but then again, they were well below grade.

"They must have escaped again," Wicks said in a whisper, his rifle high and tight against his shoulder.

"Shit," Krista snapped, getting to her feet as she broke into a sprint, keeping low. She could hear the clatter of Wicks' equipment only a few steps behind.

When her ears rang with more bursts of gunfire, she figured all of her men were now engaged, firing at will, attempting to take down Horton and the Scab Girl. "I can't believe they let them escape. Again."

The rise in terrain came quickly to her feet, causing her to slow and creep forward, in case her assumptions were wrong about what was happening ahead.

The crest of the hill brought not only the highway into view, but a scene of carnage she never expected. Scabs were everywhere, maybe fifty of them, their teeth showing and mouths snarling. Her men had dug in by the transport under the overpass, emptying their magazines at the targets moving in a circle around them.

A number of Scabs had been hit, their bodies lying motionless on the cement. A few were twisted into a heap, with limbs missing and heads exploded, their parts scattered like castoffs on a butcher shop's floor.

"We need to help them," Wicks said, bringing his rifle up after arriving in a plop next to her on the left.

"Stand down, Wicks," she said. "We'll hit our own if we fire now."

"We have to do something. We can't just leave them out there. They're going to run out of ammo."

Krista took a moment to think, running through a number of scenarios that might work. One of the choices worked itself to the top of the list. "What we need is a diversion. Draw them away."

"Divide and conquer," Wicks added, his eyes indicating he understood where she was going with her plan.

Krista pointed to the nearest side of the broken-down overpass, specifically at the hanging rebar with rubble below it. It looked like one of the cement chunks on the end of the exposed rebar was within reach. "Do you think you can get to that rebar and climb up?"

Wicks paused for a beat, his eyes running a check of the overpass. "Yeah, I think so."

"I'll draw them out so you can pick them off."

Wicks nodded.

Krista continued, "But verify your targets. And for my sake, don't miss."

"I won't."

Krista gave him her extra magazines. "Go! Now! There isn't much time."

He stuffed two into his vest, then tried to give two of them back. "You might need these."

She shook her head. "If I have to change mags, I'm dead already. It'll be up to you to keep them off me."

Wicks held his stare, but didn't respond.

"Go! That's an order!" she said, shooting him her most commanding look.

Wicks pulled the ammo back, then climbed to his feet and swung around to the right, sprinting faster than a man of his size should have been able to run. His path took him to the backside of the overpass, using it as cover until he made it to the corner. He held for a beat, then made a dash for the rebar, grabbing onto the hanging chunk of cement and pulling himself up.

When he made it to the roadway above and got into position, she pressed to her feet, then broke into the open, praying her men by the truck would see her in time and not draw down in her direction. It wasn't the best plan, but it was all she had.

"Hey you!" she screamed, shooting her rifle into the air, using a series of single trigger pulls. The barrage caught the attention of the Scabs, bringing their eyes around in a collective motion. She stopped firing and yelled, "I'm over here, you freaks!"

About half the Scabs broke off and came at her. She backpedaled, firing one round at a time, making sure each trigger pull found a target.

After she'd hit four in the head, Wicks joined the fight, taking down Scab after Scab, plinking them like target practice from his elevated position. Heads, shoulders, and legs blew apart, some even happened together on a single shot as the high-velocity rounds tore through more than one rail-thin cannibal.

Just then, a number of Scabs stopped their pursuit and turned to face Wicks' position. The rest kept advancing toward her.

Krista yelled again, wanting all of them to keep their attention on her. "Come on, you fuckers, I'm right here. Come and get me!"

Before the next breath came to her lungs, the unexpected happened—the Scab Girl flew out of the back of the transport and ran into the open, taking a direct path to the horde attacking. One of her overwatch team also climbed down from the tailgate, his hand holding a Ka-bar knife.

Helena flew onto the back of one of the male Scabs and began tearing into his neck from behind. Her hands and teeth worked in unison as she ripped his spine into bloody chunks.

Krista continued backstepping and shooting a round at a time, while Wicks kept firing, taking out more Scabs from his perch.

When Krista looked back at the truck, she saw Helena on another Scab's back, ripping and shredding him to pieces like the first.

One of the other Scabs standing close to Helena turned and went for her leg as she continued her melee on Scab number two.

Krista stopped her retreat and brought her rifle up to take out the Scab who'd grabbed onto Helena's leg. Before Krista could pull the trigger, the Scab's head exploded. The blood spray and subsequent body fall indicated the shot came from her men protecting the truck.

Krista began moving in reverse again, bringing her rifle back to the gang coming at her, shooting another one in the head, landing the shot just under the hole in the middle of his face and above the lips.

Wicks wasn't done either, taking down more of the Scabs with head and neck shots, mowing them down like cannon fodder. The malnourished flesh of the damned was no match for his heavy-grained .302 caliber rounds.

When Krista turned her attention back to Helena, she saw Horton helping her off the ground. The two of them then stood together and fought more of the attackers, his hand armed with a knife.

The gunfight went on for another few minutes, until all the Scabs were down.

Wicks left his overwatch position and joined Krista, the two of them advancing on the truck, shooting anything that was still alive on the ground.

"You guys all right?" Krista asked her men protecting the truck when she arrived.

"All good, boss."

Horton and Helena were there, too. Both of them nodded, but didn't respond.

"Good thing they didn't bring more," Wicks said, releasing the magazine from the lower receiver of his rifle. His eyes studied the rounds inside. "Almost black on ammo."

Krista brought her eyes around, looking at her team. "Who decided it was okay to cut them loose?"

One of her men stepped forward. "I did, ma'am."

"Actually, it was my idea," Horton said. "Don't blame him."

"Well, soldier?" Krista said to the member of her team claiming responsibility.

"Seemed like the right thing to do. I wasn't sure we could've stopped them all, not until you and Wicks returned. Figured there was nothing to lose at that point."

Krista took a few moments to chew on the facts. She hated the idea that any of her men disobeyed her orders, but she understood his position. Obviously, he was right, given the outcome.

"I backed his decision, boss," another one of her troops said, after taking a firm step forward.

It was gratifying to see her team unified, but it didn't change what happened. "You both disobeyed a direct order. There will have to be repercussions. I can't let it go."

"Understood," the men responded in unison.

Krista looked at Horton, holding for a beat before she spoke. "Thanks for the assist."

Horton peered at Helena, then back at Krista. "I didn't do it alone."

Krista nodded at the girl, never thinking she'd ever thank a cannibal for anything. "That was some good work out there, young lady. Well done."

Helena didn't respond, only blinking a stare, her chest heaving, taking in air rapidly.

One of Krista's other guards went to Helena with a bundle of paracord in hand, preparing to restrain her once again.

Krista stopped him with an arm bar, then turned to Horton. "Tell me this isn't necessary."

"It's not. We're all on the same side here."

Krista took a few beats to consider his body language and the tone of the man's response as she pondered the situation.

Security protocols demanded that she have both restrained for the trip back to Nirvana. They should not be trusted solely based on the fact that they fought alongside her men to repel the enemy, risking their own lives in the process. That was the right conclusion—on paper at least. However, her heart was telling her something different. And her gut, too. "All right, but I still have to assign my guards."

"I would expect nothing less," Horton said, taking Helena by the elbow and ushering her to the back of the truck. They hopped in and took a seat near the front.

"Keep an eye on them," Krista said to her men only a moment before a brilliant crack of lightning shot across the sky. It rippled in a hundred directions all at once, like the veins in a heart. When the instant, bone-rattling clap of thunder followed, everyone flinched, then covered their heads.

Krista looked at Wicks after her ears stopped ringing. She held up a stiff index finger. "If I ever tell you to stop again to piss in an uncontrolled sector, I want you to pull out your .45 and shoot me in the head."

CHAPTER 20

Summer walked with a heavy heart into Morse's lab and pointed to the spot on the floor where she wanted Sergeant Barkley to lie down and snapped her fingers.

The dog responded to her suggestion, slinging his front legs out first, then dropping his hind end down in a gingerly manner.

She rubbed the fur under his collar with fervor. "Good boy. You rest now."

Summer went to the chair behind Morse's work desk and sat down. She scooted forward on the seat with an arched back and a determined chin, then tucked her legs under and crossed them.

If she didn't know better, she would have felt as though she'd been asked to attend an important meeting. One that had been called to deal with a crisis head-on.

In some strange manner, both of those points were true. This was a meeting with the ghosts of two men she'd just lost. And the crisis was about her taking over as the head of Nirvana. So much had changed so quickly, she wasn't sure what to do first.

She kept her eyes forward as she put her hands together on the desk, then laced her fingers together, never moving the rest of her body except for the occasional blink of her eyelids.

The tears racing down her cheeks were to be expected. So was the tightness pressing on her chest. However, what she didn't expect was the overwhelming need to sit motionless in an office filled with stale air and unfinished experiments.

Perhaps it was sign of respect for a brilliant man who couldn't sit still, despite his failing body, always working on something important.

Morse had once called it Mission Critical Duty, a phase he'd coined back when Summer had first met him.

It was the type of duty he hoped would make the lives of those around him better. Duty that might lessen the pain and suffering of the cherished few who called Nirvana home. Duty that took his life, consuming what few hours and days he had remaining.

The man had many courses to choose from when he learned about his terminal cancer. And what did he do? He chose the most selfless route—

preferring to do for others, regardless of what little time he had left.

Another minute marched by, then ten more came and went, all while Summer held her statuesque pose, her mind turning in on itself, drifting deeper in thought as she cried for her lost friend.

She had no idea why she'd decided to sit alone in this room and do so in such an uncomfortable position. Some might think it was punishment for the time she'd wasted with him, not knowing that any one of those moments might be the last she'd ever share with him.

When her silent tribute reached thirty minutes, Summer took a deep breath and swallowed the pain whole. It wasn't easy, but she found the strength to turn off the tears and wipe the wetness away with her sleeve.

When she brought her eyes down, she noticed at least a hundred scratches across the surface—each one of them a faint reminder of a project long since forgotten.

Some of those ventures she'd been a part of, while others were conducted in secret, all of it exactly how Morse preferred it—both shared and private, depending on his mood at the time. Or, perhaps, his intentions at the time.

Those two reasons may have been the same thing, given who Morse was and how he lived his life. He was a simple man and a diligent observer, not just of science and fact, but of people, too. A man she'd miss more than words could ever express.

Summer sniffed twice, then uncoiled her hands to put her palms flat against the marred surface. The cold emptiness of the desktop eased into her skin, acting as a cruel reminder of what life was like in a frozen world after The Event.

She closed her eyes and let her mind conjure a vision of the two of them working together at that same desk. It was a scene from the last time she was in his lab, discussing his latest project and her most recent Seeker Mission.

They'd laughed together without a care in the world, all the while conversing like normal people, if that term meant anything anymore.

Had she known he was terminally ill, she would have made the time they had together more meaningful, before he was gone for good.

Whether it would have been an extra hug, a second kiss on the cheek, or a firm hold of his hand, it didn't matter. Something would have better than nothing. Something other than the complete selfishness she'd let consume her. The same went for

Edison too—both of her favorite men taken from her life far too soon.

Another vision flashed in her mind. This time it showed Morse's face opening his eyes right before he died and whispering the words *Red radio thirty-five* to Liz.

Liz had called the phrase nothing more than random gibberish. But Summer didn't think it was nothing. Morse always had a plan or something he wanted to teach.

Summer looked at the dog on the floor. "It has to mean something, boy. We just need to figure out what."

When her eyes came back up, she let them drift to the shortwave transmitter sitting on the corner of the worktable to her right. She got up and went to it, standing with her hands on her hips.

Morse's plan was to fix the device, then convince Edison to start making calls to see if anyone else was around. Morse seemed concerned that they shouldn't remain cut off from the rest of the planet, assuming there was a rest of the planet.

The microphone wasn't attached to the radio, which was normal. Morse kept it in the file cabinet along the back wall, not wanting to jinx anything. That was a term he'd used more than once, tipping his hat to superstition instead of being guided by the sanctity of logic.

Summer shook her head. "So much for not jinxing it."

She spun around and walked to the cabinet behind her, not far from a grease board where Morse had written a cluster of calculations in red marker ink, with the letters E. O. D. under them.

Summer opened the drawer where he kept the mic and pulled it out, having to move a white envelope and a frayed extension cord out of the way to grab it. She shut the drawer, then spun and went back to the radio, taking a seat in the chair in front of it.

A second later, the microphone was plugged into the port with a snapping click of its end. She flipped the power button on and waited for the device to roar to life with its lights blinking and cooling fan whirring.

She brought the microphone up to her mouth and was about to press the transmit button, but stopped when her mind filled with a memory of Morse preaching the words, "Patience is a virtue in all things we do."

Summer moved the mic away from her lips and put it on the worktable, then took her hands away, laying them in her lap as she stared at its cord leading to the radio. "Not until it's fixed and ready to go," she muttered, channeling something Morse had said. She peered at Sergeant Barkley. "Right, boy? We wait. When it's ready, we make the call. Not a moment before."

The dog let out a long, guttural moan that kept changing in pitch, his jaw moving as if he were trying to say something.

"Exactly," she said, laughing at the strange antics of her four-legged friend. "We just need to find someone who can fix this thing."

The only person she knew capable of such a feat was the man in the brig—Doctor Lipton. He was a total asshole, but apparently very smart. At least Lipton himself thought so, and he never let anyone forget it. "We might be able to convince him to help," she told the dog. "But Krista isn't going to allow it. I guess I'll have to make it an order."

Barkley made another one of his extended moans, this time moving his head up and down along with his jaw.

She grinned. "I knew you'd understand. You always do." Before she blinked again, a brilliant memory flash took over her mind, bringing a new idea with it.

"Hey, wait a minute," she snarked before spinning around and looking at the grease board directly behind her—the one not far from the cabinet where the microphone had been stored.

The board was covered in mathematical equations—equations written in marker ink—red marker ink, to be exact, with the number 35 circled at the bottom.

"Holy shit! Red radio thirty-five," she snapped, realizing the words weren't random gibberish after all. "That's what he meant. Red calculations with the number 35. Plus, the radio. They must all be connected somehow."

Summer flew out of the chair and went back to the file cabinet drawer. When she opened it, she saw the white envelope again, now tucked under the frayed extension cord, both of them pushed to the side where she'd moved them to grab the mic.

She dug past the cord and snatched the envelope, then pulled it out and turned it over to discover that it was sealed. There were also two letters printed on the back in blue ink—an *S* and an *L*.

Her initials.

Summer tore her finger into the adhesive strip, prying one end of it loose, then ripped the back of the envelope open with a pull of her hand.

Inside was a piece of white paper that had been tucked into itself using thirds. She opened the tri-fold to see a letter inside. The page was covered with fancy writing, the kind that was filled with loops and curls that connected each word together.

"Shit," she said, realizing she had no idea what it said since the schools had stopped teaching longhand well before she attended grade school. A letter written in cursive might as well have been in Russian.

Summer peered over at Sergeant Barkley and held the letter up. "You can probably read this better than me."

The dog moaned, changing the tone of his response along with the position of his jaw to emphasize something.

"Why would he do this to me? He had to know I couldn't read it."

CHAPTER 21

Krista waited for Wicks to open the cell door to the brig before she pushed Helena into the bar-lined space. The extra force made the cannibal take an extra-long step for balance. "Let's see if you can behave yourself for once."

"You don't have to do this," Horton said, standing next to Krista, his hands no longer bound and his face free of the blindfold.

"Oh yes, she does," Lipton said from the cell next door. "You can see it in her face."

Krista nodded. "He's right. We can't have a Scab running around this facility. There'd be chaos."

Horton's face lit up red, his upper lip tucked under. "Jesus Christ! What does she have to do to prove herself? I told you, she's not who you think she is."

Krista grabbed Horton by the collar. "You might want to check the attitude, mister. Otherwise, you'll be in there with her."

"With all due respect, ma'am, shouldn't he be anyway?" Wicks said, pushing the cell door closed with a clang before locking it with a rattle of his keychain.

"Misery loves company," Lipton snarked with a snide look on his mug.

Krista ignored Lipton's remark, keeping her focus on Wicks. "Be sure the girl gets an extra blanket and something to eat. But no meat. Don't want her getting any ideas."

"Right away, chief," Wicks said, handing the keys to Krista, then turning and heading toward the door to the brig.

"Hey, Mr. No-Neck, why don't you bring me one of those almond sandwiches while you're at it? With extra mayo and some of those little sprouts I like," Lipton said, his face covered in a full-on grin.

Wicks never acknowledged Lipton's request, continuing his march through the door and out of sight.

Horton put a hand on Krista's elbow, turning her a few degrees. "We can't just leave Helena in there all alone."

Krista pulled away in a twist, aiming her disdain at his hand for touching her without permission. "Sure we can."

"Then put me in there with her."

Krista flashed a raised eyebrow. "Are you sure that's really what you want? You just earned my trust, albeit barely."

Horton threw up his hands. "Can't you see she's scared?"

Krista peered at Helena, seeing the girl sitting on the center of the cot with her arms wrapped around her knees and pulled in close to her chest.

Helena brought her head up from its tucked position and made eye contact.

Krista studied the look in the girl's eyes, seeing only the feral display of a caged animal. An animal who was used to surviving alone. "She'll be fine. I think she's already getting used to it."

"Open the door! Right now!" Horton snapped, his tone firm and short.

"So now you're giving me orders? Really?"

"If she's going to be a prisoner, so will I."

Krista paused for a beat, then brought the keys up and slid one of them into the keyway of the door. She turned it. "If you insist." She swung the entrance open, then held out an open hand and invited him to proceed with a wave.

Horton walked in and took a seat next to Helena, who was now rocking forward and back with her eyes focused in a long stare. Horton wrapped his arm around the girl and pulled her close, changing the angle of her rocking.

"Look at that," Lipton said, breaking into a familiar melody as he sang the words, "Two lovebirds sitting in a tree—"

Krista took out her knife and rapped the handle on the bars next to Lipton's head. "Quiet!"

Lipton took a step back, stopping his cadence as Zimmer walked into the brig. The gray-haired man with the handlebar mustache stopped his feet before the ping from the metal ran out of steam.

"What did I miss?" Zimmer asked.

Krista closed the door to Helena's cell and pointed at Lipton. "Just corralling a little attitude."

"So what you're saying is same shit, different day."

"Roger that," Krista said. "Do you need something?"

"A little chat, if you have a minute?"

Krista ran a visual check of the occupied cells, taking a moment to appreciate her achievements today. At least the ones that outweighed the poor decisions she'd made. "Sure, I think things are under control here."

Krista followed Zimmer into the hallway outside, closing the door behind her. "What's up?"

"In case you haven't heard, Morse didn't make it."

Krista's shoulders slumped as a wave of depression settled in. She took in an extra few breaths, needing to collect herself. "When?"

"Not long after you left."

"How's Summer taking it?"

"Not well, from what I hear. She's pretty broken up. Then again, nobody I talked to has seen her since, so who knows."

"Shit."

"Not exactly the kind of response Nirvana needs from its new leader."

"Those two were pretty close."

"I get that, but a leader has to be strong in a time of crisis. No matter who they lose on their watch."

"Do you know if Liz had a talk with her first, or did Summer find out the hard way?"

"I think they talked, not that it should matter."

Krista paused a few beats to visualize the trauma that Summer must have gone through when she heard the news about Morse.

If Summer was anything like her, and that was a stretch when discussing most topics, then she'd need something to take her mind off the heartache. Busy hands and busy minds help keep the grief from consuming all you are. "Did Summer address the camp while I was gone?"

"No. Like I said, she just went AWOL."

"Did anyone check her quarters? She likes to hide there when things get rough."

"I did. No sign of her."

Krista paused for a few seconds, scanning her memories. This wasn't the first time the girl had gone off the grid, nor was it the first time Krista had to conduct a search for her. "I know a few spots where she might be. I'll see if I can find her."

Zimmer shook his head, looking disappointed, before he spoke again. "To offer support to someone who shouldn't need it?"

"That's the plan."

Zimmer nodded, though it looked more involuntary than a sign of agreement. His eyes darted left and right for a few moments before he spoke again. "There is another way you could handle it."

"Yeah, what's that?"

"Just let her flail away in some dark hole somewhere, then ask for a replacement vote when

Nirvana starts to fail without its newly-crowned leader. The way's she's going, she'll make it easy."

"I'd rather play this straight, Rod, if you don't mind. Got to give the girl a chance."

"Normally yes, but there's more at stake here than just her feelings."

"I agree. But let me go have a chat with her. I'm sure I can get things back on track."

"I hope you realize you're missing a golden opportunity here, if you know what I mean."

"I know full well what you mean."

"Then?"

"Then nothing," Krista said with confidence, slapping the man on the back. "Thanks for the update. I'll take it from here."

Krista brought her eyes around to Wicks, who had just entered the far end of the corridor and was walking her way with a blanket and a bowl of food in his hands.

CHAPTER 22

Summer knocked on the door to Liz's quarters and waited for a response with Sergeant Barkley at her feet. The golden shepherd had made tremendous improvement, getting stronger and nimbler with each passing hour, though he still needed a bath. Maybe two of them—the stench was now mutating into its own lifeform.

She didn't know if the dog's lack of understanding about how badly he was hurt had actually helped in his recovery or not, but she was starting to think it had.

If you know you are supposed to take much longer to heal, the power of that suggestion might actually cause that exact thing to happen. That would also mean not knowing how badly you are injured would bring about the opposite.

Her theories seemed logical; then again, maybe the canine was just a wonder mutt, built to take a beating and never slow down. Either way, she was happy her new friend was feeling better.

When Summer didn't get a response from the doctor, she knocked again, only this time twice as hard. "Hey Liz. It's me, Summer. You in there? I need to speak to you for a minute."

"Hang on," Liz said from inside, her tone heavy and terse.

Summer leaned in and listened to the sounds coming from the other side of the door. First there was a clap of wood, like a door slamming. Maybe it was a drawer closing—no way to know for sure. Then the rustle of metal on metal landed on her ears. It was lightly pitched and included several pinging sounds.

When Summer heard footsteps stacked together and getting louder, she straightened up only a split second before the door opened.

"Sorry about that," Liz said in a breathy voice, greeting Summer with an ankle-length robe wrapped around her body. Her hair was a mess and she wasn't wearing her glasses.

Summer stumbled over the words as they arrived on her tongue, hoping Liz didn't detect that she'd been eavesdropping. "Uh, sorry, did I catch you at a bad time?"

"No, just getting cleaned up. Haven't had a chance until now."

Summer looked down at the dog, then rubbed his back with a quick scrub of her fingers. "Need to do the same with him. Whew! Getting a little ripe."

"Yes, I noticed."

Summer smirked, wondering if she should issue another apology for bringing the dog along. She decided against it. Might make her sound weak in front of her friend. "Anyway, I checked medical first but you weren't there, so I thought I'd try here. Sorry for the intrusion."

"It's fine, Summer," Liz said. "What did you want to speak to me about?"

Summer held up the tri-fold piece of paper she'd found in Morse's lab. "I think I know what *Red radio thirty-five* means."

Liz paused for a moment, then turned sideways and held out her hand. "The place is a bit of mess, but come on in."

After Liz found a seat, Summer stood in front of her and unfolded the paper. "I found this hidden in his lab. The envelope had my initials on it, so I'm pretty sure Morse left this for me."

"What does it say?"

"See, that's the thing. I think it's written in longhand and they never taught us that in school, you know, before The Event," Summer gave the letter to Liz. "Can you read it for me?"

The doc took a good two minutes to peruse the words, then she stopped and wiped her cheeks, whisking away the tears that had found their way down her skin. "I don't think I've ever read anything more beautiful in my entire life."

Summer wanted to cry, too, even though she had no idea why, other than the feeling in her chest. "What does it say?"

Liz cleared her throat. "Let me read it you. But you might want to sit down first. It's rather long."

Summer took the chair next to Liz, keeping her hands on her knees. The wetness of her palms seemed to be escalating, making her squeeze the cloth covering her knees.

Liz looked at Summer for a moment and smiled, then peered down at the page and started reading the words aloud:

My Dearest Summer,

If you are reading this, it means my illness finally got the better of me. I'm sorry I didn't tell you about my condition, but the last thing I wanted was anyone's sympathy.

By the way, Stuart was never told. Neither were Krista and the rest of The Committee. I swore Liz to secrecy, so don't blame her or anyone else for not telling you. She was only doing her job and keeping my confidence.

This was my decision and mine alone. I hope you can respect that.

You've been a wonderful friend over the years and I don't want to leave this world without telling you how special you are. You mean the world to me.

You are a truly amazing young lady and I think you have a bright future ahead of you, even in this God-forsaken world of ours.

Please listen to Stuart and follow his advice. He loves you as much as I do and only wants the best for you. As do I.

The same goes for guidance you will receive from Liz, and even Krista. I know you two don't get along as well as I would have hoped, but you can always change the nature of things.

Nothing is ever set in stone. Nothing. Remember that. There are always options. Always remedies. You only have to make the conscious decision to look for them and then take action.

One of the things I've learned over my lifetime is that people can change, as can relationships. They evolve and grow, just like everything else on this planet. It starts with forgiveness, then continues with the return of hope. Hope for you and those around you.

But for that to happen, you must tend to everyone's needs and give them nourishment. That's when amazing things can and will happen. Even with something that's almost dead.

Our frozen world is a perfect example. Life always finds a way. So do human contacts and relationships. Anything can be revived with the proper amount of planning and execution.

With that preaching behind me, I need to ask you a huge favor, one I hope you will consider and then carry out in my stead. It won't be easy, but I have every faith in you.

We need to finish repairing the transmitter before it's too late. Then convince Edison to make the broadcasts. We must determine if anyone else is out there with technology or supplies we can use.

It's beyond important that we do this. In fact, it's mission critical if we hope to keep Nirvana going.

If for some reason the calculations I've written on the board in red are not yet complete, then Edison will need to finish them for me. What I have is close, but there are some variables that don't quite add up. He will explain it all once he digs into them. They will not only demonstrate how dire the situation will become; they will help convince him to make the calls. At least, that is my hope. With him, one can never be certain.

When each new day begins, I change the number circled in red. It signifies how many days I believe we have remaining and serves as a visual reminder of the work that remains to be done.

I wish I could be more forthcoming about the true nature of the calculations, but I fear that someone other than you will find this letter.

Edison will need to explain the rest, once he's had a chance to absorb all that we face. However, there's a chance Edison may not be able to complete them on his own, given that he wasn't the best student in graduate school.

If my premonition holds true, then he'll need the rainbow-colored notebook I keep under the mattress in my quarters. It contains additional observations I've made along the way, though none of them have been vetted -- yet. I'm afraid they're only conjecture at this point, but that's what science is until it's proven – nothing more than observation and theory.

Whatever else happens from here on out, you must not give up until Edison agrees to repair the radio and start making the calls.

If he refuses, you need to take it to The Committee and convince them to overrule. The very future of Nirvana is at stake.

As the final curtain draws near, I wish I had more inspirational words to share with you. Something more profound and meaningful. But as you know, I'm not the most eloquent man, especially when it comes to emotional situations or goodbyes. I tend to keep my thoughts short and emotions hidden, never to get lost in the minutiae of the moment.

In closing, let me say that I will miss you, my dearest Summer, more than any other in my lifetime. I am honored to have known you and to have called you my friend.

Please, never forget me because I will always remember you, no matter where I end up once I've taken my last breath.

I wish you Godspeed with the rest of your life.

Make it count.
Make it grand.
Make it memorable.

Don't wait until you are old and gray like me before you find your passion.

Love always,

Alex

CHAPTER 23

Krista took the next corner in the silo, pushing her feet past the bulkhead that led into the cafeteria. The bustle of citizens enjoying their daily allotment of food was almost deafening, their forks and knives clinking against the metal plates and the buzz of their high-pitched voices working against each other in a fight for auditory dominance.

The pace of her feet picked up, out of both instinct and need, wondering where Summer was hiding. The girl was always one to react first, then think, meaning she could be anywhere.

Zimmer had wanted Krista to leave the girl alone, letting her flail away in sorrow, only to use it against her when the next new crisis hit Nirvana.

His plan was valid, but only for those with certain intentions on their mind. The kind of intentions that included a planned mutiny or other underhanded actions.

Krista took the next left, then ran smack into Summer's chest. The two of them bounced off each other and spun sideways in an off-balance stumble. Krista righted herself, then lunged forward to grab Summer's elbow, spinning the girl around to face her.

"Get out of my way!" Summer shrieked, her face full of tears. Her hands went into fight mode, obviously hoping to break free and make a quick exit.

Krista doubled her grip to keep the girl under control. "I've been looking for you."

Summer twisted sideways, continuing her resistance. "Let go of me!"

Krista set her feet, adding to her strength. "No, not until we have a talk."

"Let go of her," Liz said in a huff, her face appearing in the corridor ahead. "I said, let her go!"

Krista wasn't sure why, but the tone of Liz's second command convinced her to release her grip.

Summer pulled away an instant later and resumed her emotional trek down the hall, her legs taking long, awkward steps with a trail of tears marking her path.

Liz arrived with a shortness to her breath. "You need to let her be."

"Why? What's going on?"

"She just found a letter from Alex. It was addressed to her."

"What kind of letter?"

"The kind that makes emotional young ladies even more so."

"What does that even mean?"

"It means she needs a moment to collect herself. And we need to give it to her."

"Okay, but where is she going? Her room isn't that way."

"To his quarters," Liz said. "Apparently, he left something for her. Well, actually, for all of us." Liz waved a hand at Krista to follow in the same direction as Summer. "A notebook."

When Krista and Liz arrived at Morse's quarters, they found the door open and Summer on the floor, crying in a kneeling crouch, her hands outstretched and flat.

Liz brushed past Krista and went to Summer, also dropping to her knees. Her arms went around the girl, wrapping her in a sideways hug.

Krista ran a visual sweep of the room. It was empty. Not a stitch of furniture or anything else. Certainly not a notebook. Only the bare walls and floor remained, with the smell of cleaning solution in the air, which meant only one thing. The reclamation crew had already come through, clearing and cleaning the room for sanitation reasons.

It was one of Edison's long-standing rules. Foundational rules. Rules that he and June had established back when Nirvana was first envisioned.

When someone died, their rooms were to be immediately emptied in case of lingering bio-hazard. That was the official reason. In truth, it was mostly done for personal reasons. A respect for the dead type thing.

Edison didn't want gawkers or trinket hunters to arrive, pilfering whatever remained. It's a human reaction, one in which looting becomes the norm, when everyone does without for so long.

Some would abscond with items for themselves. Others would do it for their children. All of them driven by the need to survive, gathering that extra tidbit that might help keep them alive or sane for one more day.

Edison believed by removing everything, there would be nothing left to steal. It would also render the possessions meaningless, once they were repurposed and mixed in with the supplies in inventory—all of it set to be repurposed, once the bio-hazard possibility had been ruled out.

"We have to find it," Summer cried out.

"We will," Liz answered, still holding Summer in an embrace.

"Then we better hurry," Krista said. "Some of his stuff is certainly headed for the incinerator."

Summer crawled out of Liz's hug and pushed to her feet. She turned and took a deep breath, then the look on her face morphed from one of anguish to one of seasoned confidence.

Krista stood in amazement as the emotional wreck transformed herself into someone new, and did so almost instantly, with nothing more than a bold new breath and a wipe of her cheek with her sleeve.

"This ends now," Summer said in a poised tone, holding out a hand to Liz. "Let's go."

The brunette latched onto Summer, their palms wrapped around each other. The scrawny leader of Nirvana helped the healer from the floor with only a lean and a single yank.

The pair walked toward Krista in lockstep, then Summer put out her free hand and snatched Krista's as well.

The trio marched out the door and into the hallway as a team, their feet finding a common rhythm in each step, as if the maneuver had been rehearsed for months.

Krista wasn't sure how to explain the sudden swell of pride in her chest. It was profound, almost as if the three of them had just formed an unspoken union. A female union, one in which their collective skills would now meld together and lead Nirvana into the future.

It was the strangest sensation. Plus, it had come out of nowhere, catching her both off guard and unaware. Krista had no inkling that such a cabal could ever exist, particularly if one considered their combative history and disparate backgrounds.

None of it would make sense on paper, yet it did in reality, perfectly.

Right then, Krista remembered something Edison liked to tout in moments of great doubt: *Out of tragedy, comes hope.*

More so when enemies become friends, finding that common ground that binds them all.

* * *

Fletcher led his team on foot across the twin railroad tracks and past the rusted overhang protecting the passenger bench. He remembered that seat well from his teenage years, a familiar place where riders from all over the county would gather for the next scheduled train to arrive, none of them, like him, aware of what the frozen future would entail.

They were seven minutes early for this meet with their reclusive source. A meet long overdue, and, as it turned out, mandatory before Phase Two of their mission would be granted the go-ahead.

Everything else was set. All Craven and his band of teeth needed was a time and place, both of which Fletcher would know in the next few minutes. At least, that was the plan, assuming the source had the information they'd been seeking.

Fletcher watched Dice move ahead, working the approach to the train station with his squad mates TJ Pepper, Willie Boone, and Chapa Longbow. All three had been hand-picked by Dice in an attempt to create a small, but trusted band of loyalists—men who hated Frost and welcomed the leadership change.

Sketch had held back with Fletcher, standing watch on the area behind them. Sketch was usually tasked to cover their six, a posting that, if not protected, would leave the team vulnerable to an overrun from behind. Sketch had always performed well on this duty assignment, so there was no reason for Fletcher to think this time would be any different.

Dice and his team entered the train station with rifles high, preparing to sweep the inside for threats. The source they were meeting was dangerous, but he wasn't the immediate risk. It was the rogue bands of Scabs that Fletcher knew worked this area. Scabs that Craven didn't control.

Dice had brought the Scab repellent spray, but even so, it was a limited supply and not something Fletcher wanted to use unless there was no other choice.

Plus, he didn't entirely trust the one-eyed pirate who ran The Factory. Craven could have engineered the spray to become inert over time. It would have been the tactical thing to do—get them hooked on its usefulness and then demand more in trade.

Plus, there was the possibility of a run-in with another faction of society's desperate—humans— regular humans. People who had banded together in an attempt to overpower and loot the weapons, ammo, and supplies Fletcher and his men carried.

Occasionally the looters would hit an area, not realizing who they were attacking and what the punishment would be for their actions. Frost had no patience for any of them and Fletcher didn't intend to, either.

The latter of the two possibilities hadn't been much of a problem in a while, mainly because of the lure of the Trading Post. However, now that Heston and his exchange compound were down, it was conceivable the dynamics would change. Desperation has a tendency to lead even the most passive of folk to take ambitious measures.

An effective leader never assumes the threats are contained, nor does he assume they will be the same as the last mission. Not when what's left of the world is hungry and frantic about their survival.

Dice appeared in the doorway of the station, raising his hand to give the go-ahead signal for Fletcher to close ranks and join him.

"Hold here," Fletcher told Sketch.

"Orders, sir?"

"Cover this sector and report any activity."

"Permission to engage?"

"Granted, but verify your targets," Fletcher told Sketch. "Our guy could approach from any direction and we need him in one piece."

"Copy that, boss."

"He's usually in a vehicle so he can transport the fuel, but can't rule out he'll arrive on foot. He's done that before, though I don't understand why."

Sketch nodded.

Fletcher left him behind and made quick work of the hundred yards that spanned the distance to the building. He went inside and walked to where Dice stood with the rest of his team.

"I'd like to set up overwatch, if that's acceptable with you?" Dice asked, glancing at the biggest member of his team, Willie Boone.

The muscular man had to run at least three hundred pounds. He was about twice the size of the gray-haired TJ Pepper, who was standing next to him, and about half his age. Longbow was somewhere in the middle—not small, not big—but definitely capable.

Fletcher nodded, craning his neck to study the ceiling. "Assuming the roof will hold."

Dice must have understood the remark and the reason for it, because he didn't hesitate with his response. "I'll task Pepper instead. Don't want to risk it."

"Good choice," Fletcher said, turning his attention to Longbow.

The well-built Navajo's eyes sat deep in his head and were always on alert, as if he were in perpetual hunt mode. Some of the men called the proficient tracker by the nickname of "Archer," a moniker that fit his last name and not his legendary skillset.

"So I hear you're damn good with a knife?" Fletcher asked.

"I get by," Longbow replied, his focus never wavering from Fletcher. The man grabbed the eagle's claw that hung on a homemade necklace in front of his chest, rubbing it as if he were asking it for insight, or possibly good luck.

"Show him, Archer," Boone said in an energized tone, his voice deep and full of gravel. Boone turned his eyes to Fletcher. "You gotta see this, boss. Never seen anything like it."

Longbow didn't react, his eyes still locked on Fletcher's and his fingers rubbing the trinket.

Fletcher wasn't sure if the Navajo was waiting for approval to act, or if he simply chose to ignore the demonstration request.

"Later, men. We've got work to do," Dice said, releasing the tension that had built among the group.

With that, Pepper stepped away and headed outside to take his position on the roof.

Dice pointed at two of the train station walls. "Let's get those windows covered."

Longbow and Boone split off, each taking his post at a different pane of glass.

Fletcher and Dice gathered in a huddle, turning their backs to the men.

"Once we have the location, it'll be time to dispose of the others," Fletcher said.

"Already in the works, boss. I'm going to create a new hunting party and use that as the cover."

"Do you think they'll buy it?"

"Yeah, as long as you and I are in agreement as to the need for a second group."

"Easy enough. I'll just say that with our recent losses, we need to develop redundancy for all facets of the compound."

"That'll work," Dice said.

"I've got movement over here," Boone reported from the window on the left.

Fletcher and Dice turned, scampering to his position.

Boone pointed. "Eight o'clock. Just beyond that rise. See the dust?"

Fletcher did, watching small puffs billow into the sky beyond the rise.

"It's moving too fast to be a bunch of Scabs, unless they went bionic or something," Boone said.

"Chances are, it's him," Dice added. "Unless Carr and her group somehow figured out where we are."

Boone brought his eyes down and checked the chamber of his AR-10, then released the magazine with the lever on the side. He spun the ammo holder in his hand and tapped it twice on floor to align the rounds. He peered at Fletcher as he slammed it back into the lower receiver, looking sure of himself. "Either way, I'm gonna burn 'em all."

Fletcher put a hand on the giant's shoulder. "One step at a time, Boone. I don't want any mistakes. Not today. We need this guy in one piece."

Longbow joined the conversation from his position at the other window. "What if it's Edison's group? We can't let them find us here."

Fletcher gave Longbow a stern look, needing the conversation to stop. And the paranoia. "If that happens, let me handle it. Nobody fires until I give the order. Is that clear?"

"You got it, boss," Longbow said.

"Yes, sir," Boone said, his eyes shooting to the ceiling after a pounding of footsteps raced across the roof.

"Sounds like Pepper is in position," Dice said, also following the footsteps with his eyes.

"All right, everyone stay sharp," Fletcher said, walking to the door of the train station. Dice joined him, taking position on the other side of the entrance.

Fletcher kept his body positioned behind the edge of the doorframe as he pulled his semi-automatic sidearm from the holster, then racked the slide of the 1911. He didn't want to fire the .45, but he would if he had to.

"Time to nut up or shut up," Dice said, his pistol drawn as well.

CHAPTER 24

"There he is," Dice said, seeing a dual-axle truck racing up the road, its beefy tires taking the dips and turns at high speed. "And I thought I was a lead foot."

The camo-covered truck slowed to a crawl as it began a wide circular approach. Fifty yards later, the driver rolled down the side window and held out a white flag with a red stripe on it.

"That's him," Dice said.

Fletcher turned to the men behind him, stationed at the windows. "Keep an eye on our flanks, gentlemen."

"Roger that," Boone said from his firing position.

Longbow held firm as well, his rifle high and tight against his shoulder.

The truck swung around from left to right as it drove over the train tracks and brought the passenger side door into view, coming to a stop only twenty yards in front of the station's entrance. There were smears of red on the side—either paint or blood, Dice assumed.

When the driver opened his door on the far side and hopped out, Dice's assumption about his identity was confirmed after the man walked to the hood and turned toward them, passing the front bumper. It was their leather-clad source, complete with head-to-toe garb that included a full mask and a long coat that resembled a cape.

"I see he's still carrying those damn swords," Fletcher whispered in an irreverent tone.

Dice nodded, wondering if the Nomad ever left the weapons behind. Or his mask, for that matter, never attending their meets without it.

The man looked medieval, a strange sight to be sure, his extra-thick leather costume providing armor-like protection from teeth and claws.

However, a high-velocity bullet would have no issues penetrating the animal hide, nor would a honed Ka-bar knife. Or one of the man's own swords, if Dice had to guess.

Fletcher put his pistol back into its holster and walked out the door.

Dice did the same, taking position next to his commander's left shoulder.

"Call off your dogs," the Nomad said in a firm voice, sounding the parts of both superhero and vigilante. "Just me today. Nothing different."

Fletcher craned his neck and peered up to Pepper, giving him a quick hand wave.

Pepper backed away, he and the front sight of his sniper rifle disappearing from view on the roof.

The Nomad pointed at the closest window alongside the train station. "And the others—"

Fletcher put two fingers into his mouth and let out a sharp whistle. "Stand down, men."

The Nomad leaned to the side for a moment, his eyes locked onto the window he'd just pointed at.

"Are we good?" Fletcher asked.

The Nomad nodded as he brought his focus back, the hood on his head jostling in concert with the movement.

"What do you have for us?" Fletcher asked.

The Nomad held for a moment, his upper body leaning toward the middle of the doorway, indicating he was looking beyond Fletcher and into the station. "The fuel?"

Fletcher shook his head. "Not so fast, my friend. Intel first. Then I'll have the diesel brought up."

"Not acceptable."

"It is today."

The Nomad paused, his hands resting on the handles of his twin swords, both curved and hanging on his sides in their sheaths. "Why the change?"

"After last time, when you came empty-handed, we need to be more cautious."

"A circuit board and smut magazines are not nothing."

"But you didn't bring the coordinates."

"A much harder get."

"Hence our wariness. The tougher the intel, the more vigilant we must become. How do we know you didn't show up empty-handed again?"

The Nomad took his right hand off the sword and brought it to the middle of his chest. He tapped his fingers on the leather suit, directly over his heart. "It's right here."

"Then let's have it," Fletcher said, holding out his palm.

"The fuel."

"We could always just take what we want," Dice said. "We outnumber you five to one."

"Wouldn't end well for you."

"Actually, it's the other way around."

The Nomad shook his head. "Many have tried and all have failed."

"Easy now, boys; this doesn't have to escalate," Fletcher said. "We have the fuel, as agreed. Just need to verify the intel first."

The Nomad took a step back with both hands on his weapons. "The fuel or we won't meet again."

"He's bluffing, boss," Dice said. "He needs the diesel worse than us."

"Nomad doesn't bluff," the Nomad said.

Dice looked at Fletcher. "You believe the nerve of this guy? After all this time, he doesn't trust us. I take that as a personal insult, don't you?"

"Nor does he wait," the Nomad added. "You have until the count of ten."

With that, the Nomad began a countdown, starting with the number ten and reciting the next lowest digit in one-second increments.

The three of them stood firm as the sequence continued, the air around Dice seemingly getting thicker and harder to breathe with each successive numeral.

When the Nomad reached the number four, he pulled his swords from their sheaths, as if he were starring in a slow-motion scene from a Hollywood movie.

After the tips of the blades found air, the Nomad brought them together in a crisscross pattern, his front leg bent low, with the rest of his body in ninja fighting position. "Shoot me if you must, but the intel dies with me."

"We'll just take it after we waste you," Dice said, fighting to keep his laughter under control. The Nomad had no idea what Boone was ready and willing to do. Or Longbow, for that matter. The Nomad wouldn't make it ten feet.

"It's on notepaper and wrapped around a pouch of blood. If you shoot, it'll be soaked and unreadable."

Dice found the Nomad's response a little too convenient. He'd never pulled this stunt before, wrapping paper around a sack of blood. For this tactic to be true, he would've had to have known their plans regarding the fuel ahead of time, which wasn't possible, since only he and Fletcher were in the loop. "I still say he's bluffing, boss,"

The Nomad continued the countdown. "Three . . . Two . . . One . . ."

Fletcher brought his hands up in a flash of movement. "Okay, you win. Stop the countdown."

"Countdown on hold," the Nomad announced in a deep, purposeful tone, almost as if he were narrating a scene from a cheesy science fiction book about a woman terrorist being put to death in front of a live, betting audience.

"Everyone just take a deep breath. It's all good," Fletcher said, pausing before he put his fingers into his mouth again. He let out a sharp whistle. "Pepper—"

Pepper's head appeared from above, hanging over the roofline of the train station.

"Call them in," Fletcher said to the man.

"Sure thing, boss." Pepper rose to his feet and aimed his rifle into the air. He fired one shot, then held for a few beats before firing two more in rapid succession. When the echo of the last two rounds faded, he triggered a fourth shot, then brought the rifle down.

"They're on their way," Fletcher told Nomad.

"One truck only and no more men," the Nomad said, bringing the tip of one of his swords around to face the center of his chest, directly at the spot he'd tapped earlier. "Or this ends now."

"I give you my word. The fuel is on the way, exactly as you asked."

Silence hung in the air for a minute, until Dice couldn't hold back a question weighing on his tongue. He pointed at the red smears on the side of the Nomad's truck. "Looks like you've seen some action."

"A fair amount."

"Recently."

"Very."

Just then, an explanation slammed into his mind. "That's one of Edison's, isn't it? From the Trading Post massacre."

"Yes."

"I hope you know those supplies were ours."

"That's not how I see it."

Dice looked at Fletcher, wondering why the man wasn't engaging on this topic. The Nomad stole what was supposed to be theirs. "Boss?"

"Let it be, Dice."

"But—"

"That's an order. What happened at the Trading Post wasn't anyone's fault. Let's just get this deal done and be on our way."

No more words were spoken until the transport truck arrived in a rev of its engine, then swung around wide, much like the Nomad had done, only from the opposite side.

Fletcher whistled again, then sent a hand wave to the driver. "Back it in."

The driver nodded, then performed a quick turnaround before backing the vehicle into position. When its tailgate was about two feet from the rear of the Nomad's truck, Fletcher whistled again and held up a closed fist.

The driver stopped the truck in a squeal of its brake pads, then put it into park before he slid out and walked to the rear. He unhooked the pins holding the tailgate in place and lowered it.

"Now the intel," Fletcher said, again holding out his hand.

The Nomad took a step back, put his swords away, then turned and made a direct path to the fuel truck, squeezing his frame between the open tailgate and his own truck. His head turned for a few beats as he looked inside.

Dice moved his fingers to his pistol, resting his hand on the leather of the holster. If the Nomad climbed inside, he'd have to pull the weapon and fire.

The Nomad brought his attention back, then retraced his steps, arriving within striking distance this time. His hand went inside his coat and he pulled out a folded piece of paper. There was no pouch of blood.

"Shit, I knew it," Dice mumbled.

Fletcher took the paper from the Nomad and unfolded it. His eyes lingered on the contents for a few moments, then he looked at Dice. "Looks like it's underground."

"Then Frost was right," Dice said.

"For once," Fletcher replied.

"An old missile silo," the Nomad said.

"How heavy is their security?" Fletcher asked

"Virtually none."

Fletcher held out his hand to the masked man. "It's been a pleasure doing business with you."

The Nomad ignored him and instead turned and walked to the fuel truck, his swords jostling in their sheaths along his sides.

The driver tossed him the keys as he cruised by.

The Nomad snatched them in mid-air, then climbed into the truck, started it, and drove away, taking the same route he'd used on the way in.

Dice looked at Fletcher. "I thought for sure he was going to inspect the drum."

"So did I, especially with all the tension today. Why did you push him like that?"

"Not sure, but something was off—I just couldn't put my finger on it. He seemed different somehow."

Fletcher nodded. "I got that feeling, too."

"Maybe he felt something was off about us, too. That's why he was acting different. Some kind of sixth sense."

"Could be."

"Either way, he's eventually going to figure it out."

"By then, it'll be too late."

"I hope you're right, boss. Because men like him always come looking for revenge. It's that honor thing getting in the way."

"Of course he will, and we'll be ready," Fletcher said, whistling to his men. "Let's roll out!"

CHAPTER 25

Summer leaned back in the chair in Edison's office and put her arms behind her head. She closed her eyes and drew in a quick, massive round of air and let it out just as fast, wondering if anyone else would have had the same level of anxiety she had if they were sitting in this spot instead of her, pretending to be the leader. One who'd just taken the reins with zero credibility or experience.

It was one thing to be able to sit in Edison's space and not have her chest crushed by another round of heartache after all the bloodshed and death.

But attempting to *fake it till she made it*? How did she do that when she had no clue how to even fake it?

None of her new reality made sense and yet, here she was—in his office, tasked as the person in charge of Nirvana.

So far, she thought she'd kept it all under control—well mostly, but of course it was all a lie.

Everyone, including her, knew that she was inadequate to take Edison's place.

If only her trepidation ended there. Everything around her reminded her of Stuart. Not just visually, which was to be expected. What she found odd was that she could smell him—everywhere. Even on the desk in front of her and the walls.

Sure, it was old man stink that had been sprayed with layers of humidity and wrapped inside a thick, moldy blanket.

By themselves, some might consider these fragrances disgusting, but they weren't to her and she knew why—the strange mixture was Edison. Perfectly so.

Even unpleasant smells have memories attached to them. And everywhere she looked, that's what she saw and felt—memories—fond memories—all of them flooding into her mind, each one attached to a unique aroma.

She took a moment to search her memories, but couldn't remember a time when she'd noticed his scent before. It must have been as prevalent back then as she thought it was right now. If that were true, then why couldn't she remember any of those aromas?

Perhaps it was a death thing. Something about once you leave the Earth, your stink takes over in your stead.

She thought about that idea for another minute, then flushed the theory away as stupidity. She scoffed, figuring her mind was running with lunacy, all brought forth as some form of a coping mechanism. Perhaps done to help offset the pain she was trying to bury.

Then there was his workspace.

It was hers now and she needed to do something with the mess before the reclamation team showed up to do their sweep and clear thing. She'd held them off so far, but eventually someone would notice and start questioning her motives.

Her mind switched to a new question. One she'd never thought of before.

How do you clear out a lifetime of someone else's work with nothing more than a bunch of empty boxes and a broom?

Is that all there is to one's life at the end—a pile of meaningless paperwork and a collection of junk that someone else has to callously pack up and haul away?

It was a depressing thought, but one she was sure that many had asked before her. Some might have found solace in the process, or closure, but she found it distressing.

Out of tragedy comes hope was one of Edison's favorite sayings. She wasn't sure if any of that was true, more so now as she brought her eyes down and took yet another glance around the room.

All she could hear was the rumbling hum of the air circulation system and her own heartbeat, thumping in rhythm with the passage of time.

She was certain Edison thought he had more time. Frost probably did, too. Morse, not so much, but regardless, everyone usually does. It's part of pushing ahead into the unknown, trying to accomplish something positive for the day.

Summer decided to shift her focus to the page of notepaper on the desk. The first sentence had been easy for her to write, the pen scribing it with ease. Then again, all it said was "Welcome, citizens of Nirvana."

That was an hour ago, shortly after Krista had banished her from public duty until she'd completed her speech.

Summer could have argued at the time, but chose not to—her second-in-command was correct. A public address needed to get done and for that to happen, she needed to separate herself from everything else going on in the silo.

Before her next thought arrived, three knocks came from the door and then she heard a sharp, single bark. Her eyes beamed at the entrance. "Sergeant Barkley?"

"Someone wants to see you," a female voice said from the other side of the door.

Summer recognized the voice. "Come in, Krista. It's not locked."

The door opened and the Security Chief walked in, holding a paracord leash that was attached to her new four-legged friend.

Summer smiled, seeing the firm, crisp wag of the dog's tail. Plus, his eyes looked much more alive than before.

"I think someone missed you," Krista said, letting go of the homemade restraint.

The dog strolled forward, still hampered by a limp, but the pace of his paws had improved since she'd last seen him.

He cruised around the left edge of the desk and came straight at her. Summer put her knees together before the canine landed his wet snout on top of her lap.

She rubbed him enthusiastically. "You're looking better, aren't you, boy?"

"He does seem to be improving, believe it or not."

"Yeah, he's pretty special, isn't he?"

"I have to say, I'm impressed."

"With his healing or that he hasn't bitten you yet?"

Krista grinned. "Both. I wasn't sure at first, but he seems to be adjusting to life here quite nicely."

"He just needed someone to love him," Summer said, running her hands down his back and up again. It was at that moment when she realized he didn't smell awful and his fur was fluffy. "Who gave him a bath?"

"Liz and I did," Krista said, reaching behind her back. She lifted the tail of her shirt before bringing her hand out front again. "Right after I found this." She held up a rainbow-colored notebook.

"Holy shit! You found it?" Summer snapped, scooting the mutt out of the way as she jumped to her feet. "Where?"

"A member of the reclamation team had it in his quarters."

"Thank God it wasn't incinerated," Summer said, arriving at Krista's position in a heartbeat. She pinched her forehead as a million questions burned inside. Then, a second later, one popped to the top of the list, making her feel more like a leader than a moment ago. "That's not standard procedure. He shouldn't have taken it."

"And he's been written up for it."

"Why he'd do it?"

"He couldn't answer that question. Not to my satisfaction."

Summer shrugged, pressing her lips together out of habit. "Maybe he just wanted a memento."

"That's still no excuse. Especially when it belonged to a man who just died of a horrible disease," Krista answered, holding out the notebook.

Summer went to grab it, but pulled her hand back. "Is it contagious?"

"If it was, it's not anymore."

Summer shook her head when the words didn't resonate. "What does that even mean?"

"It means Liz treated it with a strong antibacterial. She says it's as clean as it's going to be."

"That doesn't sound very safe. Maybe we should just burn it?"

"I thought of that, but since it's already made the rounds from the tech's quarters to the infirmary and now here, it's kind of too late for that."

"Is that what Liz said?" Summer asked after a pause.

"Liz said to give it to you," Krista answered, shaking the notebook. "So that's what I'm doing."

Summer took it. When she opened it, she found pages and pages of handwritten notes and diagrams, none of which she understood. At least his notes weren't written in cursive like the letter he'd left for her. "What does all this mean?"

"I have no idea. I don't speak geek."

"Liz does."

"She said microbiology isn't her thing."

"So that's what this is? Microbiology?"

"Apparently Morse was worried about something in our wastewater that he called *ravenous antibiotic eaters*. That's all Liz could figure out."

"Really? I thought doctors had to know this stuff."

"So did I, but she said they had specialists for all that back in the day. You know, labs full of geeks who got hard-ons from all this bug stuff."

"Sounds like bugs eating bugs to me," Summer quipped after scanning another page of notes. She closed the journal and held it up. "Then this is basically useless?"

Krista shrugged. "Unless you know someone else who speaks geek."

Summer nodded, running through the facts in her head. Then she remembered something she'd thought about earlier. "What about Lipton?"

"I was wondering if that asshole's name was going to come up."

"He seems to think he knows everything about everything."

"In my experience, that's usually a sign that he's just a fraud. You know the type. Some guy who's pretending to be smarter than he really is, because he has a microscopically small pecker."

Summer laughed. "Or he's one of those geeks who gets wood when he discovers something new. A tiny, insignificant amount of wood. Like a splinter or something."

Krista snickered for a bit before her face turned serious again. "I guess it couldn't hurt to ask him."

"That's what I was thinking," Summer said, giving the notebook back to Krista.

"Okay, I'll do that."

Summer walked back to Edison's desk and took her seat in his chair, resuming her scrub of the dog's fluffiness.

Krista pointed at the paper on the desk. "How's the speech coming along?"

Summer snatched the paper and held it up, turning it to face Krista. "It's not."

"Writer's block?"

"It's more like leadership block. I have no idea what I'm supposed to say."

"Want some help?"

Summer nodded, hoping that Krista would offer. "If you don't mind."

"Absolutely," Krista said, grabbing one of the extra chairs in the office and pulling it around the desk.

Summer snapped her fingers at Sergeant Barkley, then pointed at the corner.

The dog followed her command and moved out of the way, lying in the spot she'd indicated.

Krista sat down and scooted in next to Summer, putting Morse's notebook on the desk next to the stand-up picture frame.

Summer's eyes went to the photo of June as well. She scoffed after a flood of new feelings entered her body. Even though they came out of nowhere, they felt as though they'd been there the whole time. "What do you think Stuart and June would think right about now?"

"About us sitting here? Working together?"

"Yep."

"Oh, that's easy. They'd both say *it's about fucking time*."

Summer paused, letting the phrase Krista had used sink in. Her mind went back in time, seeing June standing next to her, showing her how to make one of her homemade trinkets. "I really can't imagine June would ever cuss. Or Stuart, either."

"Yeah, probably not, but then again, who knows? There are times when you need to really make a point."

Summer nodded. "Fuck yeah."

CHAPTER 26

Dice pulled the truck to the side of the mountain road and put the vehicle into park. He depressed the parking brake to keep the vehicle stationary on the steep grade, hearing at least a dozen clicks as the mechanism engaged.

The cliff to the right was imposing, but unless the majority of the embankment gave way in the next half-hour, he figured the spot he'd picked was safe.

He nodded in silence at Sketch sitting across from him in the passenger seat, before knocking on the back wall of the cab, using three raps. "All right boys, this is it."

Sketch put his pad of paper down on the seat, giving Dice a view of the artwork he'd been doodling. It was a head and shoulders portrait of a young girl with unruly, jet-black hair and a petite nose. Her jawline had a touch of fierceness to it, as did her eyes, even though she looked thin overall.

He wouldn't classify her as pretty, but she did have that girl next door look. Cute would have been one term that fit. Doable after a six-pack would have been another.

Dice let his eyes linger for another second, getting the sense that he knew her face, but he couldn't place it. His friend was a terrific artist, but sometimes the man's perception was off, almost as though Sketch had re-envisioned what the subject should have looked like, not as they appeared in the wild.

Sketch tucked the pencil under the edge of the pad, then swung his hand around to latch onto the door handle. They both opened their respective doors and got out of the truck, moving toward the rear of the vehicle.

The trees lining the mountainside seemed to be making a comeback, their leaves halfway into their sprout, offering a touch of greenery to the area. If he remembered correctly, Dice hadn't been to this location in at least a year. A lot had changed since then, with the sun beginning to break through the endless winter skies.

He wondered if the majestic oaks had waited with purpose to start their bloom, needing to make sure the newfound sunshine was not a random event.

If he were a tree, that's what he would have done. The last ten years hadn't been kind, leaving all survivors to wonder if the budding signs of progress were permanent or simply a ruse, designed to torture those who witnessed them.

He knew as well as anyone that Mother Nature had a wicked sense of humor, more so since the string of volcanos down south had taken down the planet. He'd only heard bits and pieces about the backstory, leaving him to wonder if the apocalypse was actually manmade or not. It seemed like a stretch.

Then again, he'd been known to climb down the rabbit hole on occasion, chasing the latest government conspiracy. Of course, that was before The Event, usually after reading a controversial post on one of his favorite blogs.

Those articles were a welcome break from the nightly grind at the casino. Some might have thought the long line of chicks he'd banged were the diversion, but in truth, it was his reading that became the escape.

Dice met Sketch at the rear of the truck, taking a command position in front of the eight-member team of the new hunting party. The squad looked ready, their heads covered in helmets and chests carrying tactical rigs stuffed with extra mags.

"Okay, men. Today is the first day of training. Game is known to be in the area, but it's limited. You'll have to search high and low for it. It won't be easy, but if you make it through this course, you'll be part of our prestigious backup unit, filling in for the primary when they're tasked to provide support for our new leader."

Dice hesitated, taking a read on the men standing before him. Everyone appeared to be on the same page, their eyes attentive and focused. "To cover more ground, you'll break into two teams of four. But check your sightlines, gentlemen. We don't need any incidents of friendly fire today. We're short-staffed enough as it is. Any questions?"

Nobody made a sound, each man looking alert and ready to peel out.

Dice motioned to the men on the right, who were already standing in a makeshift group, their rifles at the ready. "You four are Alpha Team. Take the east side." He pointed at an outcrop of rock, maybe three hundred yards up the hill. The protrusion appeared to be made of blue granite, its size impressive. "Work your way around that ridge and meet us at the summit in two hours."

"Roger that," one of the men said, adjusting his rucksack by the straps.

Dice peered at the other four. "Beta Team, you take west. I want you to cover the area by the old mine, about half a click up. Then meet us at the rally point. Whichever team takes down the most kills will be deemed the champions of this exercise. Extra points will be awarded for head shots, so aim small, shoot small."

Heads nodded and equipment rattled, but nobody said a word in response.

Dice continued. "Be sure to salt the meat after each kill. Each of you has a supply in your pack, so use it. We can't afford to waste anything today. Understood?"

"Yes, boss," another man said.

"All right, let's get to it," Dice said, standing firm as the teams broke into a sprint and began their hunt.

Sketch waited a full minute, then turned to Dice. "Two hours?"

"Didn't want to raise any red flags."

"I especially liked the part about extra points for head shots."

"Yeah, just hit me right then."

"Kind of hard to do with disabled firing pins," Sketch said.

"Yeah, but they don't know that."

"Good thing."

Dice agreed, his mind turning to another possibility. "Craven better come through before some rogue chipmunk decides to stick its head out."

"I wouldn't worry too much about it. I doubt there's any game up there."

"If there is, we're fucked," Dice said, reaching into his pocket and pulling out the tube of spray. He applied some on Sketch and then on himself, being sure to splash the repellent on both their fronts and backs. "This shit better still work."

Sketch craned his neck and watched the teams climb the mountain. "I wonder where Craven set his ambush."

Dice matched his friend's gaze. "We'll know soon. He was supposed to be in position a half hour ago."

"Poor bastards."

"They have no idea what's coming," Dice said.

"Welcome to the Mountain of the Scabs, where the meat is plentiful and so are the teeth."

Dice couldn't hold back a chuckle, even though his insides were doing flipflops. He figured guilt was the source of the queasiness. "At least this will keep Craven off our backs for a while."

"How many payments did we miss?"

"Only one that I know about. There could have been others before I was read in as second."

"Well, that was to be expected with the Frost situation and all."

"Still, Craven's not a man you want on your bad side, if you know what I mean."

Sketch nodded, pausing for a few beats. "How much meat do you think they take with them? You know, after the initial feeding."

"I really don't want to go up there and find out, do you?"

Sketch held for a moment, then shook his head. "Just making conversation, that's all. What about all the gear and ammo? We just going to leave it up there?"

"That's interest on the debt. Craven demanded some vig for his trouble."

"I guess that's a small price to pay."

"At least he didn't want more fuel. That we couldn't spare."

* * *

"Any trouble?" Krista asked Wicks, who was still at his post in the brig, keeping watch on the prisoners.

"None," he said, his shoulders square to the wall behind him.

Krista ran a quick visual check of the prisoners.

Horton and the Scab Girl were in the cell on the left, with the girl sitting cross-legged on the floor. Horton was a few feet away, standing adjacent to the cell door, his fingers wrapped around a pair of vertical bars.

Doc Lipton was on the cot in the other cell, lounging on his right side with his back to the door.

Krista brought her eyes back to Wicks, straining her neck to make eye contact with the man. "Why don't you go get chow? I need to have a chat with our new friends."

"Yes, ma'am," Wicks said, turning and marching out the door.

Krista walked to Lipton's cell. "Hey, asshat, you sleeping?"

"Yes, I am," Lipton said, holding up his left hand and flipping her the bird without looking.

"That's what I thought," she replied. "I need to talk to you."

"Go away. I'm asleep, remember?"

The Scab Girl was now on her feet and standing next to Horton in the adjacent cell.

"Look, I'm not going to ask again. Get up before I drag your sorry ass out of that bed. We have important business to discuss."

Lipton rolled onto his back, his gaze fixed on the ceiling. "What do you want? I'm busy."

Krista held up the rainbow-colored notebook belonging to Morse, tapping the binder on the bars. "There's something I need you to help me with."

"Let me guess. You found an old cereal box and you can't figure out how to open it."

Krista shook her head. "You might want to check the attitude, mister. Otherwise, you'll never get out of that cell."

"Who are you kidding? I'm in here for the duration."

"If you help us with this journal, that won't always be the case."

Lipton turned his head toward Krista. "What kind of journal?"

"One you might have written, if you worked for us instead of Frost."

Lipton sat up, swinging his feet around and planting them on the floor. "I'm intrigued. Go on."

"Our version of you died and left this notebook behind."

"Handwritten?"

"Yes."

"Well, what do you know? At least one of you can write."

Krista ignored his condescending babble. "We need to know what it all means."

"What's in it for me?"

"One hour of exercise on the surface. Some fresh air might do you good."

Lipton shook his head. "Me? Fresh air? Exercise? I think not. You need to sweeten the deal, if you want my help—with anything." He pointed to his head. "What's in here ain't free."

"You're really not in a position to negotiate."

"Actually, I am. You obviously need what only I possess. Otherwise, you wouldn't be here begging for it, with hat in hand like some kind of street vagrant."

Krista held her temper in check, though every word out of his mouth demanded a beatdown. "This isn't begging, pal. I'm only here as a courtesy. The boss told me to make a one-time offer, so here I am."

"Then run along and go tell that little squirrel you failed. I'm not interested."

Horton laughed from behind the bars. "Now you know what all of us have been putting up with for years."

"I can't believe Frost ever did," Krista replied.

"He didn't have a choice," Lipton said, looking sure of himself. He stood up, putting his arms out to the side as if he were preparing to give a speech to the United Nations, back when that organization still existed. "Frost knew, just as you do now, that knowledge rules the world. To that end, I say to all you peasants, step before the king and shower him with gifts."

Horton shook his head, laughing again, this time even harder.

Krista rolled her eyes at Horton, then brought them back to Lipton. "Trust me, you're no king."

"Au contraire, mon ami."

Krista paused, soaking in the arrogance standing before her. She needed to change tactics, otherwise she would be forced to either unlock the cell door and beat him senseless or walk away empty-handed. Neither result was acceptable. "Okay, I'll bite. What's it going to take?"

Lipton didn't hesitate, firing back in a millisecond. "Freedom to move about this complex, as I so choose."

Krista replied just as quickly. "Never going to happen."

"Then I guess we're done here."

"Yes, we are," Krista said, turning for the door. Before she could finish the first step, Summer walked in.

"How's it going?" the new leader asked.

Krista stopped in her tracks, holding the notebook up, then shooting a glance back at Lipton. "Dingle fuck over there thinks he's the new king."

"What?"

Lipton stepped to the bars, wrapping his fingers around them just as Horton had done. "Ah, the little squirrel returns. Maybe now we can negotiate in earnest."

Summer shot Krista a raised eyebrow. "What is he talking about?"

"He thinks if he helps us, he's getting released."

Summer walked to his cell. "Nice try, Lipton. But we're not that stupid."

"Oh, the minds of the ignorant. They shall forever live in a world of denial."

Krista continued, "I asked him what he wanted and he just spouted some bullshit about the peasants showering him with gifts."

"Sounds like isolation disease is starting to creep in," Summer quipped.

"Though technically, none of us are isolated," Horton said.

Lipton chuckled before he spoke to Summer again. "It's a metaphor, darling. Try to keep up."

Summer took the notebook from Krista and held it in front of Lipton. "Just tell us what this means. Otherwise, I'll have Wicks back here in two shakes and he'll drag you outside and tie you naked to a rock. Let's see if the overnight temperature drop teaches you who's really in charge here."

Lipton's smug expression never changed. "Then you'll never know what secrets the journal holds."

"So be it. We don't know now. I really couldn't care less at this point. Either help us or not. Your choice."

"There needs to be adequate compensation, my little squirrel. Like I told Ms. All Balls over there, my wisdom is not free."

Summer took a moment, then said, "I'll tell you what, Lipton. If you help us, I'll authorize one hour a day of roaming privileges, but under guard of course. Take it or leave it."

Lipton held out his hand. "What if the notes only contain a failed recipe for some version of soy-based cupcakes?"

Summer gave him the notebook. "Then it's a new recipe. The deal still stands. One hour a day. That's the best I can do."

"I accept. We now have a binding agreement," Lipton said, opening the notebook and studying the first few pages. "Hmmm. Interesting."

"Well?"

Lipton held up an index finger, but didn't respond as he flipped through a few more pages, his eyes taking in the notes. Several minutes went by before he spoke again. "Let me say this: Your version of me was quite thorough."

"Yeah, tell us something we don't know," Krista said.

"I'm afraid that would take the rest of my days."

"Are you gonna help us or not?" Krista snapped.

"Patience is the path to enlightenment," Lipton said, licking the tip of his finger and turning another page. A few more minutes ticked by before he finished reading and closed the journal.

"What does it mean?" Summer asked, taking the notebook from him.

"His notes make mention of additional calculations. Might I see them?"

"How do you know our version of you was a man?" Krista said. "I never said that."

"Of course he was. Don't be silly."

"What a chauvinist prick," Krista mumbled, rolling her eyes.

"The calculations?" Lipton asked Summer again.

"They're in his lab."

"I suggest you take me there. Posthaste. This truly cannot wait another minute."

CHAPTER 27

Summer stood shoulder to shoulder with the taller Lipton as the scientist stepped to the worktable in Morse's lab, humming a soft tune. Summer couldn't place the melody, but it sounded familiar, though she didn't know how or why.

Lipton's hand went to the transmitter sitting on the far end of the surface, running the tip of his finger across its metal case, almost as if it gave him sexual gratification.

So far, Krista hadn't restrained Lipton, but her chief watchdog, Wicks, was not far behind, his hands on his rifle and eyes on the prisoner.

Lipton moved his hand to the box of spare parts sitting adjacent to the radio, dipping his fingers into the disarray. He picked up a couple of circuit boards, inspecting each for a moment, before putting them back in the same location.

"The equations are over here," Summer said, pointing to the leftmost grease board in the room. "You said it was urgent, so let's stop wasting time."

Lipton followed Summer to the first board, his humming never taking a second off. Not until he decided to speak. "Well. Well. Well. It appears I need to revise my earlier assessment."

"About what?"

"Your version of me being thorough." Lipton picked up a magic marker and an eraser, wiping away one of the equations on the board and replacing it with a new one. "He needed to double-check his math. Sloppy is all I can say. And a bit hasty with his assumptions."

"Morse was usually very careful."

"Obviously not. I trust you did not put all your faith in his conclusions."

"Actually, we did. He was our go-to guy—for everything."

Lipton's face pinched, his cheeks turning a red color. "And this facility remains?"

Summer held up her hands. "Look around. What do you think?"

"I suppose a modicum of luck was to be expected. Even a blind squirrel—" Lipton said, stopping his sentence short.

Summer looked at Krista and she looked back, both of them shooting each other a *what the hell* look.

Lipton moved to the right, reviewing the next board. This time he didn't change anything after pondering the handwritten presentation.

The man continued on, moving from board to board, changing a number here, an equation there, circling some figures and underlining others.

When Lipton arrived at the last board—the one with the equations written in red—he stopped his perpetual hum and took a step back before crossing his arms over his chest. He froze in that stance, his lips fluttering without any sound.

After an extended silence, Lipton put his hand out to Summer. "Journal, please."

Summer gave it to him.

Lipton opened it, zipping past a dozen pages until he landed on one near the middle. His head tilted to the left, but his eyes remained fixed on the notes when he said, "That's what I thought."

"What?"

"Time to start packing."

"Excuse me?"

He pointed to the number thirty-five circled on the board in red, then at the three letters written after it. "Haven't you ever wondered what the E.O.D. represents?"

"Of course I do. That's why you're here."

"It means End of Days, of which, you have 35 remaining," he said, pausing with an intense look on his face. He used the eraser and pen again, this time changing the number thirty-five. "Correction, 29 days."

Summer took a few moments to process the words he'd just uttered, not wanting to accept the man's explanation. Perhaps she heard him wrong. "When you say End of Days, do you mean, like, *the* End of Days, as in the Bible?"

"More or less."

"For the planet?"

"For this complex. As I mentioned before, time to start packing."

Krista stepped forward, breaking her silence with a sharp tongue. "Explain what you mean."

Lipton walked to the worktable and sat down in the chair before putting the notebook on the surface. "It's all about the wastewater experiments he was running."

"Wastewater?" Summer asked.

"Yes, as in sewage. You do have a reclamation system in use, correct?"

"I think so," Summer answered.

"It's on Sublevel 8," Krista added.

Summer cleared her throat and sent daggers with her eyes at Krista, wishing her second-in-command hadn't told him that fact.

She turned her attention to Lipton, praying he didn't catch onto where they were or what kind of facility they were in. His face didn't give any indication he'd gleaned any information from her comment, though he was an odd duck anyway, so there was no way to know for sure.

Summer waved her hands at several of the grease boards in the room, hoping to keep his attention on something else. "What does wastewater have to do with any of this?"

Lipton opened the notebook to page three and pointed at the diagram in the middle. It was one of five charts on the page. "This tells the story of what he discovered."

"Go on."

"I'm sure you remember the days when the evening news was filled with reports about physicians over-prescribing antibiotics."

"Sure," Krista said. "Something about the diseases becoming immune."

"Actually, not the disease. The microbes. When they have time to familiarize themselves with an abundance of antibiotics, both the surrounding bacteria and their own cellular structure begin to share bits and pieces with each other about the DNA involved in the antibiotics. Specifically, the resistances they encounter."

"Are you saying they learn from each other?" Summer asked.

"In a sense, yes," Lipton answered. "But it doesn't end there. That prolonged exposure allows the microbes to develop a resistance over time, rendering the antibiotics ineffective. Eventually, the drugs administered to defeat the microbes become a food source, giving them energy to grow and evolve, becoming pathogenic. And when I say that, I mean evolve into a super pathogen. One without any method of treatment."

Summer hesitated for a bit, letting the words soak in, trying to link the pieces together from what the man had said. "Okay, I get that, but why was Morse running experiments on our sewage?"

"As most microbiologists will tell you, there are concentrated amounts of antibiotics in our soils, our water, and our sewage, especially around hospitals, farms, and anywhere else physicians hand out antibiotics like pamphlets at a political rally."

"There used to be a huge dairy farm not too far from here," Krista said. "I remember the Professor talking about it."

"Me too," Summer said. "In fact, it was one of the largest in the entire state."

"As I suspected. That was ground zero. You see, when cows process what they eat, then excrete—"

"You mean shit—" Summer added.

"Yes, and lots of it. The overuse of antibiotics and steroids by farmers on their herds eventually made its way from the excrement into the soil, with the help of rain and other natural processes, some of it contaminating the water table."

"So what you're saying is we've been drinking steroids and eating antibiotics?" Wicks asked, breaking his silence.

"No. Not even close, my huge friend. It has to do with microbes and their natural tendency to evolve inside a closed ecosystem. One that includes a sufficient amount of humidity and heat, plus sewage, bacteria, and other fundamental elements. Now, when you mix in a healthy supply of antibiotics and the biologically active nature of steroids and their effect on cell membranes, what you have is—"

"—Speak English man," Krista snapped. "Pretend we know nothing about science."

"I'm not sure any pretending is required."

"Jesus, Lipton. Just explain it already. And leave out all the geek stuff," Krista said, tucking her lip under as she spoke. "You've giving me a monster-sized headache. And I hate headaches."

"I am trying to explain," Lipton said, pausing for a beat with his eyes leering at Krista.

"Just finish what you were saying," Summer said. "In layman's terms, please."

Lipton continued. "Earlier, you mentioned Sublevel 8. Obviously, that means we're deep underground in an old missile silo, given the facts I've observed thus far."

"No, we're not," Krista fired back.

"Yes, we are. The myriad of down ladders. The industrial elevator. The dampness. The apparent thickness and shape of some of the walls. The overhead piping in the corridors. The ancient electronic equipment. The recycled air. And last, but not least, the massive springs connected to the substrate, protecting everything from earthquakes and other forms of shock. There's only one type of facility that fits those parameters and is located in this part of the country—a Titan II Missile Silo."

Summer was impressed with his powers of deduction, but didn't want to admit he was right. However, she still needed more information from the guy, so she decided some casual spin was needed. "Okay, let's assume for a moment that you're correct," Summer said, "then what—"

"It means we're inside a giant incubator, one that is surrounded by leaching soils and water, all of it tainted by years of endless drug use at the nearby farm. This, in effect, formed a concentrated shell of antibiotics around this facility and eventually some of it made its way inside," Lipton said, flipping forward in the notebook six more pages.

He pointed at another diagram. "Here your man was documenting treatment options he was considering. Treatments that would attempt to convince the always-present bacteria in the sewage to attack and consume the antibiotics leaching in, and do so before the other developing microbes took notice and evolved into pathogens."

Summer understood, though she needed confirmation. "Bacteria eating the food source of the pathogens, right?"

Lipton nodded, though he didn't look convinced. "Sure, close enough."

"That sounds like a good thing to me. So what's the problem?" Krista asked.

"The problem is it's difficult to control bacteria. They have a tendency to do what they want, not what you want, sometimes becoming far too aggressive. More so when amateurs tamper with something they don't fully grasp, like your man, Morse. Good God, the audacity."

"Are you saying Morse lost control?" Summer asked, overlooking the slam he'd just made at Morse's expense.

"Exactly. In fact, it appears from his notes that his latest treatment was extremely effective at halting the evolution of any super pathogens, until it was accidentally transmitted to your food stores and then to your botanicals. This caused a plant-based pandemic of sorts, one that will consume your food supply in thirty-five days."

"All of our food?" Summer asked.

"Yes, except his math was off. It's actually 29 days. Starvation will begin shortly thereafter."

"Can't we just get rid of the old plants and replace them?" Wicks asked. "How hard is that?"

Lipton laughed. "From what? Magic seeds that haven't been compromised?"

Wicks shrugged.

"Don't you get it? This complex is already coated by the new strain of bacteria. It's everywhere by now. Plus, if it were possible to cultivate new plants, what would you eat while the new plants grew to maturity? None of that happens overnight."

"Holy shit," Summer said, thinking of Morse's dying words. "That's why."

CHAPTER 28

The Nomad drove past another stand of frozen brush and turned at the turquoise-colored rock. It was shaped liked an overgrown refrigerator, teetering on one of its corners, almost reaching out and pointing in the direction he planned to take. He sped up, taking three more turns—two rights and a left—using landmarks along the route to guide his journey.

After taking a steep, one-way road leading up to his destination, he dodged a line of gaping holes in the pavement, then slowed the truck to a crawl, aiming the tires down an incline, crunching the remains of whatever landscaping had surrounded his colossal hideout before The Event.

He pulled forward, passing several dilapidated buildings, to the old mine entrance. Ancient prospectors had mined bat guano from the cave to make gunpowder back in the thirties, hauling in supplies and equipment for their six-story descent.

The Nomad wasn't sure how many trips they must have made to engineer the flagstone steps and handrails inside, but it must have been a taxing journey to be sure.

Next up was an etching in the rockface that said *ERIN B. WORKED HERE*. It marked where he needed to turn left, penetrating the precise center of the branches and other debris he had arranged to conceal the entrance.

He always wondered what the mountain was like before it had been transformed from a dry cave into a wet one, courtesy of the melting snow after the recent thaw began.

There were broken down signs still on the property, verifying what he already knew—the cave had been used as a popular tourist attraction. Of course, that was long before most of society had scrambled into oblivion.

He slid the truck inside the secret entrance, just missing the walls holding up the opening, then turned on the headlights, making sure he didn't smash into one of the age-old formations rising up from the floor.

The mere fact that he could drive into this hideout was a godsend, avoiding the need to park his vehicle outside in the freezing temperatures that plagued the night.

The cave was a constant seventy-one degrees regardless of what was happening beyond its walls, keeping him and his clan dry and comfortable.

He'd been in his share of caves before, most of them warmer, taking his mind back to his days in the Army. He didn't miss that period in his life, especially the ass-kicking training op known as high-altitude wilderness training.

Every soldier dreaded that exercise, needing to survive in conditions that most humans couldn't. Or wouldn't. He still couldn't believe he signed up for all that mental and physical abuse, but in the end, it made him confident in who and what he was. Mostly.

The entrance had taken its share of abuse the past decade, evidenced by the avalanche of rock and dirt littering the ground outside. He figured The Event, and the havoc it wreaked, had managed to widen the access point through erosion and other means. He wasn't sure how long it took for all that to happen, but he was thankful it did.

It never ceased to amaze him how the calcium deposits seemed to reach up with precision, aiming to lock tips with the opposite formations dangling from the ceiling. It was a symbiotic relationship of sorts, one that had started eons before he visited this place as a kid with his family.

Everywhere he looked, colors reflected with the help of his headlights, dancing between the rays as if they were alive. Every shade of gray, green, orange, and even a few browns could be seen, dazzling his vision for the briefest of moments. All of the colors unique. All of them memorable.

An equal number of shadows stood beyond the formations, displaying their own shapes and sizes, reminding him of how many acres had been consumed by this subterranean wonderland.

If he let his mind wander, some of the shadows would morph themselves into a subtle feline or Big Bird from Sesame Street. There was even an outline of a witch, pointing the way out of the labyrinth with her nose.

He wasn't an expert by any means, but he did appreciate the tapestry before him. It was a primal mix of flowstone, boxwork, and helictites, plus a litany of other rarities that held no known reference in his mind.

Somewhere inside the almost endless expanse was his clan, waiting for his return, probably worried that this latest trip would be his last. He honked once, using the shortest blast he could muster, then flashed his lights three times.

That's when he saw them—five of the six—climbing out from the recesses beyond the reach of the headlamps, their scrawny arms and legs traversing the rocks in their path. He couldn't help but smile, watching their anticipation fuel their climbing speed.

They must have missed him, an emotion he didn't think they knew, not after their prolonged captivity at the hands of the one-eyed pirate known as Craven. So much pain. So much oppression. Few could have held up after what they'd gone through.

He turned off the engine, but not the lights, then hopped out of the truck, meeting his new family just beyond the front bumper with his arms wide.

They wrapped their arms around him in kind, while the success of the most recent mission soaked into his thoughts. He'd pulled off the impossible, leaving nobody the wiser, not even the plethora of women squeezing him tight.

"All right, that's enough," he said, prying their arms loose from his leather armor. They obeyed, letting him stand alone. "Where's Two?"

The women looked at each other for a moment, then the shortest turned and pointed at the deepest part of the cave. He assumed the missing member of his cabal was sleeping, or busy with one of their mundane chores.

Nomad made a mental note to look in on her later. He turned and walked back to the entrance, taking a few minutes to reset the natural camouflage concealing their location.

The eldest of his group approached him, her mouth remaining silent. It was an odd occurrence to be sure, her lips normally flapping with another round of guttural sounds.

The Nomad waited for their eyes to meet. "You're unusually quiet today, Four. Even for you."

Four flashed a wide-eyed look at him.

He nodded. "You're worried about Seven, aren't you?"

She twisted a lip, but held her grunts.

"She'll be okay. I promise. I would never have sent her back in if I didn't think she'd be okay."

Four came a step closer and grabbed his fingers with her palm. She pulled his glove off and turned his hand over.

Her eyes went down, just as she began tracing her thumb across the creases in his palm. The path she made did not match the impressions in his skin.

Nomad recognized the pattern as she drew it over and over. It belonged to the lines in the hand of Seven. "I know you miss her, but she needs to do this. We all do. Otherwise nobody survives. Not me. Not you. Not your sisters. And certainly not your daughter."

Four stopped the rubbing, then turned and led him deeper into the cave. The others had scattered into the myriad of cracks, passageways, and other crevasses, leaving the two of them to walk alone.

He broke free of her escort as they approached the rear of the truck. "I need to unload first."

She grunted once, then pointed in the direction of a ladder leading down to his chambers. "In a bit. Gotta get this done. The truck needs fuel."

She pointed again, this time grunting louder and with spit flying from her lips.

"Remember what I taught you—always be prepared. No matter how tired or how much someone misses you. The job comes first. It's how we keep everyone safe."

Her head dropped, making her look like a lost puppy—a puppy without a nose or much of a figure, her skin hanging on her bones.

"It'll only take a few minutes, then we can eat and rest," he told her, lowering the tailgate on the truck.

The Nomad climbed in and unhooked the tiedowns that Fletcher's men had used to secure the drum. He rocked the container back and forth, using leverage to maneuver it to one end of the horizontal tailgate.

Once it was in position, he moved to the inside of the drum and gave it a firm yank along the top, sliding his feet out of the way in the process.

The steel container toppled sideways in a loud clang, then rolled off the truck and landed in the dirt.

The Nomad jumped down and stood the drum upright to gain access to its opening—a twist lock offset to one side. He retrieved a heavy duty, long-bladed screwdriver from the truck's toolset and wedged it in sideways to work the cap loose in a spin. It would have been quicker if he had the proper bung wrench, but the screwdriver would suffice with the jury-rigging.

Four brought him the battery-powered fuel pump he'd acquired at the Trading Post earlier in the year and put it on the back of the tailgate.

He took the apparatus and stuck the syphoning end of its hose into the drum before walking to the side of the truck. He twisted the fuel cap off, then slid the pour spout of the hose inside the tank, making sure it was seated properly to avoid any spillage.

When he looked back, he noticed Four bending low over the drum, her face close to the hose penetrating the cap.

The Nomad wasn't surprised. She was a curious woman, but one he'd learned to appreciate during all the grooming he'd done to make her his sidekick. She'd also become his confidant, even though she couldn't speak or offer much in the way of feedback. Not in the traditional sense.

There was tactical value in having a team of mutes at his side—those that couldn't read or write. They allowed him to share top secret facts without worrying about information leaks or betrayals, maintaining the shroud of secrecy. That veil of silence was more than just important. It was mission critical if he had any hope of completing his plan.

The Nomad scoffed as more memories replayed in his mind. Memories from his past. Memories that carried endless pain mixed with periods of joy. He had no idea how his life would change once he returned home a beaten, broken, and burned soldier. Cannibals or not, his little cabal had become his family. They were the reason he did what he did.

He popped the hood of the truck, then located the batteries. There were two—one on each side of the engine compartment. He moved to the closest battery with a pair of power leads in hand. They were color-coded red and black, much like a set of jumper cables used to start a dead vehicle.

He knew from experience that as soon as he connected them to the battery terminals, matching red to red and black to black, the fuel pump would energize and begin transferring diesel at eight gallons a minute.

The instant nature of the system meant he'd have to attach the power leads, then scurry to the spout and keep an eye on the flow, especially since there wasn't a gauge on the pump indicating how much fuel had been delivered. Overflow conditions had a mind of their own, sending fuel everywhere. He couldn't afford to waste a single drop.

The Nomad held the power connectors an inch from the battery terminals and took an extra breath, making sure he was ready.

Before he could make electrical contact, Four flew into him and knocked him over, sending the connectors out of his hands and into the dirt.

He rolled to his knees and peered at her. "What the hell are you doing?"

She kicked the cables, sending them skidding through the dirt in a tumble.

"Stop it!" he snapped, trying to understand her actions.

She grunted and pointed back at the drum, hopping on her toes in the process.

"What's gotten into you? You know I have to fuel the truck. We do this every time."

She leaned forward and snatched his hands, pulling him to his feet with a firm tug.

He pulled free of her grip, throwing his hands up with his eyes wide. "Okay, what the hell's going on?"

She led him to the drum and put her face down to the opening, then spun her neck and shook her head in a disgusted look, as if she'd just gotten a whiff of rotten eggs.

He wasn't sure what to do, watching her antics continue.

She pointed a few times, aiming her finger down the hole, then started a rant of grunts unlike anything he'd heard before.

"Okay, I get it. You don't like it. But that's how it smells."

She hopped again with flailing arms, then ran to the truck and yanked the fuel spout free, sending it flopping to the ground.

"Hey, what did I tell you about putting stuff in the dirt?"

She sprinted back to the drum and tore the hose from the opening, also tossing it airborne.

"Now you're starting to piss me off."

Four zipped past him and opened the door to the truck. Her hand went inside and came out with one of his swords.

The Nomad took a step back when she held it up.

After she stuck the tip of the blade into the drum and pulled it out, several drips of diesel ran from the metal.

When she shook her head again, he was slammed with a sudden wave of understanding. "Oh shit. They did something to the fuel," he said, holding back the urge to punch the side of the truck.

She grunted twice, her eyes telling him he was spot-on.

"That fucking Fletcher. I should have known by the way he was acting."

She held the sword out in a sideways spin, as if she were waiting for him to take it to end the charade.

"Yes, yes, yes. Your sense of smell is much better than mine," he said in a mutter, taking the blade from her. "What did they taint the fuel with? Can you tell?"

She hung in place for a moment, her arms and legs frozen until she brought her hands up and made a drinking motion with a cup of her hands.

"Water?"

Four grunted twice, confirming his guess.

The Nomad ran the scenario through in his head, crunching the facts and calculating the possible outcomes. "Water certainly wasn't their best choice, but it would work assuming I was low on fuel and filled both tanks—which, of course, I always do."

Four didn't respond, her eyes focused on him.

Nomad put the locking cap back into place and secured it with a twist of the screwdriver. "Fetch me the toolbox from the truck."

Four did as he asked, buzzing to the storage compartment along the side of the transport. Sometimes she walked erect and with perfect form. Other times, like this one, she moved more like a primate, tilting and rolling her shoulders with bent knees and exaggerated steps.

He never understood why she had two distinct styles, but it may have had something to do with her mood at the time. Perhaps all humans do that subconsciously—changing body language and strides depending on the emotions swirling within. Granted, Four seemed to be embellishing her movements, but his theory may have been valid.

He'd seen much the same thing on the battlefield, with bullets whizzing overhead and blood spraying all around. Of course, the stride in play at the time wasn't that of a primate—more of a fight-or-flight panic state, taking over and governing the troops around him.

Regardless, it was all about emotions in control. And experience, something all creatures learn to value.

The Nomad continued working through his theories as he lowered the drum on its side, keeping the twist cap's side pointing up.

Four snatched the handle of the metal box, then leaned to one side as she carried it to his position, using unbalanced steps to support the weight. She put the box at his feet, then took a hop back with her face energized in red.

"What we need is," he said, unhooking the latches on the box and flipping open the lid, "something to make a hole."

He dug through the scattering of tools and past a spool of duct tape before moving a coil of bare copper wire out of the way. A center punch sat beneath it, its wooden handle and a stout tip lying horizontal.

"This ought to work," he told Four, taking it out and putting it aside.

When his hand went back into the box, he wrapped his fingers around the rubber grip of a four-pound sledge and held it up, making sure Four had her attention focused.

"A man can accomplish a lot with a hammer and duct tape. Remember that, Four. It's the same advice my old man gave to me. God rest his soul."

She must have understood the death reference, her eyes losing their intensity an instant later. If he hadn't known better, he would have sworn he saw a welling of tears—something a cannibal never does.

But then again, Four wasn't the same meat eater he'd first rescued from The Factory. She'd evolved, like they all had in varying degrees, beginning to find their natural right of humanity. He gave her a nod, appreciating her compassion and how far she'd come.

The Nomad crouched to one knee, then took the punch and pointed its end against the drum on the same side as the twist lock cap. The tip was about an inch from what would have been the bottom of the drum, if it were standing upright. "The key here is to keep the hole small."

He brought the hammer up and slammed its head against the handle of the punch, using what he considered medium force. A loud clang ensued, but the tip never penetrated, only making a dent.

"Okay, now a little harder," he said, doubling the force of the next strike.

When the metal gave way, the punch sank deep inside, smashing his fingers against the side of the drum. He pulled the implement free, shaking his hand in the process. "Yeeeoow, that hurt."

Four kept a close watch, never flinching after his sudden outburst.

Nomad put the tools aside and stood, his fingers still throbbing. "Now for the moment of truth."

He bent down and leveraged his hands under the drum, using the strength in his thighs to tilt the container upright, keeping his movement slow and measured. "Fuel is lighter than water, so they don't mix. If we go slow, we should see the water running out first."

The hole along the bottom did its job, releasing a stream of clear fluid. He smiled at her. "Nice catch, Four." He continued tilting the drum higher until the liquid turned a darker color.

He lowered the barrel back to the dirt with the punched hole angled up. "That's it. Simple, really. All thanks to you."

She spun around in a circle, grunting over and over.

"Now we need to see if we can pump this shit into the tank without it leaking everywhere."

CHAPTER 29

Boyd Craven adjusted his eye patch before walking the length of the all-brick hallway. Thirty-eight steps later, he turned and headed into the security checkpoint.

Two pre-adolescent Scabs came forward on all fours to sniff his hand, then their handlers yanked them back on a rope-style leash. One of the guards waved him through.

When he'd first embarked on this genetic experiment, Craven had no idea how well the younger Scabs would take to tracking and reconnaissance, using their enhanced sense of smell for tactical purposes.

Plus, they didn't eat much and were easier to control—an added bonus—making them the perfect security tool. At least until their rapid aging kicked in, sending their bodies into an intense maturation process.

Craven entered the Research and Development Lab next, passing a string of tables filled with beakers, test tubes, flasks, microscopes, syringes, and surgical equipment before turning left and zipping by what he called *The Wall of Failures*.

Liquid-filled five-gallon glass jars sat next to each other on four levels of shelving, chronicling his experiments from the first attempt to the last, each one containing a bioengineered fetus.

Some were grotesque in their malformities. Others looked almost human except for their missing noses, yet all of them had suffered a cellular breakdown.

Another doorway led him into the processing plant, where the infirmed and the expired were to be converted into meat units for trade and consumption.

He nodded at the two men using their skills to carve up the day's losses and add a precise blend of seasoning and other trade secrets.

Once those steps were complete, they'd flash-bake the units and put them into the towering smoker to add the expected flavor, keeping the buyers unaware as to the true nature of the meat supply.

His pace continued, taking him to the string of observation windows that provided a close-up view into the Maturation Control Pod, or MCP.

Craven stopped to run a visual check of the beds inside, each row containing twelve bodies strapped to wire-mesh frames.

He counted only eight adults, meaning the balance of inventory belonged to what society used to call preschoolers, each of them ready to undergo their first rapid maturation process.

In the early days, the MCP team installed mattresses for comfort, but ditched that plan after learning a solid eleven percent of the Scabs would defecate when hit with the intense pain. Defecation meant more time and expense, something Craven wouldn't tolerate, not when it was easier to just hose down the floor.

The Scab closest to the first window was a dark-haired boy, his face twisting and contorting as 'The Surge' ravaged his body. The violent process resembled a helium balloon being inflated in increments, making its size and shape pulsate in heaves.

Craven watched the process reach the bones in the subject's back, then listened for the expected scream that shook the glass.

Someone else might have taken a step back when it happened, but Craven's feet held firm as a thin smile found its way to his lips. He knew the warrior stage was about to begin, increasing the value of each Scab ten-fold.

Craven held silent, watching the spectacle spread from one Scab to another, working its way across the room to the other inventory.

The last of the assets to change were the older Scabs, transforming them from warrior into food source. This was the second and final surge of their existence—the one that carried only an aging component, not a structural reconfiguration, meaning far less violence. One could argue the reduced pain was a reward for those who'd survived the first surge, having proven themselves during adulthood.

Either way, it was the final step in what Craven considered the perfect four-stage circle of life: one that ran from rapid incubation to tactical tool to warrior state to food source.

"The ultimate re-provisioning cycle," he muttered, where nothing was wasted. Just as it always should have been, if the Universe had any sense of order.

Craven made a mental note to stop here later and survey the results, when this round of surges was complete. He knew he wouldn't recognize the younger subjects, each one tripling in size and age.

The other eight would wrinkle and lose their aggressiveness, making them easier to handle for final processing. An unplanned benefit of the engineering, but he was thankful for the luck.

He turned and continued his trek, arriving at his destination—the incubation lab, the most secretive chamber in the facility.

"How're we doing?" he asked the blonde, forty-year-old chief geneticist Wilma Rice, one of only two dozen staff members in the facility. She had the biggest eyes he'd ever seen, even if they were hidden behind a thick pair of glasses.

"Batch five-twelve is nearing conclusion," she answered, her braided ponytail draped across the front of her shoulder. "My calculations indicate we'll yield another female in this round. Percentages are holding steady at eleven hundred to one. I'm not sure why that's the case, but it's too consistent to be some random event."

"No, I think not." Craven walked to the cabinet behind her and opened the pair of swing doors, where he found a pack of glass vials inside. Six, to be exact. He grabbed one and held it in front of his eyes, twisting the container for inspection. He turned to Rice. "Two are missing."

"Had a contamination issue during transfer."

"Fletcher won't be pleased. He ordered eight."

"It couldn't be helped, boss. At least this version is thirty-two percent more effective than the first. That might make up for the partial delivery."

Craven nodded, not wanting to berate her. There were more important items on the agenda and he needed her to focus. "What about your efforts to forestall The Surge?"

"I expect to see a marked improvement soon. Something north of twenty percent."

"That's damn good progress, Rice. Gives us more time for training during the docile period. Nice work."

"I appreciate the kudos, sir, but I can't take the credit. It's simply a byproduct of your groundbreaking genetics, plus a bit of unexpected evolution mixed in."

"Always the modest one, I see," Craven said, taking in the numb expression on her face. "We both know where this technology came from."

"Yet you recognized the value and took action when your former employer wouldn't."

"Good thing I did too, with The Event right around the corner. Can you imagine if I hadn't stepped up?"

"That's the mark of a visionary. Seeing the future when others can't."

"For a bunch of PhDs," Craven said, shaking his head, "they had no idea what they had. They were too busy looking for that pie-in-in-the-sky cancer treatment to ever see what they were missing. Well, I didn't and now here we are, all thanks to you."

Her shoulders dropped as her voice turned sheepish. "I'm only the facilitator, sir."

Craven shook his head, wishing she'd accept the compliment. "I may have seeded the science, but you ran with it. As far as I'm concerned, you're the brains behind this operation. So I say again, nice job."

She smiled, though only for a moment, her face turning serious once again. "If my latest adjustments prove fruitful, we may see a more sustainable output from the next round of hybrid inseminations."

Craven smiled, putting a hand on her shoulder. "Excellent. Your timing couldn't be better. I'll let the boys know to start saving up. But I have to wonder, will we see a decrease in semen production this time around, after our recent ramp-up?"

"Doubtful. Reproductive biology doesn't stop simply because you're part of an insemination chain."

"True, but I'm sure the men miss the old ways of doing things. A little one-on-one time, if you know what I mean."

"I really can't speak to that, sir."

"I'm guessing some of the crew have been hitting on you, too."

She pushed her glasses up the bridge of her nose, her cheeks flushing red. "Not that I've noticed."

"Well, I'm sure they have. Sorry about that, but those biological urges have been hardwired into us, ever since we first crawled out of the ocean."

"Even if they did, which they haven't, I prefer playing for the other team," she said as if she'd told him that fact before. There wasn't any hesitation or inflection in her voice, either. Just a matter-of-fact statement about her sexuality. Almost as if she were ordering a ham sandwich for the hundredth time.

Craven hesitated for a few beats, questioning if her somber tone was a cover-up for how she actually felt—annoyed with his preemptive apology and what it meant—or she just wanted him to know she would rather be with women over men.

Then again, perhaps she offered that spin to make it easier for him to stop the unwanted advances by the mouth breathers protecting The Factory. A little deterrence, if you will, as if that would make a difference with the men. Regardless, he decided it was best to change the subject.

"Carry on," he said, walking the length of the room with his hands behind his back.

He needed to spend some time pondering the Fletcher situation. Deal or no deal, there was a change coming. He knew it and figured Fletcher knew it; at least, that's what his gut was telling him. Especially after the carnage at the Trading Post. If he was right, then he'd need to expand his territory.

Rice cleared her throat, speaking from across the room. "As to your suggestion from yesterday, you were correct. I did need to tweak the baseline formula in the Genesis Fluid. Nice catch, boss. I think this mix has real promise. Hopefully, the male population will achieve reproductive viability soon."

"Sounds like we're getting close to a self-sustaining process. I can't tell you how happy that makes me. I definitely selected the right person for the job."

"I also have a new theory for solving the issue with their noses. Or lack thereof."

"Let's scrap that for now. In truth, I think that imperfection has actually helped us over the years. A brand of sorts, making it appear frostbite was the cause. Exactly what would've happened if our products were all natural and left to fend for themselves in the wild."

Rice nodded, but didn't respond.

"If I were a betting man, I'd lay odds that this one defect kept Edison from asking a lot of questions. Frost, too."

"A reasonable conclusion."

"I've learned over the years that sometimes the smallest imperfections can help sell the biggest cons," Craven said, pacing as he continued. "Plus, I'm sure our friends at both camps were only focused on the consistent delivery of their supply. Never once did they ask where any of it came from."

"Except Fletcher. He figured it out."

"As I intended. Sometimes you have to dangle the carrot for the rabbit to enter your snare."

"Adjusting the blend now," Rice said, clicking two switches on the control wall in front of her, then twisting a trio of dials. She moved two steps over and snatched a clipboard from a hook on the wall and turned to page three of the paperwork.

After studying the information for a few moments, she took a pencil from her front pocket and made notes, crossing out the bottom line and replacing it with different numbers.

Craven stopped his pacing, leaning in and over her shoulder to verify the new figures matched the readings from the instrument panel sitting atop a workstation. "Did security figure out how we lost containment?"

"Not yet, but they're still working on it."

"What's taking so long?"

"Not sure. Commander Stipple mentioned something about the last generation being significantly more ingenious than expected."

Craven shook his head. "Still doesn't explain the breakdown in security. Good God, it was only one."

"Technically, sir, it's been seven."

"I meant recently."

She twisted a lip but didn't respond.

Craven continued. "Regardless, this problem should never have happened. Then or now."

"I would concur, assuming they'd been there on standby, as I suggested. I tried to warn them about the possibility, but they ignored me."

"I'll talk to security and make it clear. What you say goes. You're the hammer and they are the nail. End of story."

She didn't skip a beat, continuing in the same tone, reminding him of a post-graduate lecture. "You might also want to reinforce the fact that if she hadn't been far more advanced than anything we've seen thus far, others might have joined her."

"You mean a percentage of the males."

"Yes. Much like with the initial batches, when we didn't know about The Surge and its effect."

"—Emergence."

"This new variant won't be limited to the females for long. It will cross genders. It's only a matter of time."

Craven ran the facts through his head, realizing she may have been trying to rationalize the incremental failures in the technology he'd stolen.

He chose not to dwell on it, knowing that science evolves in leaps and bounds, not in a straight-line path, more so when the original theory is not your own.

The video player in his mind flashed a flood of images, each one a twisted replay of their earliest success stories.

Even though some of his former colleges might have considered The Surge a failure, he didn't. The same could be said for the new evolutionary step they called Emergence. New paths are often blazed by happy accidents, whether the science is predicable or experimental.

Sure, some of the first batches escaped containment early on, but at the time, his team was still perfecting their protocols and adjusting to the unexpected. "Frost sure took his time to hunt them down."

"Assuming he ever did."

"Good point. We really don't know for sure."

"Either way, we need to rethink our security measures."

"Sounds prudent. Though I have to say I have a lot invested in this place, so we can't afford any more glitches. And certainly, no more detention issues, not with the Fletcher situation heating up. Everything must proceed on schedule. If not, we'll be exposed and I can't let that happen."

"Understood, but I'm not sure you're hearing me, sir."

"About what?"

"The inherent danger of these evolutionary advances. If the intelligence level continues to accelerate like we've seen, we might lose containment of entire batches. Let alone keep everything on schedule. I understand your need for a superior product, sir, but this Emergence was never factored into our original plans. Some are becoming increasingly violent as a result. I'm doing my best to compensate, but I'm afraid the incubation chambers are not designed for this. Neither is the Genesis Fluid."

"I know what's at stake, Rice. Just keep it together long enough for me to take care of business with Fletcher. We'll deal with the rest later. I need sufficient numbers and I need them now. A few DOAs here and there won't matter in the grand scheme of things."

"Yes, sir. Batches one-fifty-one through one-seventy-two are ready. Stipple has them trained and ready to go, as ordered."

CHAPTER 30

The Nomad let the tension in his neck fade as he walked farther into the cave with Four, thankful she had taken the lead. His knees stumbled along, much like his logic at the moment, mired in a molasses of thought, everything trudging ahead in slow motion.

The all-consuming saturation was unlike anything he'd ever experienced before, except for maybe during his days in spec-ops wilderness training, when only the most dedicated of the beaten-down and rewired would survive.

The past week had stolen most of his energy, leaving him a shell of his former self. He'd pushed forward despite the exhaustion, hoping he'd emerge the victor, even though he knew the odds were slim his plan would come together with the precision needed for all-out success.

Every warrior knows that most missions don't go according to plan, usually because the intel is flawed or as a result of tactical errors. When they do proceed flawlessly, it's called an ambush, something he hoped to avoid in reverse.

Now that the end was near, what he wanted most was a good night's sleep. That, and a long, hot soak in a tub. His missed the days when all that was possible, long before he became the scarred enigma he was today.

Four tugged at his hand, taking him around an outcrop of rock and past a campfire flickering to stay alive. The light from the single log gave him a view of the smoke billowing up, its ribbons of white floating into a crevasse that split the ceiling into two sections, each with its own contours and formations.

The cave was a true spectacle of wonder, showering his senses with an endless cascade of angles and styles. No two areas were the same, almost as if the entire cavern had been designed with that singular purpose in mind.

If he'd been a homicide detective, he might have figured the randomness was almost too random, leading him to believe that the serial killer had gone out of his way to appear so, hoping to throw off those hot on his trail.

Too much randomness wasn't random at all. It was something else. Something noticeable. Something that could be identified and defeated.

The Nomad wasn't sure why his mind had let itself become preoccupied with these thoughts, but it had and he couldn't stop the ideas from permeating.

Perhaps they had something to do with the next phase of his mission, trying to uncover something he'd missed. Something he'd failed to take into account. He wasn't sure, but he couldn't shake the feeling. It was there, just under his skin, waiting for him to dig it free and expose its meaning.

Four took him past a candle burning on a ledge to the left, then stopped her feet and pointed at a shadow hiding under a ridge.

Her sudden change in momentum snapped him out of his thoughts. He paused for a beat to consider the significance of their location, then latched onto the answer. "You want me to go check on Two?"

Four grunted twice, then squatted into her trademark commando pose, with her knees pressing into her non-existent chest.

Her stance was a cross between a woman taking a leak and a preschooler dropping into a half-sit, half-ready to sprint away pose.

His knees hurt just looking at her, wondering how anyone could get back up from a prolonged stance like that.

The Nomad removed his mask and leather coat, then slipped out of his body armor and the cloth padding underneath.

He swept his long, flowing locks from his face, then tucked them behind his ears, the dangling curls another reminder of days gone past. Sure, he could have chosen to keep his hair short like his days in the military, but preferred the extra concealment the shoulder-length locks provided. More so during a hand-to-hand skirmish, when anything can happen.

The deep, heavy scars across his face, arms, back, and legs were now exposed, but Four didn't react. She'd seen them all before—each night, in fact, when she crawled into bed next to him before they drifted off to sleep.

He dropped to his knees and ventured deeper into the rock-lined section that bent to the right, its opening narrowing as he crawled. He could see a flame flickering ahead, the light dancing with its own shadows, highlighting his route.

"Two? You all right?" he said, snatching one of the candles burning on a flat rock ahead. "I'm coming in."

He lowered his head and snuck the rest of his frame past a narrow shelf, taking him into the private space. It wasn't much more than a hollowed-out recess under a boulder, but he knew she called it home.

The Nomad brought the candle up to get a better view. Two was on her back with her eyes closed, her arms lying on her chest in a crisscross pattern. She appeared to be asleep, possibly unconscious, with her breaths short and choppy.

The black splotches around her lips caught his attention next. Their shape was irregular, like jagged puzzle pieces. Plus, they looked to be raised above the skin, based on the depth of shadows from the candlelight.

He brought the tip of his finger toward her mouth, planning to test if the spots were dirt or some other substance, but stopped short when the knot in his stomach tripled in size, screaming at him to keep his hand away.

The Nomad pulled his hand back and redirected it to her arm instead, letting his fingers wrap around her wrist. Her skin was warm and moist, downright clammy, and the vein on the underside of her arm pulsated like a freight train.

He brought his hand up and wiped the beads of sweat from her brow, pushing some of them together as they dripped down her temple. His touch was met with a temperature spike across her skin—almost hot.

"Looks like you're running a fever, Two. Can you open your eyes for me?"

She turned her head toward him and cracked her eyes open. They were thin slits at first, until she moaned and opened them wider.

He could only see a portion of her retinas, but she was there, looking back at him.

Two had never seen him without his mask, but like Four, she didn't react to his disfigurement. He wasn't sure if that was because she was only half-awake or perhaps her eyes weren't reporting the facts to her brain.

Either way, most people would have found his lava burns revolting, thinking he was a mutant creature from some low-budget Hollywood horror movie, one that had been experimented on in the lab of Dr. Frankenstein.

Then again, the Scabs weren't exactly beauty queens in the traditional sense. Maybe their own horrific looks had made his disfigurement more tolerable.

The idea had merit, even though he would still choose to keep his hair long and face covered—if not for them, for himself, wanting to avoid catching a glimpse of his own reflection.

Nomad went to move her arms from her chest, but she held firm and let out a sharp cry, reminding him of a lamb's scream before the slaughter.

"Okay, okay," he said, letting go and jerking his hand back.

He held his position, running the facts through his head. She was obviously sick and may have eaten something toxic. That would explain the black substance on her face.

Or she'd come into contact with a contagion and now it had spread to her face. Something bacterial or perhaps a fungus—either might cause her symptoms.

Then again, it may have started with an insect bite—as in mosquito. There had been a noticeable increase in the population, thanks to the melting ice from the mountain. The dripping moisture seemed to be everywhere, leeching its way through the rock and ending up as stagnant water.

He took another few beats to think, turning his attention to the plethora of spiders. There were thousands of them, crawling in every nook and cranny, making the walls seem alive at times.

There was nothing quiet as unnerving as when the lights went out and you could sense the walls crawling with eight-legged creatures, each one on a mission to score food for the night.

The sheer quantity and variety meant any number of toxins could be swimming in her bloodstream. The same could be said for the diseases carried by the abundant bat population, their scat dotting the floor.

The facts were both clear and confusing, yielding no single answer. Plus, it didn't help that Two was the smallest of the bunch, her weight clocking in at less than eighty pounds, leaving the girl little to fight with.

Her struggle for air and the pain across her arms could mean she was suffering from some kind of respiratory infection, or even muscular damage. Then again, it may have been neurological or even biological. He just didn't know.

What he needed was more medical training, other than the basic techniques he'd learned in spec-ops. He'd have to proceed on instinct, hoping to keep her comfortable until her own body took up the fight against whatever had invaded.

The first order of business was to get her somewhere dry and warm, far away from this enclave she slept in. His chambers were at the top of that list, though he'd have to make room for a third body in the space.

Nomad turned his neck and called out in his loudest voice, "Four, I need you in here. Now!"

CHAPTER 31

Summer stepped into the lime-green hallway that connected the command center to the missile bay, taking a direct path to her new best friend, Sergeant Barkley. She ran her hands through his golden fur, then gave him a two-armed snuggle.

"Wish me luck," she said, letting go and stepping onto the mobile platform that would serve as the podium for today's speech. She adjusted the microphone in its stand, bringing it down a few degrees toward her mouth.

Krista was to her left and Liz was on her right, the three women standing together in what they hoped was a show of unity.

Everywhere Summer looked, she saw eyes and faces. Young ones, old ones, and even a few sleepy ones. Some had tears on their cheeks and others appeared to be red-faced. An odd mix, to be sure.

Rod Zimmer was in attendance, too, standing in the back with his arms folded, looking like a

Confederate soldier standing watch over the townsfolk he'd sworn to protect.

The young pretty boy, Simmer, was next to Rod, his blonde locks and blue eyes looking more inviting than ever. His focus darted between Summer and Zimmer a few times before settling on Summer.

She made a mental note to find a job for the gorgeous hunk, one that would allow her to be around him more. A do-over was needed because of the awkward start they'd had during their initial meeting near the hydroponics bay. Perhaps he would see her differently now that she was in charge.

A few more citizens squeezed into the corridor, pushing and nestling into the mix. Neither Summer nor Krista had taken a count, but it appeared that most everyone had arrived.

The neon hue from the wall paint gave her a strange sense of calm, not so much because of the striking color, but rather because of its soothing effect. A soothing effect that came in the form of a distraction, taking her mind from the butterflies pounding at the insides of her belly.

Summer took out the paper containing her speech and put it in the center of the podium. Her hands moved to the middle of the sheet and unfolded it, pressing down on the vertical crease to make it less prominent.

In truth, it would have been a good idea to have Liz review the speech, but Krista talked her out of it, feeling that what Summer had written was sufficient.

It was short and sweet, just the way Edison would have wanted it. Plus, there wasn't time to revise another draft, not with the revelation brought forth by Lipton after he revised Morse's equations.

Even though Nirvana's problems were escalating, this address had to be done and done now, in order to quash some of the rumors swirling about Edison's death. If she didn't step up and get this over with, their concerns would fester and force morale even lower.

Summer turned her eyes to Krista, wanting to see if the security chief needed anything before she started.

Krista's lips remained pressed together in a thin line as she gave Summer a head nod, then motioned with her hand to begin.

Summer took a drink of water from the glass on the podium, then brought her eyes forward, deciding to focus on one of the massive springs lining the middle of the passageway.

She'd read in one of her how-to books that you are supposed to picture everyone naked when giving a speech. That approach didn't seem relevant, not with entire families standing before her with their eyes glued on all things Summer.

Liz cleared her throat, using a sharp, triple-clucking sound. When Summer peered in her direction, Liz flared her eyes and motioned with a shoulder to get started.

Summer nodded, reading the words from the page. "Citizens of Nirvana, my name is Summer Lane. I am the new chancellor of this facility. Some of you know me and the rest of you don't, but Professor Edison put me in charge just before he passed away from injuries he suffered in the line of duty. We were at the Trading Post for our regular meeting with Frost when the Scabs attacked in force. It wasn't long before we were overrun. Everyone fought as hard as they could, but unfortunately some of us didn't make it."

The room erupted in a chorus of mumbles and a few cuss words, many of the faces filling with tears.

Then a man's comment about her being 'a low-life opportunity seeker' came from the back, tearing a hole in Summer's heart. She brought her focus up from the paper, feeling the need to address the outburst.

However, before she could set the first word loose, Krista stepped forward with her hands out wide. "Calm down, people, and let Summer continue. This isn't easy for anyone, but we need to maintain order and get through this as a community. So let's be civil and keep the comments to ourselves."

Krista paused for a few beats with her jaw jutting out farther than before. "Let me be perfectly clear. There will be order today. One way or the other. Anyone who gets out of line will be escorted to the brig and face disciplinary action. Understood?"

Summer took a few more breaths as Krista held her position out front. A short minute later, the room found its quiet again and Krista stepped back, cueing Summer to resume.

"I know your hearts are grieving right now, as is mine. We all loved the Professor dearly, and we will all miss him more than words can express. While this loss will sting for a long time, it's important that we all pull together and push ahead, just as Stuart and his wonderful wife June would have wanted. We have a lot of work to do, but we will get through this as a team. I make that solemn promise to you."

Summer held her arms out, signaling to Krista and Liz. The women stepped closer, taking a shoulder-to-shoulder position next to her on the platform. All three locked hands and raised them in unison, before Summer continued.

"Let me introduce to you the new Ruling Triad of this facility. Together in harmony, Liz, Krista, and I will lead this facility into the future, with compassion, concern, and a united goal—to keep everyone healthy, happy, and safe."

About half of the audience cheered, while the remainder pushed their eyebrows together in a squint of confusion.

Rod Zimmer turned and stormed out of the corridor, disappearing at the far end in a flash of arms and legs. The gorgeous Simmer wasn't far behind him, shooting Summer a momentary look before turning and vanishing in a chase after Zimmer.

Summer took an extra breath, wondering why Simmer had shot that long-distance lingering look at her. "We thought it important to change a few things in order to better protect everyone. This will also help us streamline the decision-making process going forward. I'm sure you all realize that I'm new at this, but with the help of these two fine ladies, the three of us will get the job done."

More applause hit the airwaves, bringing a wave of energy to Summer's chest. She figured some of the spectators hadn't accepted the announcement yet, but Summer was confident the last bit of her speech would take care of them.

"Let me be the first to assure everyone that these changes are being done with everyone's best interest at heart. No longer will one person have overriding authority over every decision, as in the past. We think this new dynamic will allow us to achieve swifter, more agile governing, bringing us into a new era of efficiency and safety. It also allows us to spread out the workload and complete important tasks faster. We hope you'll agree and will champion this change."

More cheers and applause came forth. Summer took a quick visual survey and it appeared all but the one man who'd heckled her had gotten on board.

She brought her arms down and let go of Liz and Krista's hands. Her two co-leaders stepped off the podium and returned to their positions along the side of the platform.

Summer closed her speech paper along the same fold as before, knowing the rest by heart. "In closing, we will be holding services for all those who have been lost. Everyone who'd like to pay their respects can do so at that time. The wall behind you has information regarding how rotations will be handled. Please keep your visitation short, as I'm sure there will be many behind you, waiting to do the same. That's it for now. Thank you for coming." She raised both hands in the air with closed fists; so did Krista and Liz, just as they had planned. "Long live Nirvana!"

Most of the crowd did the same with their arms and hands, answering back tenfold. "Long live Nirvana!"

CHAPTER 32

Rod Zimmer pushed the door open to the locker room with a jam of his forearm, then walked the middle aisle, taking him past two guards who were bent over, lacing their combat boots on a raised bench. "Where's your boss?"

The larger of the two craned his neck to look up as he pointed to the right, aiming his finger at the door leading to the armory. "In there. But you might want to wait until she's done."

"This can't wait," Zimmer said, his arms pumping to match the speed of his walk. He plowed through the second door, using the same stab maneuver he'd used on the first.

"There you are," he said when Krista's face came into view. "I've been looking for you."

"Well, you found me," she said, putting a pistol on the staging rack and grabbing the one next to it.

"What the hell is going on? Why wasn't I told?"

"About what?" she said, pressing the magazine release button, then racking the slide. It locked open. She checked the contents of the chamber, then freed the slide before putting the magazine back into the weapon and slotting it in the rack.

"About this new Triad Council—"

"—Ruling Triad."

"Okay, Ruling Triad, or whatever the hell you three are calling it."

She shrugged. "Your consult wasn't needed, Rod."

"You can't do an end run like that. I'm a member of The Committee, in case you've forgotten. All major decisions require a vote. In other words, they must go through me."

"Not anymore. That's been disbanded."

Zimmer sucked in a lip, holding back what he really wanted to say. "You can't do that, Krista."

"Well, we just did. What's done is done."

Zimmer wasn't sure how to respond, her words and her tone taking him by surprise.

Krista continued inspecting pistols, looking more interested in her routine weapons check than in dealing with the heat in his words. She pinched her brow, never taking her eyes from the gun in her hand.

"Nirvana needed a new direction, Rod. Something to galvanize the citizens and serve as a distraction with all that's happened. So we girls got together and decided to make a few changes. For the greater good."

Rod snorted a breathy huff. "You know, history is full of power-hungry dictators making changes that were supposed to be *for the greater good*. Like Germany of the 1940s. And we all know how well that worked out—*for the greater good.*"

"All we did was form a new ruling team. That's all. Nothing sinister, I promise you."

"No, what you did was choose Summer over me."

"Relax, Rod. You're completely misreading the situation. Nothing is going to change. I simply convinced Liz that it would be better if we grabbed some of the power from Summer while we could. You know, all in the name of showing a softer side with a woman-led team."

"Yeah, I get that part. I was there for the announcement, remember."

"Once she and I explained to Summer that a three-headed approach would help alleviate some of the anxiety in the ranks, the girl agreed. She's not exactly the most confident leader right now. I had to move while I could."

"And you just tossed me aside in the process? I thought you and I were partners."

"We are. But there's a new dynamic at play after what happened at the Trading Post. And with Morse's cancer. Summer is vulnerable right now. I had to do this, before she found her footing. An all-woman council seemed like the easiest way to work myself inside."

"So where does that leave me?"

"Your job hasn't changed, except you'll be reporting directly to me."

"That's unacceptable. I demand to be heard."

"By whom? All that's left of the Committee is Liz and me. And now Summer."

"That little snot—" Zimmer said.

"This keeps me close to her and in the loop. Isn't that what you wanted? For me to keep her in line?

"Yes, but—"

"This is the most effective way, Rod. Whatever you need can go through me. I'll take care of it. She'll be none the wiser."

He paced the room, walking from one end to the other and back again, turning every five steps.

Krista stopped him with an arm grab. "Don't make a big stink about it. Otherwise, all the groundwork I'm laying will be for nothing. I know what I'm doing."

Zimmer appreciated her candor and her softer tone, both working to calm the fire inside him. "You better be right about this."

"I am, trust me. This is how it needs to be. We stay close and lead from within. Right now, I'm in her circle of trust and I plan to stay there."

"Which is a good thing."

"She's constantly asking for my advice, so this seemed like the right move at the right time, Krista said. "As long as she thinks I'm on her side and have her back, I'll be able to control things. Isn't that exactly what you wanted?"

"Actually, what I wanted was for you to be in charge. We talked about that."

"That was before Edison's dying wish. Don't forget the Rules of Succession, Rod. What's done is done. If I don't follow the rules, someone will notice. Now is not the time to start breaking traditions."

"I still don't like this one bit. Especially with Liz involved. She's just another one of Edison's clones, all kumbaya and hugs. You know how that'll play out."

"Don't worry about Liz. I can handle her, too. Her mind is in a million places right now, with Stuart's death and all. They were more than friends, in case you didn't know. That, too, makes her pliable. This is our shot, Rod. Right here and right now. I had to take it."

Zimmer nodded, but held his tongue.

Krista let go of his arm. "You need to take a breath and let this go. I'll work our agenda from the inside. Then we'll reposition as we go. It's the only way to get where we want to be."

"Okay, I'll let you run with this and see how it goes."

"Don't forget, Summer will be busy learning her new job and trying to deal with the aftermath of Edison's death. You'll be free to work your magic while nobody is looking. There's real value in that."

"True," Zimmer said, pausing while the scenario played out in his head. "But let me make one thing perfectly clear. If I sense, even for a second, that this is spinning out of control, I'm going to take that little shit out. And I don't want you standing in the way when I do."

"I understand. In fact, if my plan doesn't work, I'll hand you the gun and step aside."

"Fair enough. I'll be watching."

* * *

Krista walked into the cafeteria, taking a hard right toward the table in the back, where she saw Summer sitting with Nick Simms—aka Simmer.

When Krista arrived, Summer brought her head up. "There you are."

"You wanted to see me?"

Summer pointed at the nice-looking blonde kid. "You remember Nick."

Krista nodded at him. "Yeah, one of my new guys."

"Not any more. I've just promoted him to administrative assistant. We need to start cross-training."

"Cross-training?"

"You know, in case something happens to me."

"Ah, well, I'm not sure he's the best choice," Krista said, turning her eyes to the boy. "No offense."

Simms shrugged. "None taken. I was shocked, too."

Summer continued, "Like you and Liz said, we need an entirely new direction with Edison and Morse gone. I thought it would be good to start with a cross-training program, where everyone mentors an assistant to take over in case something happens to them. You never know with what's going on out there. Or in here, for that matter."

"Not a bad idea," Krista said, wondering how this greenhorn leader came up with such a plan. Perhaps it was Simms, batting his pretty blue eyes at her and working himself a new job. "Just curious, Summer, how did you come up with this?"

"Read it in one of my books. Something about prepping for the worst-case scenario. As in total government collapse."

"I might have to read this book."

"That would be a little tough to do. It's in a secret library on Frost's side of the line."

Krista took the girl's words in and let them percolate for a few beats. That was when her mind latched onto a new revelation. "So that's where you went all those times."

"Yes. My little home away from home."

"Did this book suggest anything else?"

"Yeah, lots of stuff. But I think we should start with this first, until we deal with that other thing."

"What other thing?" Krista asked, her mind conjuring a list of items needing their attention.

"The EOD thing in Morse's lab."

"Right. Right," Krista said. "In fact, that's what I thought you wanted to speak to me about."

"I do, but first, I want you to start training a new assistant, too. Do you have anyone in mind?"

Krista held for a few beats, searching the names on her list of guards. "Wicks is the obvious choice."

"The Neanderthal?"

"He's the most senior."

"A bit of a 'shoot first and ask questions later' type, don't you think?"

"On the surface, yes. But I can work with him."

"I don't know about that one."

"Is it my choice as a member of the new Ruling Triad, or are you making all the decisions now?"

Summer hesitated, bringing her eyes to Simms.

The kid shrugged, then nodded.

Summer did as well before focusing her eyes on Krista once again. "It's your choice."

"Then he's my pick."

"Okay then, it's settled. We go with Wicks— for now. But he really needs to think before he acts. I don't want any more situations like what happened with me and him."

"No offense, boss, but some of that was you, too. Not just Wicks."

"I admit I played my part in it. That's why I'm letting you choose him. A second chance type thing."

Krista held back a roll of her eyes after the comment about Summer *letting her choose*. "I appreciate the support, boss."

Summer looked at Simms. "Why don't you go check on the dog for me? Take him for a walk to get his legs moving. Otherwise, he won't get stronger. I need to speak to Krista for a moment. In private."

Simms stood from his chair. "All right, later."

When he left the room, Krista took his seat. "Walk the dog? That's your idea of cross-training?"

"He's got to start somewhere," Summer said, her face flushing red.

"I'll admit, he's damn cute. I can see why you chose him."

"That's not it at all," Summer shot back.

"Well, it's not up to me. He's your assistant," Krista replied, pausing. "But we do need to deal with that other thing."

"What do you think about Lipton?"

"He seems capable."

"I guess it's time to find out if he's as good as he says he is."

"If not, then we're screwed."

Summer smiled, looking proud of herself. "Good thing we didn't leave them out there, back on that road."

"Roger that," Krista said, wishing she didn't have to agree, but she couldn't deny it. "Sometimes we get lucky, even if the decision is tactically wrong."

"Nothing wrong with a little good luck now and then."

"No, there's not. But the problem with relying on luck is that the luck always runs out, eventually."

"Then we'd better make this one count."

CHAPTER 33

Nathan Wicks escorted Doc Lipton into what used to be Morse's lab with Krista leading the way, while their new boss, Summer, brought up the rear.

There was a strong vibe in the room, one Wicks could only describe as impending doom. The hairs on the back of his neck sprang to attention, putting his situational awareness skills on high alert. He could feel Summer's eyes focused on him from behind. It was almost as if her thoughts had tunneled a hole into his skull, burrowing their way to the center of his brain.

He couldn't shake the sensation, wondering if she would soon take revenge for what happened earlier in the brig, when he'd gotten rough with her. Perhaps she had already taken out a blade and was about to jam it into the back of his neck.

Wicks spun his head, peering back at Summer.

"Something wrong?" she asked after a casual smile.

Wicks stuttered through a few mumbles, trying to corral the words on his tongue. "Well, uh, no ma'am. Just making sure you're okay back there."

"All good here. Thanks for the concern. Just keep an eye on Lipton."

Wicks brought his eyes forward, pretending to study the body language of the prisoner. Even though the sense of peril still lingered across his skin, he decided to let it go and trust that Summer was not trying to gut him.

Summer moved ahead and took the lead from Krista as the group neared the worktable in the lab. Krista took a position next to her, the pair bracketing the radio in the middle.

Summer held out a hand, pointing to the device. "Here it is, Doc. Same place as before."

Lipton came forward and activated the power switch on the radio. The unit roared to life, its cooling fan whirling and lights flashing.

After the speaker crackled with static, Lipton took what looked like a measured path around the back side of the table, stopping at the rear of the transmitter. He remained there for at least ten seconds, his eyes scanning the back of the case before he continued on, stopping again at the cardboard box holding a stack of electronic parts.

Krista was the closest to the man, leaning in and holding her gaze as his hands went into the fray and sifted around.

Lipton pulled out a green-colored circuit board with a smattering of raised parts across its surface—most of them black. Wicks wasn't familiar with them, each about three times the size of the normal diodes and capacitors he'd expected to see.

Wicks took a step forward to better observe the box and its contents. The other boards didn't appear to have the same distinctive look as the one Lipton grabbed, making him think the sheer oddity of its components was the reason Lipton had selected it.

Lipton held the board up. "I saw this earlier. Apparently, your man didn't."

"What is it?" Summer asked.

"The answer to the problem."

"How could you possibly know that?" Krista asked, her eyes burning with intensity. "You barely even checked out the radio."

"First things first," Lipton said, holding out his empty palm. "Where's the mic?"

"I'll get it," Summer said, turning and cruising to the desk parked along the back wall. She opened a drawer and pulled out a microphone and its cord before returning in a flash. "Here, but it's not going to work."

Lipton plugged its adapter into the port on the device, then played with several of the dials and switches, as if he were searching for something. He brought the microphone up to his mouth and pressed the transmit button. "Mayday. Mayday. This is Doc Lipton. I'm being held prisoner—"

Krista shot forward and ripped the mic from his hand. "I knew you'd try something like that."

"Relax, Ms. All-balls. It was only a joke. Nothing was ever going to be transmitted," Lipton said, putting the circuit board down on the table. He sat in the chair and peered up at her, as if he were about to deliver a joke.

Krista looked at Summer, her eyes holding tight. "Maybe we should rethink this idea, boss?"

Summer shook her head, pushing her lips together into a tight line before she spoke. "Don't really have a choice, now do we?"

"Like I said, you people need to chill," Lipton added. "And loosen up a bit. It was a joke. As in levity."

Silence hung in the air until Lipton spoke again, this time changing his tone and his accent, sounding as though he had been raised in a backwoods town somewhere in the Deep South. "What we have here is a failure to communicate."

"Cool Hand Luke," Wicks said, recognizing the catchphrase.

"Precisely, my giant friend," Lipton quipped, looking smug.

"What does that old movie have to do with any of this?" Krista asked.

"Not a damn thing. Just trying to lighten the mood. You people are simply wound much too tight to think straight."

"Okay then, explain it to us," Summer said. "You seem to know everything."

Lipton pointed at the radio. "Simple reasoning, my little squirrel. First, your man Morse was somewhat capable, though a little sloppy with his math, as I mentioned earlier. Therefore, it's reasonable to assume that he had tested the power supply, the base circuitry, and the components responsible for transmitting before hitting a roadblock. Those are the normal steps when first performing a diagnosis on a non-functioning electronic device."

"Okay, I get that," Summer said. "Sort of."

Lipton pointed to the box in front of Krista. "It also means he assembled those parts thinking he might need them at some point, whether now or in the fut—"

"Actually, I collected them," Summer said.

"Interesting," Lipton replied, holding his tongue for a long pause. "Regardless, one can further deduce that those parts are loosely related to this device, otherwise he would not have saved them when space in this silo is at a premium. Now factor in their close proximity to the radio and it means they are specifically designed for this unit, having been vetted through whatever research was available to him. Otherwise, they'd be on a shelf somewhere, collecting dust."

"Okay, I get that," Summer said.

"Therefore, there's a good chance they hold the missing solution, given the quantity of parts and their apparent condition. Excellent, I might add."

"I only bring back the best," Summer said.

Lipton resumed, "I can also reasonably conclude that your man would have run through a set of secondary checks next, eliminating each of the parts that were working correctly. Otherwise, he would have been nothing more than a complete incompetent."

"Well, he wasn't," Summer said. "In fact, if he were still alive today, he'd give your sorry ass a run for your money in the intelligence department."

"So you claim, my little squirrel."

"Stop calling me that!"

"Do you want me to step in, boss?" Wicks asked Krista, wondering if he might receive the green light to step forward and pummel the man until he stopped flapping his gums.

"Stand down, Wicks," Krista said, using a look that said, "I'm with you, but we can't."

Lipton continued, not skipping a breath. "With that as a basis, I scanned the box of components, looking for something we might use, something that would solve a more obscure problem with the transmitter. Something your man probably overlooked."

"Wow, that's a huge frickin' leap," Krista said after a roll of her eyes.

"Actually not. I find that lesser minds are often too close to the problem to see the solution. They become obsessed, almost myopic, in their reasoning, missing a critical piece of data that reveals the solution."

Krista threw up her hands, shooting a glare at Wicks, then at Summer. "My God, does this man ever stop talking?"

"Get to the point already," Summer said.

"When I inspected the back of the unit, I noticed a number of screws were missing from the casing. In fact, there's only one still seated in place. Morse must have decided on a partial reassembly, to save time during his repeated attempts to triage the problem. Since that leads us to know he dug into the internals, looking for the cause of the transmission failure, we can begin our diagnosis elsewhere."

"What do you mean by elsewhere?" Wicks said, not able to contain his words.

"Elsewhere, as in not inside the case."

"That doesn't make any sense," Krista snapped. "Of course, the problem is inside. Where else can it be?"

"You think far too one-dimensionally," Lipton said.

"One-dimensionally?" Krista asked. "What the hell does that mean?"

"It means I would suggest listening to my words more carefully, just as I chose them."

"I am listening, but you're just being the pompous ass that you are."

"In the world of science, every word matters, especially how they are used in context. It's how we distinguish theory from fact, after the research has been done."

"He's just stalling, boss," Wicks said to Krista, wanting to help lessen her obvious frustration.

"Bottom line it for me, Lipton. Can you fix it or not?" Summer asked.

"Yes. But I'll need a few things first."

"Name it," she said. "Because we don't have time for this."

"Let's start with pen and paper. Then I'll make a list, assuming you all can read."

CHAPTER 34

Dice moved past a trio of men loading out with tactical vests and combat boots for today's op, his heart full of expectation. His feet seemed to be on a mission of their own, pounding at the floor with purpose. After months of planning, the time had come. And not a second too soon.

This was always his favorite part of a rollout—the sound of eager men and their equipment clattering. Especially the mil-spec weapons and related gear, adding to the anticipation filling the air in Frost's compound. Wait, check that, Fletcher's compound, even though the new boss hadn't had a chance to put his own spin on the place.

It's hard to break old habits and coin new terms when you've been indoctrinated for years under a single command structure. One bolstered by the color red and a blade-first mentality.

After Dice passed a bank of empty lockers that used to be full of gear and personal memorabilia, his mind connected to a set of memories related to the ambush he'd helped orchestrate.

In truth, it was Fletcher's assassination plan, but one that was needed to cull the men loyal to Frost. It was a tough step, but he was on board with the operation. Leading it, in fact, something he'd have to reconcile in the days that would follow. He knew he could handle the guilt, but only after a few ghosts paid him visits in his sleep.

When he landed a step in the next hallway, he ran into Fletcher marching in the opposite direction. "Hey boss. Got a minute?"

"Sure. But make it quick," Fletcher replied. "We've got a mission to complete."

"That's what I wanted to talk to you about."

"Is there a problem?"

"Not exactly. Just wanted to be clear about the objectives today."

"It's simple. We shoot anything that doesn't surrender."

"That's my point. Why not shoot everyone? End it once and for all, instead of these half-measures. I worry they'll come back to bite us in the ass."

"I thought of that initially and it would certainly be easier, but there is tactical value in keeping some alive."

"Assuming our advance force doesn't wipe them all out. They're not exactly a well-trained army."

"True on both counts, but a few of the enemy will certainly take refuge during the invasion. Count on it. There's zero chance they won't have fallback positions already established, where they can hunker down and ride out an assault like this."

Just then, a new thought penetrated his mind, taking Dice down a new path of thinking. "Oh, that's why you'd been syphoning off all the explosives when Frost wasn't looking."

Fletcher slapped Dice on the back. "You catch on quick, my young friend."

"Just doing my part, sir."

"Once we've liberated the holdouts, we'll interrogate them. Someone has to know where they've stashed their advanced technology. And you know there will be plenty of it. That compound has to be full of it."

"Too bad Lipton isn't here. We could use his eye for the better stuff."

"We'll make do. I'm sure the valuable stuff will be easy to spot."

"And if it isn't?"

"We leave it behind."

"Especially with the limited space in the transports."

"Our primary goal is to find something to help with the refinery issues."

"Or someone."

Fletcher nodded, his eyes full of determination. "In the end, no matter how this plays out, we'll adapt and overcome. Like we always do."

Dice pounded a closed fist on his chest, amplifying his voice. "Together, victory is at hand."

Fletcher made the same gesture. "Nothing, and I mean nothing, is going to stop us now. This is what we've been working for."

"And sacrificing."

"Roger that. Let's roll out. Time to finish this thing."

* * *

Wilma Rice walked the remaining steps to Craven's private kitchen and went inside, where she found her boss standing at a prep counter with a meat cleaver in his hand.

The smear of red across the front of his pants caught her attention, running vertically from just above his knee to the front pocket on his right side.

The cutting board in front of him held a stack of sliced meat about the size of a shoebox, each slice with a precise width no wider than a quarter-inch. It appeared Craven had been at it for a while, taking his time to prepare every portion, almost as if the carvings were a work of art.

Craven brought his eyes up from the cutting surface, stopping the work of the blade. "Report?"

Rice took a seat in a high-back swiveling stool. She brought her legs around to face him, keeping her feet in tight to avoid smacking into the cabinet. "Commander Stipple's runner just arrived. They're almost in position."

"Excellent. He made good time."

"Stipple or the runner?"

"Both," Craven said, running his fingers down the blade before bringing them up to his lips. He opened his mouth and stuck the tip of his thumb inside, licking off a drip of red.

Wilma cast her eyes downward and didn't respond, acting as if she hadn't noticed his lack of sanitation. Or his culinary decision.

Craven brought the knife back to the slab of meat, continuing his work. "It's good to know the training worked. I was wondering if he could convince a Scab to stay on task and not get distracted on the way here."

"The man works wonders. You chose him well, sir."

"Now we'll see how well the latest enhancements perform in the field."

"My guess is the success rate will be far superior than the last."

"For us, it better be," Craven said, pointing the tip of the knife in her direction. "Otherwise, questions will be raised. And we both know what that will mean. Especially now, heading into the next phase."

Rice agreed, but chose not to further his line of self-reinforcing paranoia. He was obviously looking for validation. "Stipple has been working the troops hard, so to speak."

"I swear, that man never sleeps."

"It comes with the job, sir. Though I do worry about that heart of his. Word has it, he passed out again the other night. I think his condition is getting worse."

Craven scoffed. "He'll be fine. Nothing he can't handle."

She nodded, but didn't respond.

Craven turned to the wash sink on his right, running a stream of water over the knife. The new coating of blood rinsed off and disappeared into the drain, along with a wedge of meat that had been clinging to the glistening edge. "I'm sure you'll agree, Wilma. Never in my wildest dreams would I have ever thought we'd be here right now, about to share a meal on the eve of our greatest accomplishment."

"Actually, boss, we did discuss this. Four years ago. Don't you remember? It was right after that incubator suffered a meltdown, nearly taking out the lab. You turned to me and said that it wouldn't always be like this. That one day, we'd be raising a glass to toast our success."

Craven held still for a few moments. "Oh yes, that's right. What a long night. How could I forget?"

"I'm sure the lack of sleep didn't help with your memory at the time."

"For any of us," Craven said.

"I think you sensed my doubt that night, about whether I was the right woman for the job."

"Sometimes setbacks happen and I didn't want you to lose confidence. Especially when we were breaking new ground."

"I'll never forget how that made me feel, sir. That one statement really made a world of difference. I was about to tender my resignation."

A smile took over his face, then it vanished a moment later, almost as if her gratitude had struck a nervous tone within him. Or perhaps it was her admission of almost quitting.

Craven put the knife down next to the edge of the sink. "Actually, the time period I was referring to was just after graduation, when I was still struggling to make a name for myself. If it weren't for a few lucky breaks back then, I never would have landed that first job." He smirked, then laughed again. "It's amazing how life unfolds."

"That's an interesting comment, given all we've been up to."

Craven seemed to ignore her reference, his eyes now focused on the meat waiting for him on the counter. "Think about what that really means, Wilma. One simple decision to apply for that first job affected the flow of history. And not just mine, either. For the entire planet."

"What's left of it."

"True, that did help narrow the possible outcomes a bit."

"That it did, sir."

"But it still doesn't change the fact that we are here, right now, together, on the eve of sheer greatness."

She nodded, but chose not to respond.

He picked up the cutting board and held it out in front of her.

She studied the enormous size of the slices leaning against each other, but never put her hand out. "How about a smaller piece? I'm watching my weight."

His eyes scanned her figure before he put the board down and picked up the knife, hacking off a sliver of meat from one of the corners. He used the tip of his finger to tilt the piece up and onto the flat side of the blade. Then he held it out in her direction.

She took the quarter-sized portion and put it into her mouth, beginning to chew.

Craven picked up one of the full-sized slices and slid it into his mouth, folding it over with a stab of his finger. His words ran together into a garble. "I couldn't imagine sharing this with anyone else. You've never let me down, Wilma. Not once. And I want you to know how much I appreciate all you've done."

When he turned his head away, she opened her mouth and let the hunk drop to her lap, landing in the palm of her hand. She managed to stuff the mangled piece into her pocket before he brought his eyes back to her. She continued her chewing, hoping her simulation rang true. "Thank you, sir. It's been an honor."

CHAPTER 35

Krista took a step back in Morse's lab as the snot-nosed recruit, Simmer, appeared with Sergeant Barkley on a leash, the two of them cruising past her on their way to Summer's position by the radio.

For some reason, the animal had decided to stare at her with his tail low, making her wonder if Barkley had forgotten who she was, or if he was in the process of sizing her up for a skin sandwich.

She thought they had been getting along okay, even after her initial apprehension about a vicious dog who used to do Frost's bidding. Trust is hard-earned, even for a canine whose recent bath had made him far less menacing.

Her new boss had managed to tame the beast, but like all creatures, you could never be sure what was boiling inside their brain.

That was true for the two-legged varieties, as well as the four-legged, but Summer seemed to have a special connection with the mutt, able to control him when nobody else could. Or wanted to.

When the boy passed by Lipton, the animal lunged and snapped its jaws at him.

Lipton stopped his work in a twisted lurch, pulling his feet, legs, and arms back at all once. "What the hell is that thing doing here?"

Simmer leaned back and tugged with his arms, straining to control the dog. "Down, boy. Down."

Barkley reared on his hind legs and began to bark as if Lipton were an intruder, spit flying from his mouth.

Lipton pushed the rolling chair back with his feet. "Keep that mangy animal away from me!"

Summer rushed over, taking a position between Lipton and the dog. She knelt down, holding her hand out to the animal. "It's okay, boy. He's our friend."

"You're damn right I am," Lipton said. "At least until I get this radio working, which won't happen if that fleabag doesn't watch itself."

Krista laughed. "Yeah, right, Lipton. If Simmer let go of him right now, you'd probably scream like the little bitch you are."

"Might be fun to watch," Wicks said from his guard position, breaking his silence.

Lipton shot a piercing look up at Wicks, then over at Krista. "Trust me, all of you would scream, too, if that thing was trying to rip you apart."

"It wasn't that bad," Summer said in a light tone, wrapping the dog in one of her hugs. "He probably just got scared or something." She brought her attention from Lipton to the fur bag. "Right, boy? You don't want to hurt anyone, now do you?"

Lipton scoffed as he scooted his chair back into position. "Actually, this isn't the first time. That dog has had it in for me since day one."

Krista understood why. "I knew there was something that I liked about that dog."

Lipton peered at Barkley, then at Krista. "Spoken like the true caveman you are—"

"Cavewoman," Krista quipped.

"Like semantics matter at this point."

"I thought you preferred accuracy."

"On things that matter, not when classifying another species of the lowbrow community."

Krista held out her hands. "So who exactly put you in charge of that task?"

"I did," Lipton said. "Nobody more qualified than me."

"So you say."

"Yes, I do," Lipton replied, his focus on the antics of Barkley and his display of teeth. "As I was saying, you and Cujo over there would make a good husband and wife team. All fangs, stench, and temperament. None of it good, by the way."

Summer held out a turned-down hand and shot Krista a look that told her to stand down.

Krista decided to honor Summer's wishes and keep her lips silent as she folded her arms and leaned a shoulder against the wall. Under normal circumstances, she'd never back down from any man, especially one like this whose only weapon was his arsenal of verbal jabs. Jabs bolstered by a self-anointed sanctimonious viewpoint that made her want to rip his face off and feed it to the dog.

Summer may have had command over her, but not over the instincts of the dog, whose chomping teeth demanded attention of their own. Certainly Lipton's.

On one hand, she enjoyed watching the dog get the better of the man who thought he was superior to everyone.

On the other, she knew the constant threat of a bite would be a distraction and slow the work down.

Right on cue, Lipton turned to Summer. "Look, if you want me to finish this, then take that rabid mongrel out of here. I won't spend another minute on this repair until you do."

Summer held for a moment, then turned to Simmer. "Why don't you take him for another walk?"

"And miss all the fun?" Simmer said, a smile beaming from his lips.

Summer stood and touched a hand on the young man's arm. "I know how you feel. We all do. But all kidding aside, we need to finish this."

Lipton crossed his arms over his chest, matching Krista's pose, then raised an eyebrow. "Which I won't, until that *Canis lupus familiaris* is outta here. It's him or me."

Simmer looked at Krista, his eyes waiting for approval.

"Go on, like she said," Krista said to Simmer, wishing she could have selected Lipton as the one to be hauled away on a leash, instead of the dog. "He really doesn't need to be in here anyway."

Simmer turned and dragged the dog away, the shepherd's four paws skidding across the floor in defiance.

Krista held for a moment, running the recent events through her logic. That's when a new idea tunneled into her mind, arriving with the force of a grenade.

She walked to Wicks and motioned for the giant to lean down. He did, bringing his ear close to her lips as she delivered her words. "I've got an errand for you."

"Whatever you need, chief."

"Fetch Horton and bring him here. On the double."

"What about the Scab Girl?" the guard asked in a whisper.

"She never leaves that cell. Ever. Is that clear?"

"Roger that," Wicks said, straightening his spine. He repositioned his rifle to the side, then pulled his sidearm from its holster and gave it to her. "You might need this."

Krista took the weapon before Wicks left the room in a march. Once he was outside, she went to Summer. "You got a minute?"

"Sure."

Krista used her eyes to motion for Summer to follow her to the corner. She did, where the two of them began a covert chat, using a close proximity huddle to conceal their lips.

"What is it?" Summer asked.

Krista kept her eyes on Lipton as she spoke in a dull tone, just above a whisper. "Do you buy this whole *I can fix the radio* thing?"

"Seems like he is, why?"

"I'm not sure, but he's not using that circuit board he pulled from the box."

"Except the one part he unsoldered."

"But why is it still sitting on the table?"

Summer shrugged. "Maybe he changed his mind."

"That's what I'm worried about. What if he's just stalling until he can figure something else out?"

"Like what? Escape?"

"I don't know, but my gut is telling me something is off here. Plus, the way your dog reacted tells me there's more going on here than we know."

"Maybe Sergeant Barkley got that same gut feeling you did."

"If he did, then I'm liking that dog more and more."

"I told you you would. Just had to give him a chance."

"That's not what I meant. I meant tactically. As in adding to our ranks, like any member of the team should do. Otherwise, if they can't provide some value, they're just a drain on resources."

Summer nodded, peering back at Lipton, then bringing her eyes to Krista. "Where did Wicks go?"

"To get Horton. I want to see if he'll provide a new perspective on all this."

"Another gut thing?" Summer asked.

"Yep. I've learned over the years to trust my instincts."

"Sort of like the dog."

"Exactly."

"So, other than wasting our time, how does Lipton's stalling matter?"

"If he's up to something, we really need to know what it is. Especially if he *does* get that transmitter working."

"He has to, or we're all screwed."

"I get that, but he's not to be trusted. Once we break radio silence, there's no turning back. We don't know who might be out there, listening."

"You mean like Fletcher?"

"Or worse."

Summer tilted her head with her eyes pinched. "You still don't trust Fletcher, do you?"

"Not really. He was Frost's second-in–command, after all, and involved in everything."

"Yet he did help us at the Trading Post."

"But why? He could have just let us die like everyone else. Then he would've had the city all to himself."

"Maybe he's not like Frost?"

"Which would be a good thing, unless it's not."

"What does that mean?"

"It means things can always get worse. It wouldn't be the first time."

"I appreciate what you're saying, Krista, but maybe there's just a little too much paranoia creeping in."

"Maybe. But I think it's prudent to be sure, if there's a source available."

"Which is why you sent for Horton."

"Exactly. Can't hurt to ask."

"Besides," Summer added after a pause. "He does seem willing to help us."

"And I don't think he cares for Lipton too much."

Summer nodded. "Yeah, who does?"

"Then it's settled?"

"Sure, do what you need to do. Just don't get in the way in case Lipton can actually fix the radio. Either way, we need that done," Summer said, leaving their huddle and returning to Lipton.

Krista moved to the door, keeping an eye on Lipton with the pistol in hand.

Wicks walked back in a few minutes later, leading Horton with a hand on the man's shoulder and the muzzle of his rifle pointed at his back. "Prisoner delivered as ordered, ma'am."

"So I'm still a prisoner?" Horton asked Krista, his hands unrestrained.

"For now."

"I thought I proved myself."

"Partially. But trust takes time to earn."

"I've already told you everything I know. Even risked my own life to help you out there. Doesn't that count for something?"

"It's a good start."

"But you want more."

Krista waved the man closer and pointed at Lipton, whose head was buried in the repair of the microphone. "What can you tell me about all that?"

"What do you mean?"

"Can he fix it or not?"

"How am I supposed to know?"

"You've worked with him for years, right?"

"Not directly. He always kept to himself in his lab. Nobody really knew what he did in there."

"Does he always deliver, or does he find excuses more times than not?"

"With Frost, there were no failures. It wasn't an option."

"So he did deliver?"

"As far as I know, yes. But I don't—" Horton said, stopping in mid-sentence.

"What is it?" Krista asked.

"That radio. It looks familiar," Horton said, walking three paces to the left and angling himself at a distance.

Krista followed, taking a position next to him.

Horton leaned into her ear and whispered, "You see the scratch mark running diagonally across the back of the casing, and the three dents in the corner?"

"Yeah, what about them?"

"I made those dents when I dropped the unit on the way to Heston's place."

"The Trading Post?"

"Yep."

"As in you traded it away?"

"Couple of weeks ago, if I remember it right."

"Shit. If I remember right, that's where we got it from. Cost us a bushel of tomatoes from our food stores."

Horton continued, turning away from Lipton's vantage point. "It used to be sitting in the corner of his lab."

"Wait a minute, his lab?"

Horton didn't hesitate, turning away even more. "It was his radio. I saw it a couple of times when I'd bring him food."

"I knew it," Krista snapped, swinging her eyes around and letting them burrow a hole into Lipton. "Was it operational?"

"I don't remember seeing any lights or anything. It was just sitting in the corner, like a bunch of other stuff he had piled up there. But then again, I really don't know. He may have gotten it working and never told anyone. Like I said, he was alone a lot."

"Do you think he used it to contact someone outside?"

"Possibly. Nobody ever knew what he was really doing in that lab, except maybe Frost. Lipton would chase everyone out."

Krista ran the facts through her mind, matching them with the memories of recent events with Horton. "Maybe that's why you ran into him out there. He was on his way to someplace else."

"Wouldn't surprise me," Horton said. "Though he did say specifically that he was looking for me."

"Did you believe him?"

"At the time, yes. But in reality, who knows?"

"Well, if that radio was working and he contacted someone else out there, why couldn't our guy get it working?"

"I'm sure my dropping it didn't help."

"Or Lipton sabotaged the thing before it was taken to the Trading Post."

"Makes sense," Horton said. "Probably worth the same in trade whether it was working or not. Heston's crew rarely checked to see if anything worked. They let the traders work all that out."

"Plus, if he did contact someone out there, he wouldn't want to share that discovery with anyone else. What better way to protect that secret than to disable the only method to contact them?"

"Come to think of it, I think Fletcher did mention that Lipton was the one who said to trade it in. Something about needing more steel for the refinery repairs. I never thought twice about it."

Krista sucked in a lip as a wave of pressure built in her chest. "That's how he knew what was wrong with it without ever looking at it. He sabotaged it. Damn it, I should have known."

"He's a sneaky bastard, that's for sure."

"Thanks for your help," Krista said to Horton, before waving Wicks over. "Escort him back to the cell. Make sure he gets an extra ration for his trouble."

"Right away, boss," Wicks said, grabbing Horton by the arm and taking him away.

CHAPTER 36

Summer kept an eye on Horton as Wicks pushed him through the door and out into the hallway. She couldn't hear what Krista and Horton had just talked about, but it looked important. The bearded man seemed to have been focused on the radio the whole time. Or perhaps Lipton. Maybe both.

Krista walked to Summer with her head angled down, as if she were in a deep state of thought.

"What's going on?" Summer asked when she arrived.

"Just checking a few things."

"And?"

"Nothing you need to be concerned about."

"Ah, in case you forgot, I'm in charge here."

"I haven't forgotten. Though technically, I'm part of the new Ruling Triad. Along with Liz and you. We all have a say."

"Yeah, we all have a say. But for that to happen, we all need to know."

"And you will. I just need to vet the information first. So please be patient while I figure a few things out. Don't want to worry you or Liz about something that may turn out to be a great big nothing burger. The last thing we need is to waste our time on a witch hunt."

"Does it have something to do with the radio?"

"Yes, but I don't know why."

Summer wasn't sure how to take those words. They seemed out of place, at least based on the twist of ideas floating inside her head. "If you'll just clue me in, I might be able to help."

"Normally I would, but I need to ask for some leeway here. I need to run with this for a bit first."

Summer wanted to know, but in the spirit of their new alliance, she decided to not press the issue. "If you think you need to—"

"I do. This is precisely in my wheelhouse and I need to see where it goes. If anywhere. I don't want to waste your time, or Liz's. You two have enough on your plates."

Summer hesitated for a few beats. She didn't like all the secrecy but figured Edison would have given Krista the latitude to check and make sure.

"Okay, but as soon as you have something, let me and Liz know."

"I will. You have my word."

Krista turned and walked back to her post by the door, keeping the pistol angled down at her waist.

"Okay, that should do it," Lipton said, pulling his hands free from the radio. His back arched and he yawned, stretching his arms high into the air. His head turned in Summer's direction. "Time to light the fires and kick the tires."

"Yeah, I saw that movie," Summer said in a sarcastic tone. "When I was like seven. Edison had the DVD at his house."

Lipton brought his arms down. "What movie?"

"The movie with that rapper guy. Can't remember his name, though. But he was cute," she said, thinking of Fletcher and his chiseled physique.

Lipton held still for a moment. "I don't know what you're talking about."

"You know, the one with the aliens and their ships over the cities, right before they attacked."

Lipton's face ran blank, but at least his lips weren't flapping.

"Never mind," Summer said, walking to the worktable, standing only a foot from the man. She picked up the microphone and held it out. "Show me how this thing works."

"It's simple, little squirrel. Once the frequency is set," he said, pointing, "all you need to do is press the transmit button and say what you need to say. If someone's in range and listening, they'll hear you."

"Don't we need a big antenna or something?"

"It would certainly help extend the range."

"What about the Command and Control Center?" Krista said, leaving her position at the door and joining them. "They had a lot of comms back in the day. I'm sure one of those leads connects to something on the surface."

"Good idea," Lipton said, standing from the chair. "Someone will need to carry the unit, though. That's not in my job description."

Just then, Wicks returned to the lab, his rifle slung diagonally across his chest from high to low.

"Ask and ye shall receive," Lipton said. "I love it when a plan comes together."

Summer recognized the latter of those two phrases, too, but chose not to mention it, even though a vision of a man with a cigar and a decked-out van danced in her memories. They had work to do and it started now. Anything else was a waste of time.

Krista turned to Wicks. "Need you to carry the transmitter up to C-n-C."

"You got it, boss."

* * *

Summer carried a set of twelve-foot-long electrical wires in her hand as she walked around the aging command chair in the former Missile Control Center.

That chair was once the single most important duty station in the entire complex. A place where Air Force personnel used to sit for hours on end, watching the blinking lights and performing drills as they ran through countless checklists, all the while waiting for an Encrypted Action Message to come through the squawk box.

Summer was thankful none of those orders were ever issued, but she admired the men who remained vigilant all those years in this underground bunker.

They were obviously well-trained and mentally prepared, needing to select one of three targets pre-programmed into the computer system, assuming what Edison had taught her was correct.

Fire and fury would ensue once they pressed the launch button, incinerating thousands of people at ground zero when the three-hundred-thousand-pound Titan II missile delivered its nuclear payload. Somewhere in Russia she figured, given the Cold War that dominated the geopolitical spectrum back then.

Lipton spun his backside and took a seat in the command chair as Wicks deposited the radio on the surface in front of him. The mountain of a man turned it a few degrees before he bent down and plugged the power cord into an outlet not far from the command station.

Wicks then turned and went to his post near the exit that spilled into the connecting corridor. The man never said much, but Summer found it comforting to know he was there, keeping an eye on everything.

Sure, they'd had their altercations in the past, but now that she was in charge, she needed to rise above the pettiness and keep Nirvana moving forward. Wicks, like Krista and Liz, would be an integral part of the process.

More so now that they needed to solve the bacteria problem killing their food supply. The EOD number would continue to tick down to zero, bringing them ever closer to their own version of Armageddon.

She knew there would have to be some hard choices made in the coming month, unless this transmitter experiment brought them some new possibilities.

Summer stopped in front of the wall of equipment and held up the wires. "Where do I connect them?"

Lipton pointed another foot to her right, toward the end of the electronics bank. "That junction box over there."

Summer went to it and popped the latch open on the side, allowing the door to swing open. A plethora of wires was hanging free inside, with a hunk of metal running vertically down the middle. It was the size of a chalkboard eraser.

"Connect them to the terminals," Lipton said, his tone confident. "They're part of the bar down the center."

She bent down and brought the bare ends of the wires to the center, but held before contact. "Does it matter which end goes where?"

"Red on top. Black on the bottom," Lipton said, giving Krista a pair of alligator clips. "She'll need these."

Krista brought them over and held them out in the palm of her hand. "You're supposed to use these."

"Thanks," Summer said, taking the connectors. She pinched the end of the first one, using its open jaws to connect the red wire to the screw at the top, then did the same with the bare end of the black wire, only this time she pinched it to the bottom. "Okay, all set."

Summer returned to Lipton, her elbow brushing against his shoulder. She could have stood farther away, but wanted to send him a message.

"Ah, excuse me. Personal space," Lipton said in a snort, looking up at her.

"Actually, you're in my seat," Summer said.

Lipton shook his head. "I fixed the radio. I get to be the one who makes the call."

Krista came over and waved her hand at the man. "You heard her. Get your ass out of that seat."

Lipton held for a moment, his expression one of defiance.

Wicks walked three steps closer, bringing his rifle into position, aiming it at Lipton's forehead. "Move, asshole."

"I'd suggest you do as he says," Summer said, giving Wicks a wink in appreciation.

Lipton got to his feet, taking a position to the right.

Summer sat down and brought her hands to the controls on the radio. "What frequency should I try first?"

"Already set," Lipton answered, leaning forward and turning on the power. "Just use the mic and say what you need to say."

"Like what? I've never done this before."

Krista put a hand on Summer's shoulder. "Anything you want. Just don't give away our position or too many details."

"Which is it? Anything I want or not too many details?"

Lipton looked at Krista. "Maybe someone with a little more experience ought to be initiating. For security reasons and whatnot."

"Who, like you?" Krista asked.

"I was thinking you. She's obviously a novice. There are probably a hundred other tactical reasons, I'm sure."

"He's right," Summer said, standing in a flash. "I don't want to say the wrong thing."

Krista held for a second, then took Summer's seat and grabbed the mic, bringing it close to her mouth. She pressed the transmit button and appeared ready to speak, but then let go of the transmit button and moved the mic away.

"Something wrong?" Summer asked.

Krista turned her neck and peered up at Lipton. "I don't know; you tell me."

Lipton pinched his eyebrows, his face looking as though it was about to swallow itself. "I don't know what you're talking about."

"The frequency you chose."

"What about it?"

Krista pointed at the indicators, seeing it set to twenty-three-thirty kilohertz. "Why that one?"

"We have to start somewhere."

"I know that, but why set it ahead of time and why that specific one?"

"Simple logic, really."

Krista huffed, shaking her head. "Bullshit."

Lipton didn't waste a second, his words arriving with force. "It's one of FEMA's emergency frequencies."

"FEMA?" Summer asked.

"It stands for Federal Emergency Management Agency. The key word being emergency."

Summer nodded. "Oh, a federal government thing. Makes sense."

"Precisely," he said, bringing his eyes from Summer to Krista. "You see, the little squirrel gets it. Too bad we can't say the same thing for you."

"No," Krista said with a sharp tongue. "We're not falling for it."

"You're much too paranoid," he replied.

"With good reason. You *want* us to use that frequency."

"Of course I do; that's the point. To make contact. It's the most likely."

Krista shook her head. "Not if you wanted us to only hear static."

Lipton threw up his hands. "Again, total and complete lunacy." He brought his eyes to Summer. "You see what I'm constantly dealing with here? It makes it impossible to do my work."

Krista stood from the chair and grabbed the man by the collar, pushing him back until his spine slammed into the wall. She twisted the fabric in her hands, lifting him up to his toes. "You already made contact, you son of a bitch. And now you don't want us to."

Lipton struggled for air as he replied, "That doesn't make any sense. How could I have made contact? You've been with me the whole time. Have you seen me transmit or contact anyone?"

"He's right. He couldn't. You're reading too much into it," Summer said, stepping forward and grabbing Krista's hands. She worked them free, allowing Lipton to step away and cough as the air stormed back into his lungs.

Krista spun to face Summer, pointing at the radio. "Don't you get it? That's his."

"No, it's not. You're insane," Lipton snapped.

Krista never took her eyes from Summer. "Horton told me he remembered seeing it in his lab. Just a few weeks ago."

Lipton laughed. "He's a Neanderthal, like the others. That man couldn't remember what he had for breakfast this morning, let alone recall a specific piece of electronic equipment he allegedly saw way back when."

Summer needed clarification from Krista. "Okay, so what if it is his? What does it matter?"

"It's not mine. Why isn't anyone listening to me?"

"Because you're a fucking liar," Krista said, turning from Summer and taking steps toward the man.

Summer scampered to get in front of her, using two hands to stop her advance. "Is this what you needed to vet?"

"Roger that. I knew something was up," Krista said. "But I had to be sure. And now I am. This man can't be trusted."

Lipton smirked. "Once again, the lunatics are running the asylum."

"He wants us to fail," Krista said. "Don't you see that?"

"But why?" Summer asked.

"Because he's already made a deal with someone out there. That's why he left Frost's camp and ran into Horton and the girl. He was on his way to meet up with someone that he doesn't want us to know about."

"Wow, that's what I call a big reach," Lipton said, looking smug. "It doesn't matter what I do, everyone assumes the worst."

Krista raised a fist at him. "Because that's who you are. A man who's only in it for himself."

"Except I did fix your radio."

"Only because you're the one who disabled it first."

"I suppose Horton told you that, too?"

"No, we figured that out together."

"Well, good for you two. But as usual, you're both wrong. I keep telling you, that's not my radio. I've never seen it before in my life."

Summer waited for Krista's eyes to return to her. "Is there some way we can verify any of this?"

Krista's eyes dropped their focus to the floor, darting back and forth before she brought them back up. "No. And that's exactly what he's hoping for. He wants us to only get static; that's why he chose the frequency ahead of time."

Summer understood. "So he could sneak off and go meet up with whoever he made a deal with."

Lipton shook his head. "Sneak off? When exactly would that happen? You have me under armed guard 24/7."

Krista ignored the man's response, keeping her eyes trained on Summer. "Yes, he'd slip away as soon as we weren't paying attention."

"So what do we do?"

"We change the frequency. That's what we do."

Lipton's tone turned cynical as he moved a step closer to Summer. "You see, here's where her delusion falls apart. There are nearly endless frequencies. Even if I did all that you say I did, which I didn't, you'd never know which one I used to make contact. You'd spend months trying to figure that out, and that's assuming anyone was still listening on that frequency at the exact moment when you happened to try it."

"He's right," Summer said.

"Why don't you try the frequency and find out? Got nothing to lose, according to her thinking," Lipton said, his eyes glued to Summer. "Then again, it won't prove anything if you only hear static. In my world, it's called *circular logic*, trying to use the absence of a negative as some kind of proof."

Summer looked at him, letting the facts percolate in her brain. His face was a jumbled mess of smugness mixed together with twitches and a sour expression that never seemed to go away. But she was starting to believe him.

Lipton continued before Summer could speak again. "I'll tell you what. To prove I'm on the up-and-up, if you fetch me some paper, I'll write down all the FEMA frequencies for you. I committed all seventy plus to memory a long time ago, just in case the need ever presented itself."

"You see what I mean? Seventy frequencies," Krista said. "Who in their right mind does that? He's up to something, I tell you."

Summer nodded, but needed to slow her Security Chief down. "Maybe, but we have to start somewhere. He's willing to give us a list. What could it hurt?"

Krista didn't respond right away, her eyes alternating between Summer and Lipton. "Okay, fine. But I'm making the calls. Same as before, just in case he hopes we'll give our position away or something."

"Sure. That seems like a smart approach," Summer said. "Just don't use the name Nirvana."

"Wasn't planning to. I was thinking Eagle Base."

"Why that?"

"Why not?"

"It's a good American name," Wicks added.

"It is, assuming this doesn't backfire," Krista said.

"Trust me, you're making the right decision," Lipton said to Summer.

Summer walked to Lipton and stood close, her breath washing over his face. "So help me God, if this is some kind of trick, I'll have Wicks carve you up and feed you to the Scab Girl. One piece at a time."

CHAPTER 37

"This is useless," Krista said to Summer in the Command and Control Center as she put down the microphone and sat back in the chair, letting out a sigh. "We've been at this for hours. There's nobody out there."

"Why am I not surprised?" Lipton said.

"That nobody's out there?"

"No, that you'd give up so easily. It's obvious. You are a woman of weak character."

Krista ignored the man, even though she wanted to thump him every time he opened his mouth. Instead, she brought her attention to Summer. "It's time to call it quits and focus on more important things. Like figuring out what we're going to do about the impending food shortage and that damn bacteria."

"Which is precisely why we're doing this," Lipton said.

Krista shot Lipton daggers with her eyes. "Look, asshat, you're not part of *us*. So don't be including yourself in this 'we' business."

"I beg to differ. Your survival is *my* survival."

"Assuming we decide to keep you around longer than an hour from now."

"For your sake, you may need to rethink that position. Especially now that your man Morse is no longer viable."

Krista shook her head, forcing the tension in her chest to remain where it was. "No longer viable? Seriously? That's what you call the horrible death of one of our closest friends?" She looked at Summer. "This is what happens when we listen to a man who has his own agenda. Nothing but a giant waste of time. Talk about diarrhea of the mouth."

Summer twisted her lips, tapping a hand on Krista's back. "We still have a few channels left. Let's give them a try, then we'll decide. As a group."

"Then we'll need to bring Liz in on this."

"Of course," Summer said, turning to Wicks, who was still at his post by the exit. "Go get Liz. Tell her we need her."

"Roger that," Wicks said, turning on the heels of his combat boots and disappearing in a flash.

Ten minutes later, after two more failed attempts, Krista reset the transmitter to use the last frequency on Lipton's list. She picked up the microphone. "Mayday. Mayday. This is Eagle Base. Is anyone out there? Please respond. This is Eagle Base broadcasting a general distress call to anyone in range. Please respond. Over."

The speaker on the radio resumed its chorus of crackling static, as the group waited for someone to respond.

After another minute ticked by, Krista picked up the mic and sent the same message across the airwaves, this time deciding to ramp up the intensity in her voice. If this was to be the last attempt, she wanted it to be louder and more urgent. Not because she expected someone to answer; more so to finish with her best attempt, before getting up and calling it quits.

"I've got a question," Summer said to Lipton.

"Sure, fire away."

"How do we know our signal is getting out?"

"It is, trust me."

"I'd like to, but what if those connector clips I used on the terminals aren't attached properly? Wouldn't that screw up the antenna side of things?"

"Possibly."

"Maybe we should check?"

Lipton flared an eyebrow. "I take it you mean me. I should check."

"Yep."

Lipton walked to the junction box and bent down, using his fingers to inspect the alligator clips. He popped back up a second later. "No issues here."

"Like I said, this is pointless," Krista said, just as the static on the speaker changed. It was no longer random bits of hiss. There were now quiet segments interrupting the noise, with a few squelched pops mixed in.

"Hold on," Summer said, leaning in close to the unit. "Do you hear that? It's different."

"Try again," Lipton said in a hurried voice, his forehead creased.

Krista used the mic. "This is Eagle Base. Is anyone there? Please respond. We need your assistance. Over."

"We read you, Eagle Base. This is Blackstone. Come back. Over," a man's voice responded, just cutting through the static.

Krista scooted forward in the chair, her heartbeat shooting to double its normal level. "Yes, we read you, Blackstone. But your signal is weak. Can you boost? Over."

Summer put a hand on Krista's wrist, pushing the microphone away. "I don't like the sound of that."

"What?"

"Blackstone. Is that a person or base?"

"Good question."

"You realize it doesn't matter," Lipton said. "We need their help either way."

"Yes, it does matter," Krista answered. "We need to know who we're dealing with. That's why Edison was against this from the start. We don't know who's left out there or what risk they might pose."

"Just so you know, Morse always thought he could get Stuart to change his mind," Summer said.

"Never would've happened," Krista said. "I'm pretty sure he only let Morse work on the radio to keep him busy. He would have never authorized its use. It was too big a threat."

"Well, obviously things have changed. On so many levels," Summer said.

The frequency came alive again, this time with more signal strength than before. "Eagle Base. Eagle Base. This is Blackstone. How's the signal now? Over."

Krista held back her excitement, making sure her voice remained calm and consistent. "We read you five by five. Over."

"We didn't think anyone was on this frequency. Over."

Krista pressed the transmit button again. "Well, we are and we're damn glad to hear your voice, Blackstone. Over."

"What kind of emergency are you experiencing? Over."

"Food stores are running low and we have mouths to feed, including women and children. Can you assist? Over."

"Hold on," the man said, the speaker returning to its uneven melody of hiss.

"I wonder where they are?" Summer asked.

"Could be clear across the country," Lipton said, "assuming that antenna is doing its job. Possibly farther."

"Let's hope not, otherwise there's no chance of getting help anytime soon," Krista said.

"Eagle Base, are you still receiving? Over." the man on the radio asked.

"Yes, Blackstone. Standing by. Over."

"I've talked to my commander and she's willing to discuss a possible trade. Over."

"His commander?" Summer asked, just as Wicks arrived with Liz.

"What did I miss?" Liz asked.

"We just contacted a base called Blackstone," Summer said. "And it's run by a woman. Just like us. How about that?"

"A base? Where?" Liz asked.

"Let's find out," Krista said, bringing the mic back to her mouth. "What's your twenty, Blackstone? Over."

There was a pause before the frequency came alive again. "I'm sorry, but I can't divulge that information. Over."

Krista swung her eyes to Summer. "And I thought we were paranoid."

Summer shrugged. "Can you blame them? They probably never expected anyone to ever be out here."

"You're wasting your breath. They're never going to tell you," Lipton said. "Would you?"

"Wanna bet?" Krista said, looking at him for a few beats before bringing the mic back into position. "Blackstone, this is Eagle Base. Can you give us a general idea of your location? Are you in the USA? Over."

"Roger that, Eagle Base. Pacific Northwest. What's your twenty? Over."

Summer put her hand over the microphone and wrapped her fingers around Krista's. "Wait a minute. Let's think about this. What if this is some kind of trap? I mean, who calls themselves Blackstone anyway?"

"Probably a black site," Wicks said, "as in CIA. Don't trust them."

"He's right," Liz added.

"That's assuming any part of the government still remains," Lipton said. "I really doubt the CIA survived what happened out there. It's not like there's much of a need anymore."

Krista brought her eyes around and studied Lipton. The man's face usually carried a hint of arrogance, as if he knew something that everyone else didn't. But right now, it looked as though he was forcing his expression to be something different. Like a bad poker player trying to hide his tell.

Lipton must have noticed her noticing him because he turned his head and stared at the empty wall, running his hand over his chin.

That was when Krista saw his fingers twitching. It brought a new idea into her brain. She let the words fly at him, no longer willing to temper her thoughts. "You son of a bitch. I knew it."

"What?" Summer asked.

Krista looked at Summer. "Think about it. What are the odds that the very last frequency on the list is the one we make contact on?"

Lipton brought his focus back to the group. "It's called a statistical anomaly. Otherwise known as dumb luck."

"I doubt that," Krista said to Summer. "He knew we'd make contact on this one. That's why he wrote them down in the order he did."

Krista held the paper up and showed it to Summer, her fingers scanning the list from top to bottom. "Why else would they be out of order like this? If he's the super brain he says he is, and he memorized them, they'd be in numerical order. Not this mess."

Summer swung her eyes from Krista to Lipton and back again. "I see your point."

"That doesn't mean anything. It's called random memory recall. Look it up," Lipton said.

Krista pointed at him. "Look at him, boss. He's squirming. He knows I'm on to him. He knew they'd be listening; that's why he put it at the bottom of the list, hoping we'd give up long before we got to it."

Summer nodded. "And we almost did."

Krista was surer than ever. "Oh yeah, these are the people he contacted before."

"That's your theory?" Lipton asked, shaking his head. "That I'd be dumb enough to include the one frequency actually being monitored, hoping you'd give up long before you ever tried it?"

"Yep. No doubt about it."

"Look, if I didn't want you to make contact, all I had to do was leave that one frequency off the list. You never would have known it was missing," he said to Krista before turning his gaze to Summer. "Tell me you're not buying her logic. Or lack thereof."

Summer didn't answer.

Lipton continued, "She's just trying to invent a narrative that fits her agenda. One that justifies her hatred of me. And her distrust. This is insanity."

"Or it's brilliant," Krista said in a matter-of-fact way. "Think about it. No matter how it turns out, he's covered. Either we never make it to the end of the list and give up, or we make contact, at which time he can use this preplanned excuse about not leaving it off the list to cover his ass. He's playing both ends like the conniving asshole he is."

Wick stepped forward, raising his rifle at Lipton. "I can put a bullet in him right now, chief. Just give the order."

Liz stepped in front of Wicks with her hands out. "Okay, I've heard enough. Everyone needs to calm down. This is getting out of hand. We have more pressing business to handle right now."

"She's right," Summer said. "We can deal with Lipton later. Let's get back to the radio. Either way, we need their help."

Lipton tilted his head, his face showing its usual expression of smugness. "As I said."

Krista agreed with Summer and Liz, though it was clear her gut was more on fire than theirs. She engaged the mic once again. "Blackstone, this is Eagle Base. You mentioned a trade. What do you have in mind? Over."

"We need supplies and someone to help with repairs. Over."

Lipton pointed at the radio. "There you have it. Quid pro quo. A simple proposition."

Krista held the mic steady. "What kind of repairs? Over."

"We need someone with a background in science. Advanced physics, preferably. Over."

Krista whipped her eyes around to Lipton. "That figures."

Lipton smiled, turning her insides raw as his lips began to flap again. "Good thing you have exactly what you need. As in me."

Krista held her eye lock on him. Blackstone's need for a scientist fit her suspicions, proving in her mind that she'd been right all along. They were looking for a geek like Lipton. That's why they would have worked out a deal with him when he talked to them covertly.

"Ask them about the supplies," Summer said, breaking Krista's focus on Lipton.

"What kind of supplies are you looking for, Blackstone? Ours are limited. Over," Krista said, grabbing a pencil and slip of paper to jot down what she assumed was a long list.

"Equipment mainly. Over."

"Please explain, over."

"A Geiger counter if you have one. Plus, a spectrometer would be helpful. And some protective gear. Over."

Krista looked at Summer, then at Lipton, shooting him a raised eyebrow and a look that told him to explain their needs.

"Do I really have to lay it out for you?" he snarked.

"Humor us," Krista said, figuring he already knew the answer. Perhaps his words might convince Summer that this was all a ruse, set up long before today.

Lipton pointed at the transmitter. "They have a radiation leak, obviously, and need someone to repair whatever device is causing it."

"Can you do it?" Summer asked.

"Impossible to know. Not without more specifics."

Krista turned to Summer. "Do we have a Geiger counter?"

"Yeah, there's one in the basement, along with a bunch of old suits, but I don't know if they are the right kind of protective gear."

"You know it doesn't matter, right?" Lipton said.

"Which part?" Summer asked.

"The gear. Whatever is going on has already become critical. That's why they're reaching out and risking a reveal of their location on an open frequency."

"He makes a good point," Wicks added.

Krista shook her head at Lipton. "There you go. You just made one of those miraculous leaps again. It confirms what I said earlier."

"That I already knew the answer?"

"Roger that."

"It's simple logic, not some kind of setup," Lipton replied. "Just think about it. Otherwise, why would anyone ever take the chance to reach out and expose themselves? They didn't have a choice."

"Like us and our problems," Summer said.

Lipton nodded. "Exactly. They are desperate. Their needs list proves as much. You don't ask for protective gear and a Geiger counter unless you have a radiation leak."

"Maybe we can use that to our advantage," Wicks said. "Even if it is a trap."

"Possibly," Krista said, taking a moment to think. She brought the mic back up. "Blackstone, this is Eagle Base. We have the items you need. Over."

"Even the scientist? Over."

"See? They don't know I exist," Lipton said.

"Actually," Krista said, "they don't know that we know you. That you're here and not somewhere else."

"You're right," Summer said.

"Like I said, this is all a setup."

"Damn, I just can't win, can I?" Lipton asked.

"You should probably answer them," Liz told Krista.

"Right. Right," Krista said, bringing the mic back to her lips. "Ten-four, Blackstone. We have everything you need and would be willing to trade, if you can reciprocate. Over."

"What do you need, Eagle Base? Over."

Krista looked at Liz and then at Summer, ready to scribble more items on the paper. "Okay, ladies. Time for a list. Make it count. We only get one shot at this."

"Vegetable plants, that's what you need. Uninfected stock and a resupply of seed," Lipton said.

"I hate to admit it," Liz said. "But he's right."

"I agree," Summer said.

"What about the bacteria?" Wicks asked. "It's everywhere, right?"

"We'll need chemicals to keep the new plants from being infected," Liz added.

"What kind?"

"Not sure yet."

"Ask for a centrifuge and some testing equipment," Lipton added. "We'll need those as well."

"There he goes with that 'we' business again," Krista said, wishing the others in the room had the same level of concern as her. But she was outnumbered two-to-one, if she chose to discount Wicks, who would agree with her no matter what. She needed to save her objections for a better opportunity. It seemed likely that Lipton would hang himself, if she just gave him a little more rope with which to do so.

"And a more powerful microscope," Liz said. "What we have isn't powerful enough."

"Is that all?" Krista said, scribbling down the last two items. "That's a lot."

"I'm worth it," Lipton said, tugging on his shirt collar, looking the part of both politician and thief.

"I hope you realize this means you'll have to leave Nirvana," Liz said.

Lipton shrugged. "I'm not welcome here anyway. A fresh start will be beneficial for everyone, mainly me."

"You just can't wait to get there, can you?" Krista asked.

"It's always nice to be appreciated," Lipton said. "Obviously, that'll never happen here."

Krista started to reply, but held her words when the lights overhead flickered and dimmed before changing their luminance to red.

A siren went off a moment later, filling her ears with a high-pitched squeal that tunneled its way into her brain.

Everyone flinched, including Krista, as the whooping continued.

"What the hell is that?" Summer asked before covering her ears with her hands.

"Intruder alert!" Krista said as she shot out of the chair. She ran to Wicks, grabbing the guard by his camo-colored sleeve. "Follow me."

CHAPTER 38

Fletcher took a step forward in the stairwell, leaning his torso over the handrail to look down. He could see several more flights of stairs leading down to what he assumed was the entrance level of the missile silo.

His second-in-command, Dice, moved past him and took charge, giving his three-man team a hand signal to take point.

They did as he instructed, keeping low with their backpacks loaded with C-4 explosives. Their boots made quick work of the steps, pounding rubber to metal until they vanished into what appeared to be a connecting corridor far below.

"Hope you brought enough," Commander Stipple said from his position next to Fletcher.

"We did," Fletcher replied. "All of it, actually."

"Plus thermite," Dice added, pointing to a satchel he carried over his shoulder.

"A little something Doc Lipton cooked up," Fletcher said, scanning the horde of Scabs packed in behind Stipple. The man stood there with a look of confidence, as if his stance of feet wide and arms out could somehow hold back the force of all the Scabs.

Fletcher craned his neck and peered up, seeing the same thing on every level. Nothing but ravenous eyes and drooling mouths—hundreds of them.

He had expected Craven to send an entire squad to hold back the swarm, but he only sent Stipple with a whistle around his neck and a sidearm on his hip.

"Fire in the hole," a man said from below, just as the advance team ran back into view and scampered into a protective recess near a run of cabling and pipes.

Fletcher backed up to the wall and bent low to cover his ears. An instant later, an explosion ripped the air apart, the compression wave sending him back a step.

After the smoke cleared, Dice followed Fletcher to the handrail, where both of them looked down.

One of the men below came into view and cupped his hands around his mouth, looking up. "We're in."

Fletcher grabbed Dice and pulled him to the wall before focusing his eyes on Stipple. "Let them go, Commander."

Stipple brought his arms down and stood aside, then grabbed the whistle dangling in front of his chest. He spun to face the cannibals and blew into the noise maker, filling the shaft with three ear-piercing shrieks.

The army of Scabs broke lose in a stampede of feet, arms, and teeth, tearing down the stairwell and disappearing into the entrance of the silo.

"God help those inside," Stipple said.

"God won't save them," Fletcher said in a firm tone. "Not today."

TO BE CONTINUED in
Silo: Nomad's Revenge
Book 3
Frozen World Series

Get Cool Free SILO Stuff

Get your official copy the U.S. Air Force Titan II Missile Silo Schematics and other amazing insider information and photos by joining our newsletter.

These are the same plans Edison reviewed before he purchased and rebuilt the silo into Nirvana. It's all free, so signup today. Here's the link:

http://MCPWorlds.com/silo1

At one time, these plans and photos were "Top Secret" and the former U.S.S.R. dispatched spies to retrieve them.

Because you're a follower of the SILO Series, we'll send these directly to your email in just minutes without having to risk your neck or go undercover.

Please Leave a Review

Help spread the word about this book and the Frozen World Series by posting a quick review on Amazon and Goodreads. Here's the link:

http://MCPWorlds.com/silo1

Help Support Our Veterans

Visit MCPBrigade.com and show your support for military veterans by purchasing official Brigade merchandise.

100% of the profits are donated to the veterans charities, such as the Oscar Mike Foundation for disabled veterans.

Here's the link:

http://MCPBrigade.com

Join us in showing support for those in uniform. They have sacrificed so much to protect our freedoms and need our assistance.

Join us on Facebook

Be part of a growing community of fans who interact with each other and with their favorite authors. Our exclusive Facebook group is the place to be for news, contests, discounts, and plenty of fun. So what are you waiting for? Join today. Here's the link:

http://facebook.com/MCPBrigade

Books in the Frozen World Series

Silo: Summer's End
Silo: Hope's Return
Silo: Nomad's Revenge

More From Mission Critical Publishing

Visit MCP Worlds for more information on other books available or coming soon from Mission Critical Publishing. Here's the website link:

http://MCPWorlds.com

About the Authors

Jay J. Falconer

Mr. Falconer is an award-winning screenwriter and Amazon #1 Bestselling Author in Action & Adventure, Military Sci-Fi, Post-Apocalyptic, Young Adult, and Men's Adventure fiction. He lives in the high mountains of northern Arizona where the brisk, clean air and stunning views inspire his day.

When he's not busy working on his next writing project, he's out training, shooting, hunting, or preparing for whatever comes next.

You may connect with Mr. Falconer by visiting his website at:

http://JayFalconer.com

AWARDS AND ACCOLADES

2018 Best Sci-Fi Screenplay, Los Angeles Film Awards

2018 Best Feature Screenplay, New York Film Awards

2018 Best Screenplay, Skyline Indie Film Awards

2018 Best Screenplay, Top Indie Film Awards

2018 Best Screenplay Finalist, Action on Film Awards

2018 Best Feature Screenplay, Festigious International Film Festival - Los Angeles

2017 Gold Medalist: Best Young Adult Action, Readers' Favorite International Book Awards

2016 Gold Medalist: Best Dystopia Book, Readers' Favorite International Book Awards

M. L. Banner

Mr. Banner owns and runs several businesses and has written business articles for years. In 2014, he jumped—head first—into the warm waters of science fiction and self-published his first novel: Stone Age, which became a #1 best-seller on Amazon for post-apocalyptic and dystopian fiction.

Since then, he's self-published numerous novels that have been #1 best-sellers and one an international #1 best-seller, as well as released two short-stories and a number of audio books.

His books have been featured on Amazon's Daily Deal, Monthly Deal, and Big Deal and they've garnered acclaim by Readers Favorite and multiple bloggers, receiving well over 500 five-star ratings from Amazon & Goodreads readers.

He's an avid consumer of sci-fi books & movies, especially those with dystopian/apocalyptic themes. You may connect with Mr. Banner by visiting his website at:

    http://mlbanner.com

Made in the USA
Columbia, SC
09 May 2020

96681410R10237